Symphony

Cassandra Frew

This is dedicated to my wonderful 'forever' friends,

namely Jason, David, Geoffrey, Troi, Hellen, Peta,

Alex, Kari, Poida, Marie, Melayne, Tom and Di,

Melissa and John, and to the township of

Abermain NSW, who held and cared for me when I

lost my Chris.

As with my other supportive and wonderful

friends, your names are forever emblazoned via

the character names here in print.

And, as always, to my late husband Chris.

Without your love and support, this series of

books would never have eventuated.

Commenced 8 March 2010
Completed 6 April 2010

Covers designed by Microsoft® Clip Art and used with permission by Microsoft.
Microsoft, Encarta, MSN, and Windows are either registered trademarks or trademarks of Microsoft Corporation in the United States and/or other countries.

Symphony - Copyright © Cassandra Frew 2020 ISBN 978-0-6488635-4-0

TABLE OF CONTENTS

PREFACE

AFTER SIXTEEN YEARS of continual studying, seventeen for me including my repeated fifth grade attempt, Lorien and I were taking twelve months off now that we'd both completed our Bachelor of Music; Lorien of course as the dux of the course. Elijah was still only halfway through his Bachelor of Medicine, with another two years of theory and a final year of practical before he got his wings.

Lorien and I had talked about travelling, hanging out and just being sloths or possibly looking for part-time work. The only thing we'd decided on at present was we didn't want to leave the bedroom. But, that was a decision we'd reached over five years ago. As it was, when we first got together, was now still the case - insatiable.

Lorien had been composing music through our entire three-year course and had managed to sell quite a few songs to an up-and-coming Castlebrook band, not to mention an already established Castlebrook band that were now internationally renowned. His name as a talented young song writer/musician was becoming well known throughout the music industry. Neither of us had managed to meet any of these famous people, only the business managers and staff. In time that would change... we hoped.

With Lorien's self-made monetary comfort and the fact that we'd now finished our BMs, I decided to uphold a bargain I'd made with him at the onset of our first Uni term and casually threw away my birth control pills...

FALLING

The Stranger

"Surprise is the only thing you can't see coming,
Better start running..."

L Standish, 'Stranger in a Strange Town'

"WE'RE GOING TO BE LATE!" I called up the stairs to the twins. We were due at Michael's in less than fifteen minutes, and it was a twenty-minute drive. I hated to be late. The thunder on the stairs announced their arrivals and I watched as they hit the lounge room floor, jumping over the last few steps. "It's supposed to be a woman that runs late, not twenty-two year old men," I tsked at them, my arms folded over my chest.

"Sorry Baby," Lorien gushed then grabbed me to him, tickling at my sides to change the faux anger on my face. He knew if we'd bounced out of bed an hour ago like he suggested we'd have been on time, but he allowed me to blame him in front of his brother. I was unsure as to what Elijah's hold-up had been.

He'd been single for nearly three years now, having broken up with Keren not long after he started Uni, so he certainly wasn't up there tripping the light fantastic. The pressure of their ever-eroding connection plus the scads of work involved in his Bachelor of Medicine became his main priority, and he decided to leave relationships until he was finished with his studies, although he did still date on a rare occasion. Everyone has needs...

I realised this is what he'd probably been doing in his room, just that last-minute bit of work, just five minutes more... As if reading my mind he said, "I really should stay here and get some more work done..."

"What you need is a night out, Elijah," I told him. "You're cooped up in your room too much. You need some fun."

"Yes Ma'am," he said and saluted.

"What he needs," Lorien started, throwing his twin a calculating glance, "is to get laid!"

"I'm sure you're getting enough for both of us Lori," he sighed and grabbed the car-keys off the island bench.

Lorien nuzzled into me from behind and breathed into my ear, making me break instantly into goose bumps, ready to race him back to our room for the next round of lovemaking. I turned in his arms to face him and smiled, leaning up to kiss him. "I'll be in the car when you guys are ready..." Elijah said and went to the front door.

"Wait," I said, breaking the kiss.

"Baby," Lorien groaned, not happy with the cruel interruption to his feasting. I kissed him on the nose before wrangling free from his grasp.

"Where's your bag Elijah? We're staying at Michael's tonight."

"I really can't Ash," he complained.

"I think you can Elijah," I responded in a mockingly similar whine. "Surely one night off won't put you too far behind?" I reasoned.

"No... I suppose not." He went back upstairs to grab his gear.

"Alone again Baby," Lorien crooned, closing the distance between us, taking me into his embrace once again.

"Where's *our* bag lover?"

"Upstairs," he grimaced, knowing he was not getting his kiss.

"I'll be right back," I said and headed for the stairs.

Bree met us at Michael's door with a huge grin on her face. "Michael has someone for you to meet," she said elusively and stood back to let us enter. A mid-twenties, handsome, blond man was standing talking to Simon at the kitchen sink, a beer in each of their hands. Simon looked up and nodded to us. The handsome stranger smiled politely and looked around the room for Michael. "Michael, the twins and Ash are here!" Bree called out and Michael instantly appeared from the back patio, smiling at us widely.

"'The time has come...' Michael started. "Glen Bailey, I'd like you to meet Lorien and Elijah Standish..." He pointed to each in turn, and it must have been *killing* him to be actually using their names for once instead of the usual reference of 'twin'. Glen and the twins met halfway across the floor and each shook Glen's hand in turn. "And this is Ashlyn Mercy, my other best friend." Glen leant down and gave me a peck on the cheek,

"I've heard a *lot* about you," he said, smiling cheekily.

"I'm sure you have." I looked at Michael and frowned, then went to him and hugged him fiercely. "It's about bloody time!" I was so happy for him and was full of questions: where they'd met, how long they'd been going out; the usual standard enquiries for a new relationship, but I didn't want to embarrass Glen by barraging Michael with them now. I would talk to Bree later if I didn't get a chance to speak with Michael privately.

Glen went to the fridge and grabbed us each a beer before Michael led us out to the patio. I couldn't stop smiling at him. "Knock it off Mercy," he told me and grinned, knowing how much I was enjoying his happiness. This sparked off even more questions for him, like whether his parents and Wally knew, what they thought… had they done 'it' yet, adding them to my growing list for later. "Does this bother any of you?" Michael asked, and made a big show of taking Glen's hand and putting it on his thigh, covering it with his own. It didn't worry me, and the twins laughed loudly.

"We grew up in Sydney guys, it's nothing we haven't seen before," Elijah said. "And I assume Ash has told you at some stage about our breakfasts there?" Elijah looked at me and I shook my head. I hadn't divulged the fact they'd been propositioned on several occasions when they were younger. "Who knew you were such a great keeper of secrets!" he said and smiled at me.

"What secrets?" Simon asked, pulling Bree onto his lap. None of them were aware, not even Bree. They were all looking at me for the explanation.

"That's for the twins to tell you," I said. It wasn't up to me to be the newscaster now that they were both sitting here with us. Lorien and Elijah outlined their liaisons to the crowd, and it was met with great amusement, not only by our gay friends, but also by Simon and Bree. Simon in particular seemed to be totally entertained by it.

"What a waste," Glen laughed.

"I don't think so," I retorted and Lorien smiled at me, drawing me to him for a kiss.

"These are the gooey pair I'm guessing?" Glen asked Michael.

"Yes, and don't think you'll ever get used to it. It can be rather nauseating at times…" Michael answered. I looked around for something to throw at him and came up with nothing. "I've removed all possible missiles from the area Ash, good luck," Michael said and winked at me. I grinned back, so happy for him. It seemed he'd met someone with a similar sense of humour, and I knew I was going to love Glen. In fact, anyone that Michael chose would be someone I'd always be certain to love.

"So, you must also be the muso?" Glen asked Lorien.

"Trying to be," he answered, and they then proceeded to talk the talk. Glen was the DJ at the top Castlebrook gay nightclub, 'Snipers'.

"You'll have to come in one night," he offered.

"It's the best dance music you'll ever hear," Lorien said. Glen raised his eyebrows and smiled at him, impressed with his knowledge of this.

"Have you ever tried to get a band together?" Glen asked.

"Ah, we don't talk about that..." Michael interjected.

"It's OK Michael," Lorien told him and looked at me, placing a kiss at my temple. I nodded and smiled lovingly at him. If Glen was to be part of our little family, there was no point in keeping things from him. "We had a band in Year 12 – 'Listening at Keyholes'. Ash played violin and Eli was on bass. It was an unusual sound and we seemed well received. However, I stuffed it up and was unfaithful to Ash one night and we decided, well actually our *parents* decided, our schoolwork was suffering and we were shut down after two gigs."

"Wow, and you're still together... What you have must be pretty special," Glen said. Lorien's gaze warmed my heart and the magnets in our heads drew our lips to each other's, blocking out the rest of the world.

"It's pretty special," Elijah said. "You should try living in a room next to them." The loud laughter brought us back to the present. Lorien hugged me tightly and turned to the laughing faces with a broad grin.

"Have you thought about starting another band?" Glen asked.

"No, now I want to be a father." He smiled up at me so lovingly, his dark brown eyes liquid and full of love. I knew my blue ones reflected his tenderness.

"So, when is this majestic experience going to take place Ash?" Michael asked.

"We're trying."

"Very bloody trying, most of the time," Michael quipped.

"We are?" Lorien shrilled incredulously. I looked at Elijah who responded to my grin with a smile. He already knew about this as I'd asked him how long it would take the pill to be out of my system. We were at 'fertile city' stage. "Will you excuse us for a second," Lorien said and took my hand, leading me inside.

"You're not going to impregnate her now are you?" Michael called out as we closed the sliding door behind us, muffling their laughter.

"Baby girl, when did this happen?" He lowered me onto his lap and pressed his lips to my forehead before drawing back to look deeply into my eyes. I smiled at him shyly and dropped my face a little, unsure why I was embarrassed. Hooking his finger under my chin, he brought my face back to his, leaning in to kiss me so softly, so sweetly. "Ash," he breathed, "this is great news..."

"We're not pregnant yet," I laughed. "It will take more than the want to make it happen."

"I'd like to have a go right now," he purred. "Not that I don't want it from you morning, noon and night anyway, sexy boxers." I laughed with him.

"If we concentrate too hard it could make it more difficult to conceive so I want you to relax. OK?" He grinned at me and nodded. "I wasn't going to tell you at all, but Elijah said you should know about it before we fall."

"Why were you discussing this with Eli?" Lorien asked, a confused look on his face.

"I wanted to know how long before the pill wore off and we'd be able to conceive."

"And?"

"Now, Sweetheart."

"Right this second?"

"Yes, but can you wait until we get home?" I laughed.

"Can we go home now?"

"No." I kissed him on the nose, and he pouted at me.

It was a long and difficult evening. When Lorien wasn't trying to seduce me into another room, he was taking drinks from my hand, instructing me on the dangers of alcohol. I ended up *begging* Elijah to have a word with him, to make him realise he was being overprotective. "Sorry Ash, but I have to agree with Lori. There's no harm in your *not* drinking prior to conception."

"What if we don't get pregnant for six months? Surely no mother—in-waiting takes on this kind of ruthlessness before actually falling pregnant?"

"I'm just telling you, it won't hurt you, but it won't hurt you not to either..."

"Thanks Elijah, you've been a great help." He grinned at me, knowing he hadn't told me what I wanted to hear.

Glen excused himself at one stage and I scurried over to Michael, eager for a chance to ask him some of my brewing questions. "Come on Michael, give me all the goss!" I said. He laughed and looked at Bree who also made her way over; she was obviously waiting to hear the news too.

"We met at the club about six weeks ago and have been seeing each other since."

"So, is this *love*?" I asked in a Michael undertone, trying to embarrass him as he had done so many times to me over the years. His simple answer shocked me a little with its sincerity.

"Yes."

"Wow," Bree said, "that's great Michael!"

"Have you told your parents yet?" I asked.

"More than that, they all met him last weekend. We went out for dinner. Even Dad came."

"So why are we the last to find out?" Bree asked.

"Because *you* are the ones I love the most and I knew it wouldn't be an issue with any of you. I wanted to get the formalities out of the way so we could relax and start the beginning of our lives together." He grinned at us and took each of our hands. "I love you two, you know that?" We did.

"I'm so happy for you Michael," I said and kissed him on the cheek.

"Mum moved in with Wally three weeks ago which leaves Glen free to move in here."

"And is he?" Bree asked.

"I haven't run it by him yet, but I'm going to."

"Sweet," she said.

"I was also wondering if you and Simon were ready to take the next step. There's plenty of room here now if you were looking at finding a place together."

"We haven't really talked about it, but thanks for thinking of us Michael. I'll get back to you." I would be very surprised if Bree and Simon didn't end up moving in with Michael. They'd been together for years and they now had somewhere to go without uprooting their lives so completely. Michael, Bree and I had all grown up at each other's homes and they would be more than comfortable living here.

"Can I ask you a personal question?" I asked Michael, a little coyly. He laughed, possibly knowing what was to come. "Have you had sex yet?" I whispered.

"Yes," he said and laughed again.

"Did it hurt?"

"Did it hurt when you lost your virginity?"

"It's different though, surely?"

"Yes, it is, but I suggest you try it. It may surprise you!" I doubted it. I didn't have a prostate. I saw Michael wink and turned to see Glen was back at the door. "We're talking about anal sex," Michael told him, and I went purple. The twins and Simon burst out laughing and I slunk back to Lorien, still blushing furiously.

"Aw bashful Angel," he crooned and held me tightly. I could feel his smile against my cheek. "Do you want to give it a go sometime Baby?" he asked, not all that quietly. I surveyed the smiling faces, waiting expectantly on my answer.

"Not right this second, but thanks for asking," was all I could respond. It was enough for them to have a fit of the giggles regardless. I looked at Lorien and narrowed my eyes, knowing he had done this deliberately to stir me. He loved it when I was flustered. I was sure it turned him on; everything turned him on. "It's impossible for me to get pregnant if you aren't firing into the right orifice you know," I whispered through clenched teeth. His response was a broad grin, and he lowered my face down to his, kissing me deeply. One of them obviously counted them in, as after a few seconds they called in unison,

"Gooey!" and Lorien drew back, smiling at me widely. *I love you*, he mouthed to me.

"Gooey!" they all called again, laughing loudly, having caught the interaction. I didn't care though. I leant down to kiss him again, confirming that I loved him too.

After dinner, Simon approached me with a smart-arse grin plastered all over his face. "So where are you two sleeping tonight?" he asked casually.

"Why?" I asked.

"I want a front row seat." He flashed his teeth at me, and his eyes slid past my vision, looking at Lorien who I now assumed was standing behind me, feeling his arms slip around my waist. Simon's grin broadened and I turned quickly to see what reaction Lorien had on his face.

"Don't even think about it Lorien!" I warned.

"What? I didn't say a word!"

"You didn't have to."

"I brought our own sheets," he whispered into my ear, his hands playing across my stomach as his lips grazed up the side of my neck to my ear. He sighed breathily. It was going to be hard work to keep away from him tonight...

We ended up sleeping on the lounge room floor as we had done so many years ago when I was still with Elijah. The knowledge of this was yet another factor I considered in my pursuit *not* to conceive tonight. Bree and Simon were on the other side of the room, as was Elijah. Michael was upstairs in his room with Glen.

At some wee hour of the morning, I woke to Lorien whispering in my ear. "Baby, are you awake?"

"No," I grumbled. He'd been lying behind me and now rolled me to face him. His soft lips found mine and his hands worked into my hair. His throaty moans stirred me immediately and my vocabulary shortened extensively; the word 'no' disappearing altogether. I was weak and I wanted him just as much, but not here, not in front of everyone. "Lorien, I can't do this here," I whispered, his mouth now working its way down my throat. It had a date with the hand holding my pyjama top out of the way, apparently.

"It's OK Baby, we don't have to...," he murmured, his hands lightly pressing my breasts together, his tongue lazing across my nipples.

"But I thought..."

"Like I need an excuse to make love to you." He stopped his tormenting and sat up, looking into my eyes through the half-light of the night.

"I want to..."

"Hmmm!" he purred and leant down to kiss me again, stoking the fires into the inferno that would then have to burn out of control. Nothing would extinguish it.

"But not here..."

He was making it hard for me to stop him as his hand worked past the elastic of my pyjama bottoms. His fingers aligned themselves to my vertical heat, teasing and circling against me gently whilst his mouth fed on mine. For several moments, all that could be heard was our coarse breathing, slowly rising and escalating, working into hushed moans. Lowering himself down my body, he caught the sides of my PJ bottoms with his movement, and ensuring we were covered, flitted under the covers so he was solely a mass outlined beneath them. I heard someone stirring and it wasn't me.

The figure sat up and whispered angrily, "Lorien!" It was Elijah. I froze but Lorien was unconcerned, and I drew his head from between my thighs. This was *way* too public.

"Good on you Elijah," Simon muttered from the corner. He'd obviously been awake too and had not intended to interrupt our foreplay.

"You're such a voyeur Simon!" I whispered harshly.

We were now all stirring downstairs, some of us more than others, with the exception of Bree. It would take World War III to raise her from sleep. Lorien didn't come out from under the covers; however, he had stopped working his lips and tongue against me. No one spoke, no one knew what to say to each other in the pre-dawn, but no one was going back to sleep either. Without moving his body, Lorien nuzzled back towards me, slyly working his fingertips against me. He couldn't care less about the early morning rabblers. I however did. "Come out from under there," I ordered in a whisper.

"Will you guys hold it down, I'm trying to sleep here," Lorien said and laughed. Simon joined him and now we were all *wide*-awake.

I made sure my clothes were properly adjusted then took great delight in whipping the covers from both Lorien and myself. "Hey Baby!" he called, rolling onto his stomach to disclose his obvious erection. Not that anyone could see it in the near dark. But, he knew it was there and he knew that they all knew what we'd been up to.

"I'm making tea. Anyone?" I asked, sliding out of bed.

"I may as well go back to sleep," Simon muttered. Elijah was silent. "What time is it anyway?" I checked the clock on my phone,

"Nearly 4.00 am," I told him.

"I'm definitely going back to sleep."

Lorien had joined me in the kitchen and looked at me with his eyebrows raised, coming to me and taking me in his arms. I kissed him until the kettle boiled and then pulled away, smiling up at him slightly. Now was the time to find another location... "Want me to turn on the washing machine?" he suggested playfully, and I laughed quietly before kissing him.

"No."

"How about the vacuum cleaner?" I had to stifle the laugh that wanted to bubble from me. "Are you really making tea?" he complained. I nodded and leant back against his chest as his hands found their way into my PJ bottoms again. "Why Baby? You don't feel dry enough to need tea..." he chuckled, starting to stroke me gently, the tea now forgotten. "Where can we go?" he whispered urgently into my ear, his hot breath sending a lick of electricity through my body. Right here would do!

I turned to him and we kissed deeply, writhing our hips against each other. My hands worked through his hair, holding our faces together. "Ash," he sighed, running his warm hands down my back and fitting them to the curves of my rear, pulling me tightly against him. "Where can we go?" He moaned slightly as I worked my tongue against his earlobe, drawing it lightly into my mouth.

"Outside…"

He leered down at me and took my hand, dragging me through the laundry to the back door. He led me all the way to the top entertainment deck and pulled his boxers off before sitting on one of the padded chairs. "Climb aboard Baby," he encouraged, patting his thighs. I hooked my thumbs into my PJ bottoms, ready to remove them when he interrupted me. "Let me help you with those," he offered, drawing my pyjama bottoms down my legs, which I stepped out of as they hit the ground. "Hmmm," he purred, his face pressed into my stomach. He slowly slid his hands up my legs, savouring the curves before pulling me forward to straddle him.

"I love you Lorien," I exhaled, my breath now racing toward a pant as he filled me so completely.

"Not as much as I love you," he whispered, raising my arms to remove my pyjama top, lowering me backwards slightly so he could tease at my nipples with his tongue.

We rocked back and forth, for what seemed like an hour. His control was always reined in, although he could go off like a firecracker when time was of the essence. The delicious grind was taking its toll on me however, and a few minutes later, I leant to his ear and whispered, "I'm ready Baby." No sooner were the words out of my mouth than my orgasm hit. Lorien quickened his pace and shortly joined me in our shared intensity, trying to stifle our collective groans. He pulled me against him tightly and laid his head to my chest, his breathing still harried, and his hot breath coursed across my nipple. His mischievous tongue darted out to torment me before he drew back and looked up, grinning.

"Orgasm?" he smiled cheekily, his hands running across my back in a slow caress.

"Thanks, already had one." He chuckled,

"Want another?" and slid his palm between us, teasing against my still straddled pose. I sealed my mouth against his as he worked me into the next waves of desire.

Ten days later, I got my period.

The Question

"Every question I've ever asked you
Was answered honestly
But this one's worth a million
And will effect eternity."

L Standish, 'Sleep on it'

WE WERE BOTH DISAPPOINTED. We were ready to get pregnant and have this baby as soon as possible. This baby would certainly be a lucky child when he or she arrived. Lorien and I were discussing this in the kitchen after one of our 'menstrual cycle shower sex' liaisons, and his comment stunned me. "I'm sort of glad in a way..."

"Are you having second thoughts?" I asked, a little worried that he might be.

"No, nothing like that." He held me tightly with one arm around my waist and the other around my shoulders. Locked to him, he eased his hand softly into my hair. His silence was concerning me. There was something wrong, as the grip he had on me also seemed to confirm.

"Lorien?" I drew back and he smiled down at me, a serene smile, a loving smile... Nothing was wrong? He dropped to one knee... *Oh my God, he's going to propose*! I thought, seconds before he opened his mouth. He gazed up at me and took my hands in his.

"You look terrified, are you OK?" he asked. This was not the question I was expecting, and I laughed, nodding my head.

"I'm fine. I thought you were going to ask me to marry you." I felt like a dill, and laughed again, shaking my head.

"Will you marry me Ashlyn Diane Mercy?"

He lifted his eyes slowly to meet mine; all humour now drained from them. I watched him reach into his pocket and pull out a small satin covered box, which he opened to reveal a classic-cut diamond ring. I was speechless and just stood there looking at him, looking at the ring, looking back to him. "Well?" he smiled, "Do I get an answer?"

"Yes Lorien, of course I'll marry you!" He slipped the ring onto my engagement finger and I pulled my hand back to get the full view of it twinkling under the incandescent lights. "It's so beautiful Sweetheart, I love it."

"I was going to ask you then let you pick your own..."

"No, this is perfect. I would rather you chose it; it means more this way..." I couldn't stop looking at it and I twirled around in excitement. I was *engaged* if you could believe that!

When I regained my senses, Lorien was leaning against the island bench, watching me with amusement. I blushed as he approached and took me into his arms, kissing me intensely as he carried me up the stairs to our room to solidify our agreement.

We planned to tell his family during dinner that evening and were taken aback when Cara and Nick beat us to the punch with their news. "Well family. Do you think you'll be able to get along by yourselves for twelve months or so?" Nick asked. The twins looked at each other in confusion, their eyebrows slightly drawn. I felt Lorien squeeze my left hand under the table, the hand sporting the engagement ring.

"What's happening?" Lorien asked.

"Your mother is taking long service leave and I'm taking twelve months off too. We're going to travel around Australia, maybe going a little further if we're so inclined." Nick looked at Cara and she beamed at him, they were obviously looking forward to this very much.

"When?" Elijah asked.

"In about six weeks when your mother breaks at the end of term for Easter. We'll be heading off shortly thereafter. Are you all OK with this?" It warmed me no end that Nick's gaze not only met his sons, but mine also, considering me in the response. I smiled at him, which he returned. They were my second family now, unaware how shortly this would actually become fact.

"Can Ash and I move into your room?" Lorien asked.

"Lorien!" I chastised and he grinned broadly at his parents, who laughed in response.

"We can talk about that later," Cara said and reached over to tousle his hair. He still kept it long; I didn't give him any other option.

"Well, it's certainly a surprise," Elijah said, "but good on you. Make sure you keep in touch."

"Of course we will," Nick said and reached across the table to take his wife's hand in his.

"Don't bring home another set of twins with you," Lorien said, laughing.

"I think we're a little past that son," Nick said.

"Rubbish," Lorien told him and winked at his father. His mother seemed to blush a little but said nothing. He pulled me to him closely, saying, "We have some news too…" Nick and Cara smiled at me, possibly guessing what Lorien was about to tell them. Elijah was grinning, thinking he knew what this news was, but he was wrong. Lorien looked at me as he addressed his family, "I've asked Ashlyn to marry me, and she said yes." He leant in to kiss me briefly.

"Welcome to the family," Cara said, coming over to give us both a hug.

"Come to papa," Nick said, and I went to him. The bear hug from my soon to be father-in-law nearly cracked my ribs. "What wonderful news kids, you've made my day." He clapped Lorien on the shoulder as I went to hug the now standing Elijah, his arms open to me.

"Can I start calling you sis?" he asked, and I laughed. We all took our seats again and I showed them the ring.

"It's beautiful Ashlyn," Cara commented, holding my hand in hers to admire it properly. "You have good taste Lori," she told her second-born.

"But wait, there's more," Lorien added in his best infomercial presenter voice.

"You get a set of steak knives for an additional ninety-nine cents?" Nick asked and we all laughed.

"No, we're trying for a baby." The laughter stopped.

"Oh, my baby boy!" Cara cried and came to take Lorien in her arms, tears streaming down her face. This wasn't the reaction I was expecting. "You're going to make me a grandmother!" I stood as she came to me, taking me in her arms too, hugging me fiercely as Nick took Lorien into his.

"That's great son," he mumbled, wiping his damp eyes with the back of his hand.

When we'd been released, we all took our seats once again, giving his parents a little time to refocus their emotions before continuing with the conversation. Lorien smiled warmly at me and drew me back to his side.

"When is all of this to take place?" Cara asked.

"We haven't told my parents yet," I told her. "We'd better do that tomorrow," I said to Lorien. "Mum will want to start making plans no doubt."

"Whatever you want Ash, it's your day," he said.

"No Lorien, it's *our* day," I smiled at him. He kissed me lightly and then asked his parents about dates, considering their upcoming travel plans.

"Don't worry about that son," Nick told him. "We'll be back for the wedding if we're already on the road."

"And for the birth," Cara added and patted my hand warmly. "What will your parent's reaction be to this Ashlyn?"

"They were married young and had me young so I'm not sure what they'll think initially. They knew Lorien and I were likely to travel this road sooner or later..."

"You seem a little worried Ashlyn," Cara said, looking concerned.

"No, not really. I know they'll be happy, if not a little surprised at first."

"From what I know of Anna and Dom, I'm sure they'll be delighted," she offered. I hoped so. We would find out tomorrow.

I was nervous as we drove home to Warden the next day, fiddling with my engagement ring and twisting it roughly around and around my finger. "Do you want to take it off until we tell them?" Lorien asked.

"Oh no, Lorien," I smiled at him. "I'm thinking we might just mention our engagement today though and leave the baby for another occasion, like when we're pregnant..."

"If that's what you want Ash, but do you think they'll be that upset over it?"

"I really don't know. I suppose I can gauge their reaction to the first download of news and see where it takes us. Mum has always talked about how young they were when they had me, and I know she wanted me to have so much more before I became a mother."

"Do you?"

"No, I want to have a family, and as soon as possible." He smiled at me sweetly and took my hand. I knew we agreed on this.

"I'll let you lead OK?"

"OK."

They knew we were coming for a visit and opened the door before we were even out of the car. "We miss you Honey," Dad said and hugged me.

"I miss you two, too," I told him and then hugged Mum to me. Lorien also got one. No sense beating around the bush. "We have some news," I told them.

"Come inside first," Dad said, and we took a seat on the sofa. They looked at me expectantly and I glanced nervously at Lorien. He smiled with his dark eyes full of so much love, and drew his arm around me, taking my left hand in his. I opened my mouth to speak, and Mum beat me to it.

"Oh my God!" she shrilled when she saw the ring. "You're engaged?" I smiled at her, not knowing where this was going. "My baby girl is getting married!" she said and came to hug us both.

"Congratulations kids, Lorien, we couldn't be happier," Dad said as Lorien rose to shake his hand, ending in a male back-clapping embrace.

"I'm glad you're OK with this," I said, hugging him.

"Why wouldn't we be?" Dad asked.

"I was a little worried about it since you two always said you were too young when you got married."

"You're nearly twenty-three Ashlyn. We knew you'd be telling us this news at some stage," he answered.

"You're not pregnant, are you?" Mum asked, her face betraying the shock that this would imbue if it were true. I looked at Lorien before answering, noting that we were *not* going to be discussing this with them today. I also felt relief in knowing I wasn't about to lie to them.

"No."

"Whew!" she exhaled, "So when's the big day?"

"We haven't set a date yet Anna. We wanted to tell you both and Mum and Dad before we started making any plans. Spring maybe...?" I smiled and nodded. Spring would be perfect.

"Have you told your parents?" Mum asked.

"Last night," Lorien said.

"I must ring Cara immediately," she said and went to the phone.

"Looks like the hens will be cackling it up," Dad laughed. "Are you staying tonight?"

"We can," I told him.

"I think your mother would like that, and we can have a toast!" he said.

"Dad, it's 11.00 am."

"It's a special occasion." He went to the fridge and pulled out a bottle of wine. "I think we need something more special than this. I'll be right back." I smiled at Lorien.

"We're not going to mention the baby, I'm thinking," he whispered.

"No." I shook my head at him and leant in to kiss him, breaking apart only when I heard Mum get off the phone.

"Where's your father?"

"I think he's gone to the bottle shop, he wants to make a toast." She smiled at me.

"We have a lot to discuss kids."

By the time we went to bed that night, Mum was ready to kill me. I had very little in the way of input to her many questions and the frustration of my not being able to answer her adroitly was mounting. "At the very least Ashlyn, you need to set a date," she complained.

"Mum, we've only been engaged for twenty-four hours. Lorien and I need to work out a few things before we can go booking a caterer. We'll talk it over tonight and get back to you in the morning with what we've decided so far." She smiled at me wanly and let it go for now. However, I noticed that Dad cooked dinner, leaving her free to let her fingers do the walking through the trusty Yellow Pages online.

Dad insisted we be treated like true guests and refused to let us help clean up after dinner, so, Lorien and I sat on the sofa watching a current affairs programme whilst Mum and Dad tackled the kitchen. "What was that?" Lorien said startled, sitting up.

"What?" I asked, listening for a sound. When I turned to face him, he was grinning at me and leant down to kiss me, turning my stewing thoughts solely back to him.

"Must have been my imagination," he mumbled through the kiss and I realised he'd heard nothing. I started to giggle. "It's hard to kiss you when you're laughing Baby girl," he mumbled again, making me laugh even harder.

"I'm sorry Lorien, I'm OK now." As his lips found mine again, I tried to stop them from curling back into a smile. The more I fought it, the less successful I was and Lorien finally drew back with a sigh. "It's your fault," I told him. "No point in getting cranky with me."

"I didn't think you'd find it quite so hilarious," he said, moving to lie across the length of the sofa with his head on my lap. He gazed up at me and I ran my hands through his soft curls; a warm smile was my reward. He brought his hand to the back of my head and lowered me to him, attempting another kiss.

I didn't laugh this time, and found myself running my hand over his chest and down his stomach, my other hand cradled under his neck. When my fingers started to trace his contours through his shorts, he hissed, "Ashlyn! Your parents are three metres away!" I smiled down at him as I drew back, having left him in a rather compromising position and he sat up abruptly, trying to hide his straining alter ego. I laughed again. I couldn't help it. "You're certainly in a humorous mood this evening Baby," he said and pulled me onto his lap. "How about I stoke your fires up and see how you feel about it?" He brushed his fingers across my breast, lightly rolling my nipple between his thumb and forefinger. "Hmmm? How does that feel under your parent's close proximity?"

"Wonderful," I sighed and kissed him properly.

His busy fingers were not assisting in deflating him, if anything the solid silver beneath me was growing at an alarming rate. "Still like you're sixteen," I heard Dad say. Lorien snatched his hand away and I looked up. Dad had a banana split in each hand, obviously meant for us. I felt Lorien stiffen under me and not in the usual sense of the word; he was already in that situation. His entire body flexed with the concern of being caught... in my parent's home, with me on his lap, with him sporting a full-blown erection.

"Should we sit at the table?" I asked lightly, alluding to getting up. Lorien held my hips to him tightly, solidifying the lock he had around my waist. He did not intend on letting me up. I smiled demurely at him and shifted again; he flexed again - eyes wide and his brow drawn. My smile broke into a grin and I laughed. "Or maybe we'll just eat them here?" Lorien's hand shot out to take the dessert from my father before any further conversation could take place.

"Eat them there Honey, no need to move." Dad walked back into the kitchen.

"Do you want coffee?" Mum called out; we both did. Well I did, Lorien may have just wanted to keep them in the kitchen for a while longer. I sat there poking the ice cream into my mouth, smiling through the spoonfuls as I stared intently at the TV. He put his mouth directly to my ear and whispered,

"You are in *so* much trouble!" I ignored him and continued to eat.

"Hmmm, this is good," I said. He chuckled lowly and started to make a dent in his own.

We made our excuses around 10.30 pm and went to bed. We'd had a great day with my parents, regardless of Mum's one-track mind, and I was glad we had decided to stay the night. When I came out of the bathroom Lorien was already stripped off and in bed waiting for me, patting the space next to him and grinning cheekily. The grin faded. He was not expecting me to start fiddling around in my cupboard, going through the rest of my stuff that I hadn't moved into his room.

"What are you *doing* Baby?" he groaned, rolling onto his side.

"I should really sort through this whilst I'm here and throw away what I haven't needed so far. It's mostly old school papers and junk. It won't take me long." I was right; I was at it for about five seconds before I felt his arms around me, dragging me away as he closed the cupboard door with his foot.

"Not tonight."

"But…"

"You can do it in the morning." I sighed in defeat and leant back against his chest, his hands rippling lightly across my stomach, dipping into my PJ bottoms and slowly working them down. He eased between my thighs and purred softly into my ear, bringing me in line with his ideals. "That's better," he whispered, noting my response to him was now ready, willing and able. I turned in his arms to kiss him, and we locked at the mouth as he manoeuvred me back to the bed. Alas, it was not meant to be…

As soon as the dormant springs started to squeak in protest at being woken from their slumber, I found myself laughing again. Lorien was not as amused as I. We initially tried it on each remote area of the bed, then with him sitting on its very edge and me straddling him and finally, me lying across the bed with him kneeling on the floor. Those springs were like a tattle-tailing little sibling, wanting to alert my parents that the big sister was fooling around in her bedroom, alone with a boy. It was pure comedy and finally Lorien exhaled deeply, flumping back onto the bed, acceptant.

I sat on its edge, putting my pyjamas back on, and started to bounce up and down, making them squeal again. I grinned at him as he looked at me in horror, "What are you doing Ash?"

"Making my parents think we're having sex."

"Why? That's the reason we aren't currently having sex! Please Baby, this is really frustrating, and you aren't helping."

"Aw, poor Lorien," I leant over and kissed him, stopping the sound effects. I knew how I could make it up to him and without the need to squeak. I bustled under the covers and tended to his hurt ego personally.

Laying in his arms sometime later, a smile back on his face, he surprised me by saying, "I'm going to talk to Eli tomorrow."

"And this is relevant to what I just did... how?" He chuckled and dropped a kiss to my forehead, pulling me tightly against him.

"I've been reading up on falling pregnant and I want to run a few things by him."

"OK, care to tell me what they are?"

"Just the basics. Is there anything you want to ask him?"

"How it works."

"How it works?" he asked in sincere curiosity.

"How to get pregnant."

"How to get *pregnant*?"

"You know, how conception happens."

"How *conception* happens?" he asked in disbelief.

"Stop repeating everything I say, it's really annoying!" I was smiling widely when he pulled back to look at me, not sure whether my mood was amusement or flippancy. He shook his head lightly when he realised I was teasing him again.

"You're a regular laugh-riot today Baby," he chuckled and drew me back to him.

"It would be pretty funny asking him about the birds and the bees then hearing him explain it."

"That it would," he laughed.

"We're supposed to be talking about the wedding," I sighed.

"You're a little reluctant, aren't you?"

"Only with my mother. She'll want to turn this into a three-ring circus and that's not the type of wedding I want."

"We don't have to do anything you don't want to."

"You try telling her that. I'm going to hold her at arm's length for as long as I can though."

"Shouldn't we at least decide on a date?" Lorien sat up and I moved up with him, "Give her a little something to cling to?"

"I like what I'm clinging to right now," I told him and snuggled into his side further, tracing my fingers lightly over his pecs.

"You'll get no complaints from me," he said, motioning down to his newfound hardness. I laughed quietly,

"This must be driving you crazy."

"Not really, I think we have too much sex."

"What?" I asked, sitting fully up next to him. "What on earth does that mean?"

"Apparently when you're trying to conceive, you should only make love every other day. We make love roughly three to six times over that period; I think we're having too much sex."

"It's not always rough," I teased.

"Roughly as in approximately, not forcefully, you little minx," he laughed, lying back down on the bed.

"Now I really want to talk to Elijah. It sounds ridiculous. Where did you come by that information?"

"I read it."

"In a journal published in 1975?" He smiled at me and went to draw me down against him. I sat back up. "I don't think I can do it Lorien."

"What, cut back to once every second day?"

"Exactly. It's like living in Atlantis and then finding out you've been evicted and can only take a shower every two days in comparison. I don't want to leave my underwater Eden."

"I love you," he chuckled. I wanted him to love me right now.

"Let's not make any snap decisions until we talk to Elijah OK?"

"Alright Baby. Now what about a date?" I sighed,

"I thought I had slipped that past you."

"Come on Ash, we need to have something to give to your mother tomorrow."

"How about the thirty-eighth of October?"

"Ashlyn," he admonished, and I tried again.

"What's your lucky number?'

"'My lucky number's one'," he said laughing. When I questioned his mirth, he explained it was an old song from the 70s; I should have known.

"Mine's six, so the first month we come across with a Saturday on either of those dates will *be* the date." He laughed but realised it was as good an answer as any. "But it has to be more than three months away. Mum will flip otherwise."

"OK, we'll check a calendar in the morning before we speak to her."

"Pass me my phone," I told him and switched on the bedside lamp. I opened the calendar app and scrolled through the months. "And the lucky date will be… the first of August." I started to laugh again and had to adjust the volume. Lorien had no idea what tickled me so greatly about this date and I explained this was also the annual horse's birthday.

"I still don't get it Ash," he said but his expression changed when I started to glide my hand over him.

"Well my little thoroughbred," I teased, "you are rather equine in some ways."

"And you're rather asinine," he laughed. "Want to saddle up Ma'am?"

"Hmmm," I purred and rolled on top of him.

Through the act of simply removing my clothes, the bed reminded us again of its presence. "Damn it," Lorien whispered, "I forgot about that!" I grabbed a pillow and spread out on the floor.

"Come to me Phar Lap," I crooned, and he was beside me immediately; shortly thereafter, was galloping for first place in the Cup. It was an excellent victory for both the horse and the jockey.

We sought out Elijah the second we got home but had to wait for three long hours before he returned from Uni. We were both rather agitated by the time he arrived; Elijah looked tired. I was sure the last thing he wanted to do was field sex questions from his brother and me, but I had to know if what Lorien had said last night was in any way true.

We left Elijah alone for half an hour, him casting us odd looks every now and then, aware that something was going on. However, when we heard the shower stop, we could wait no longer. Lorien knocked lightly on his side of the bathroom door a few minutes later. "Yeah," he called out and we both slipped through the door. He was sitting on his bed with a towel wrapped around his waist, flipping through a textbook. "What are you two up to?" he asked with a grin on his face, closing the book. Lorien sat next to him and I took a seat in the pappadum.

"We want to ask you a few questions," Lorien told him.

"About what?"

"Pregnancy."

"Before, during or after?"

"Before."

"No."

"Why not?" Lorien asked. "You're my brother and I trust you more than any website or medical journal."

"Who do you think writes the medical journals Lori?" he asked, running a hand over his face.

"But I want to ask *you*."

"You do realise that this could be really difficult? I don't want to know what you two get up to."

"How about if we pose the questions to you in a simple yes or no answer format?"

"OK, give them to me..." he sighed and rolled his eyes, waiting.

"Ash," Lorien prompted, and I launched into my only question.

"Can you have too much sex?" Elijah looked at me oddly before saying,

"What do you mean by *too* much sex?" I nodded at Lorien to continue; I did not intend to explain this any further to him. Lorien picked up where I left off but was a lot more open with the information than I certainly would have been.

"On average we have sex about twice a day and I read..."

"Hold it," Elijah interrupted him. "This is in the area of 'I don't want to know', OK?"

"Let me try again. I read you should only have sex once every two days, is this correct."

"No."

"So, it doesn't matter how much sex you have when you're trying to conceive, it doesn't 'dilute' the potency?" Elijah laughed, then answered,

"No," *Whew,* I thought, that was a relief to know. "Especially when we're talking about young healthy adults."

"OK, is there any substance to the boxers versus briefs philosophy?"

"No."

"Good. See this isn't too hard." Elijah grimaced at him. "Now, ovulation takes place fourteen days prior to Ash's period starting?"

"Yes."

"And conception around this period is most prominent...?"

"That's not a yes or no answer," Elijah reminded him.

"Come on Eli," Lorien moaned.

"Several days leading up to it," he sighed. "But if you're having as much sex as you said, all that is irrelevant. You'll be copulating when Ash is fertile anyway."

Lorien and I looked at each other and burst out laughing at his use of the word copulating. It took us back to when my mother gave me the birth control speech in front of Lorien. Instead of copulating however, her word de jour was 'intercourse', a word we still used playfully from time to time. It had tickled us so, and we now had another to add to our list. "OK, that's it, no more." Lorien tried to apologise but it didn't sound all that sincere with a burst of laughter emanating from his mouth during his request for forgiveness. "Seriously Lorien, out!" Elijah ordered. "Sorry Ash," he smiled at me.

I grabbed the still-laughing Lorien's hand to drag him off the bed, but he struggled against me. The hilarity I had found last night now seemed to be instilled in him. I leant to his ear and whispered, "I want you Baby," and he jumped up immediately, throwing me over his shoulder to march out of the room. "Sorry!" I called, holding myself upwards with my hands across the small of Lorien's back, trying to look Elijah in the eye. He just shook his head at me and smiled as we faded into the bathroom.

The Henhouse

"When the chicks take over the henhouse,
The rooster ends up in trouble, always in trouble...."

L Standish, 'Battle of the Sexes'

THIS WHOLE WEDDING THING was starting to drive me crazy. Mum was driving me crazy. Cara had obviously picked up on my mood whenever the wedding was mentioned lately, so chose to keep as many comments as possible, to herself. I didn't ask for her input and she didn't offer it anymore. I felt terrible about this though; it was her son's wedding too. I discussed it with Lorien that night in bed to see what he thought of it, to see what kind of bitch he thought I was becoming. His reaction stunned me greatly, he laughed. "Mum will be as involved as *you* want her to be. You have to remember, she doesn't have a daughter."

"But she was someone's daughter, and by *not* having a daughter, this may mean more to her than you know."

"Don't stress over it Ash, really. She would have mentioned something to me if not someone else if it was a problem..." I chewed his words over, finally swallowing them and feeling better. I turned to him and noticed his slight smile.

"What?"

"Do you need to use the bathroom?" he asked, and I laughed.

"I suppose so. I always seem to need to go lately. Why? Do you have a three-hour bout in store for me?"

"Come with me first..."

He took my hand and led me into the bathroom. What on earth was he doing? It's not like I hadn't used the toilet in front of him over our many years, but he'd never *purposefully* brought me to the bathroom when I needed to go.

He sat me down on the closed toilet seat and leant against the cabinet, his legs crossed at the ankle, his hands lightly holding the vanity. He smiled at me again. "What?" I asked, not getting where he was going with this.

"Feeling better?" he asked. I looked at him curiously. I *had* been a little off-colour for the past few days but didn't really think too much of it. It was very mild passing nausea.

"I suppose so," I answered again and looked at him quizzically.

"Now for the sake of not wanting to get my head bitten off, but I have to mention... you've been having a lot of mood swings the past few days, and your breasts are a little tender." I scowled at him.

"My stupid period is due again." I crossed my arms in front of me in a huff and turned my anger towards the blank tiled floor. I heard him open one of the cabinet drawers and I looked up to see what he had taken from it.

"You're overdue Ash. I think you might be pregnant." He had a home pregnancy test in his hands, but it clattered to the ground shortly after as I launched myself into his arms.

"Do you think so? Aren't these symptoms a little premature?" He was always *so* aware of my cycles, moreso since we'd decided to become pregnant. He nodded and leant in to kiss me softly.

"I really do think so Mummy," he murmured into my hair. "There's nothing set in stone when it comes to the individual mother." I drew back from him and looked to the door on Elijah's side of the bathroom. "I don't think we need him for this Ash, just like he wasn't needed for the conception," he chuckled into my ear.

"But aren't we supposed to use the first urine of the day for the best results? I just wanted to ask him..."

"You can wait until morning - you don't have to do it now, but it is a multi-pack," he said, picking it up off the floor to show me.

"I want to do it now!" My eyes flashed, excited. Waiting for another several hours was too much to bear.

"Well then, use it. You can try again in the morning if necessary." He kissed me once more and went to leave me with my privacy. I stopped him.

"I don't mind if you stay." I didn't want him to leave.

"I'll stay then," he smiled at me.

He read the packaging and the enclosed literature whilst I did my business and then we waited, so breathlessly, for the results to show. "Looks like two lines to me," Lorien said finally. The line in the test window couldn't be more obvious if it had been drawn in ink.

"We're pregnant," I gushed and threw him an elated smile. He smiled back and as I thought he was reaching to take me in his arms, was surprised to see him knocking on Elijah's bathroom door.

The door slid open, and Elijah looked at his twin curiously. I thrust the test stick at him, and his curiosity turned into a broad grin. "Well, looks like it might finally be congratulations to you both." He hugged his brother and clapped him on the back, then swooped down to plant a kiss on my cheek, hugging me lightly. What he'd said confused me though.

"What do you mean by 'might' Elijah?"

"There are a lot of variables Ash," he explained. "You need to get it confirmed by a doctor."

"Can't you do it?"

"Not legally, no."

"Can't you do it?" I asked again.

"I don't have a lab at home Ash. You may as well go and see Dr Wood when you can get in, and it makes more sense." He smiled at me, knowing how eager both Lorien and I were to have this confirmed. "Are you going to tell Mum and Dad?" he asked.

"No, not yet. It will be our secret for the moment, OK?" Lorien answered.

"What about my parents?" I asked. "Mum will want to know why I'm making an appointment." Mum worked as the receptionist at my local doctor's surgery. There was no *way* we were going to get this past her.

"Dr Wood can't divulge patient information," Elijah told me.

"I know that, but she'll *smell* it on me, trust me." The twins laughed and Lorien drew his arms around me from behind, cradling me to him.

"Come on, Mrs up-the-duff, let's go to bed. We can worry about that in the morning." Lorien said.

"You can only get her *so* pregnant you know," Elijah teased. I smiled at him as Lorien backed me out of the door, sliding it closed behind us. His eyes were glinting at me in the darkness of the room; a glint that I knew would contain an intense amount of smouldering if I'd been able to see into them more clearly.

The second Lorien and I walked into Dr Wood's surgery Mum was around the reception desk in a flash, a load of magazines and papers in her arms. "Hi kids," she chirped and handed the pile to me before giving us both a kiss.

"What's all this Mum?" I asked laughing, and then frowned when I saw the cover of the top magazine was 'Bride Guide Worldwide'. A quick flick through the bundle confirmed that it was all relevant to weddings: dresses, caterers, florists, venues, cake decorators... arrrghhh!

"Now this one..." she said, pulling at a magazine from mid-pile. When it started to teeter, Lorien took the offending top section from me to allow her to take it with ease, "...shows you all the best places to hire luxury cars. And *this* one," she started re-sorting through the armful I had left, "lists all the photographers in the area and their prices."

"Mum, put the brakes on." I looked around and a few of the waiting patients were smiling at us bemusedly. Lorien interrupted in his usual smooth tact,

"We'll have a good look through these when we get home Anna, thanks. We appreciate your effort in making this easier for us."

"Thank you Lorien, it's good to see *one* of you is taking this seriously. I don't know Ashlyn. You just seem to be elsewhere at the moment." I certainly was, and when Dr Wood poked his head around the door to call me, I was hoping it was about to be officially confirmed.

"What can I do for you today Ashlyn?" Dr Wood asked.

"I want you to test me for pregnancy Doctor," I said a little shyly. Lorien took my hand, noting my difficulty, understanding that this man had been my family physician for over ten years.

"I see, and what makes you think you're pregnant?" he asked, reaching for a medi-swab and needle. I assumed he was going to be taking some blood.

"I took a home pregnancy test last night and it was positive."

"She's also been having mood swings, not sleeping the best and has breast tenderness," Lorien added.

"I didn't know I wasn't sleeping."

"You've been a little restless the last few nights Ash."

"Good, good, these are all likely symptoms and the pregnancy test being positive is a pretty good guide. However, they aren't always accurate," Dr Wood told us.

"Elijah said we should come and see you to make sure," I said.

"And how is he doing at Uni?"

"Fine Sir," Lorien said. "It's his second last year and he's already been accepted at Byrong Hospital for his internship.

"Excellent. Please tell him I said hello and when he's licensed, to come and see me. I can always do with an extra pair of hands."

"We will, thanks," I said and rolled up my sleeve.

At home, I was flipping through one of the magazines at the dining room table, muttering under my breath and turning the pages so violently I was nearly tearing them from the binding. "I hate seeing you like this Ash," Lorien said, coming to sit with me, a coffee in both of his hands.

"Thanks Lorien," I said, taking the mug from him and leaning over to kiss him lightly. I sighed deeply before taking a sip, then smiled at him and rolled my eyes.

"You don't have to do this on your own, Baby girl," he said, removing the mug from my hand and putting it on the table, taking my hands in his as he shifted around so he was facing me.

"I don't want to do this at all!" I said. "Surely there's an easier way."

"There can be…"

"Like?"

"Are you happy with me taking over?"

"It's all yours lover!" I laughed. "What do I need to do?"

"Find your dress and anything else personal, like your bouquet, and get in the car when it arrives on the eighteenth of April. I'll do the rest."

"Bringing the date forward? You're game."

"If we're taking the reins on this Ash, does it really matter if we move it forward?"

"Not at all, but why so eager?"

"If you *are* pregnant you won't be showing much in another couple of weeks."

"Good point. You think of everything don't you Sweetheart?"

"I try to," he said and leant down to kiss me again.

"Have you thought about how we're going to break the news to my mother?" I mumbled through the kiss. He drew back and smiled.

"Not yet. We also need to let Mum and Dad know too. They're due to take off on their holiday this weekend. No time like the present though?" He handed me the phone and I grimaced at him as he took to the stairs, off to break the good news to his parents.

"Coward!" I shouted and he shot me a smug grin.

Lorien came back down the stairs a few minutes later, his parents in tow. I was still on the phone with Mum, and I smiled at him weakly. I hadn't spoken for a few minutes as Mum was still in persuasion mode, assuming that the decision was not yet concrete. *Do you want me to talk to her?* he mouthed, holding out his hand for the phone. I shook my head at him; there was no point. "Mum…" I tried to interrupt again, but to no avail, so I let her continue her side of the debate. I saw Cara speak to Lorien out of my earshot and was surprised to find her then in front of me, holding her hand out for the phone, her eyebrows slightly raised and a smile on her lips. She wanted to speak to my mother. "Hang on Mum, Cara wants to talk to you." I handed her the phone and joined Lorien and Nick on the sofa.

"Cara has a little more patience with your mother perhaps Ashlyn?" Nick asked with a laugh.

"Yes, a little more, definitely," I said, laughing with him. I perched myself on Lorien's lap, waiting on the outcome.

Nick stood and headed into the kitchen and Lorien asked him to pass the pile of wedding literature. "Do we have to do this now?" I asked.

"You don't have to do anything," he told me, sorting the pile into two stacks, one much larger than the other. He handed me the small one. "Flowers and dresses, that's all you have to concern yourself with. This is my pile and I have just over two weeks. I need to get a start," he said. "Well, in a few minutes," he whispered and drew me down to kiss him, which lasted until I heard Cara in front of us, discreetly clearing her throat. She sat with us on the sofa, letting us know the gist of the conversation.

"Anna's not elated as you know Ashlyn, but she has accepted it and will do what you want her to. Now, can I ask what the rush is? Obviously we were coming back for the wedding anyway, but I would like to know why you've brought the date forward by so much." I couldn't believe Lorien hadn't told her we were pregnant.

"Mainly because Mum was already driving me crazy, Cara. I'm sorry this has effected your and Nick's departure plans." Nick smiled at me as he brought in a coffee for himself and his wife.

"That's nothing to worry about. We have twelve months to get to wherever it is we're going." I looked at Lorien and nodded, giving him the privilege of informing his mother of her ensuing grandmother status.

"We're also pregnant," he told her. I couldn't help but laugh as I watched Nick take the mug back from Cara as she came at Lorien and me, hugging us both at once in our double-storey.

"How wonderful. When are you due Ashlyn?"

"We're not totally confirmed yet, but it'll be around mid-December from my calculations."

"A Christmas baby, there is no greater joy. Nick, we're going to be grandparents," she said and went to hug him. It looked funny with him hugging her back with his forearms solely; he still had the mugs in his hands.

"I know Cara, we're a blessed family." He winked at us over her shoulder.

"I haven't told my parents yet." I blurted out; worried that Mum would assume this was the reason for bringing the date forward.

"Why ever not Ashlyn?" Cara asked and I explained as best as I could, hoping she would be in agreement with me. "I understand, but I think you're under-estimating your mother, Ashlyn. But it's your decision." I was glad that we'd discussed it with Lorien's parents at least.

Lying in bed later that night, recovering from our celebratory sexual romp, Lorien brought the wedding back to the front of my mind. "I have to ask you some questions Ash," he said when I started to complain. "I need to know a few things, like who I have to invite from your side of the family."

"Mum and Dad," was my short response.

"That's it?" he asked.

"Well, I'll be there too," I smiled and kissed him again.

"You'd better be, woman!" he said. "But there's no one else, no one that would be offended if they weren't invited?"

"Sweetheart, I'll be happy with your and my immediate families and our closest friends."

"OK, and what…"

"No more questions Lorien, not tonight."

"I have one more and then I'll ask you no more questions, period."

"Alright then, shoot."

"Do you have any preference as to the reception, wedding cars, catering or photographer?"

"That's four questions." He just smiled at me.

"No, no input, it's all up to you. Whatever you decide is OK with me."

"Fine then, no further questions, your Honour." I laughed, I kissed him, we made love again.

The Unexpected Venue

"So take my hand and come with me, Baby.
The promises I make, I won't break,
You're everything to me."

L Standish, 'There's Only Two'

THE LATEST LEXUS pulled into my parent's driveway at 10.15 am on Saturday, the eighteenth of April, decked out in bridal ribbons. It was sleek and stylish and just the thing needed without overdue flashiness. My dress was a white satin, knee length, empire-sweetheart style and my mother's tiara was threaded into my swept-up curls. I had no bouquet - my mother was to lead me down the aisle on my other arm instead. I thought this was the least I could do to make it up to her, and she was delighted in being a dual escort with my father. I also had no veil.

My dress was new, the tiara old and borrowed, and I wore Cyndi's blue garter that Lorien had caught at her and Frankie's wedding, which covered the pre-requisites. I was ready to get married and I couldn't wait to see Lorien, wherever this car was going to take me. "Haven't you forgotten something?" Mum reminded me. She had Lorien's wedding ring in her hand and passed it to me, smiling. I slipped it onto my index finger to keep it safe. This would normally be the best man's job, which Elijah was, but Lorien had decided to leave the formal pillow play out of the ceremony and be responsible for each other's rings. I also had no bridesmaid to remind me; Elijah formed the only other part of our small bridal party.

I'd been having a difficult time in choosing between Michael and Bree to be my significant other, and not wanting to increase the bridal party size to four, decided to not have a bridesmaid at all. They were both acceptant of this fact and understood where I was coming from. I was glad, as I didn't want to hurt either of their feelings.

As I stepped from the car, Dad took my hand and I looked down the grassy area toward Glassread baths. A red carpet had been laid in advance, forming an aisle from the car door to the beginning of the wooden platform of the baths. At the far end, Lorien was waiting for me, and I found myself wanting to run to him.

He was wearing a white collared shirt, open to the waist, and a pair of rolled calico pants, also in white. His feet were bare. The lake breeze captured the fabric of his shirt like a sail, causing it to billow out behind him, his hair also moving in this gentle caress.

Elijah stood behind him, dressed the same; our friends and his parents were scattered across the boards, watching me, beaming smiles on all of their faces. Mum took my left arm and Dad the right as I kicked off my shoes and started the walk down the carpet to my waiting fiancée.

Tradition played no part in this ceremony; it was purely about the two of us. Lorien started to walk toward me, meeting me halfway down the baths. "Excuse me Dom, sorry," he muttered to my father with an apologetic smile as he took me in his arms and kissed me tenderly. Mum and Dad slipped past us and joined the rest of our small congregation and we stood there, suspended in time with each other. He finally drew back and looked deeply into my eyes, a broad smile on his face. "I love you Ashlyn," he whispered.

"I love *you* Lorien." He took my arm and escorted me the final few metres to the waiting celebrant.

The only thing I remember about our actual nuptials was his dark eyes and warm smile, which widened into a grin when he prompted me to answer the celebrant. "Oh, I do!" I answered and blushed, slipping the wedding rings onto each other's fingers. Then, we were married, and he took me back into his embrace, confirming our bond with another intimate kiss.

It started simply, with only our hands holding each other's, but my arms eventually wound around his neck as he wrapped his form against me, holding me tightly to him. The crowd clapped and cheered; it seemed to be in a wind tunnel and so far away. All I concentrated on was Lorien, Lorien and me.

Eventually Nick approached and tapped him on the shoulder, causing us to break our kiss. "I'd like to kiss the bride too if you don't mind." Lorien grinned at me and stepped away, allowing our guests free passage, and to him also. Hands were shaken and cheeks were kissed, all in a hazy sheen of surrealism. I was so glad we married in this fashion, so relaxed and peaceful with all the people we loved the most here.

We left Glassread together in the Lexus and I was curious when he took the Warden turnoff instead of the main road back to Sommersett. "Where are we going husband?" I asked with a smile on my face.

"To your parent's place, wife."

"Why?"

"Because I want to consummate this *right now*," he said and raised his arm so I could draw against him for the drive home.

"Won't they be expecting us?"

"Don't stress, they think we're off getting photos taken and I knew no one would be home at your place today." He winked salaciously and I laughed loudly. Who was supposed to be taking these photos? What were we going to show them when the time came for their curiosity to remind them of our temporary departure? I knew the mothers would want to see them at some stage, as would Bree and Michael at the very least. "We'll cross that bridge when we come to it," he said as we pulled into my driveway and turned off the ignition.

I went to climb out of the car, but he stopped me, running around the front to lift me from my seat, ready to carry me over the first of three thresholds. "Got the house keys?" he asked.

"No, they're at your place."

"I didn't think this out too well did I?" I just raised my eyebrows at him and smiled. He looked thoughtful for a moment and took me to the side gate, raising me high enough so I could reach over and unbolt it, swinging it open before us. "Is this OK with you?" he asked. I nodded slightly, caught up in his lust and wanting to consummate this also, now we were here and alone. Tonight could be the main course, I was happy with a handful of entrées for now. "Any blind spots out here I don't know about?"

"Over near the clothesline is the most secluded area."

He looked around and spotted a rug folded across one of the patio chairs and grinned at me widely, grabbing it in one hand and doing his best to spread it out on the ground, still standing, still with me in his arms. "You can put me down if you like lover."

"I don't like. Your feet aren't hitting the ground until we get through my front door and then our bedroom door."

"Wow, great service!"

"You'd better believe it Baby." He knelt and lowered me to the blanket gracefully, following my trajectory with his body, leaning down to kiss me.

"I can't believe I'm kissing a married man!" I laughed, several minutes later.

"Mrs Standish..."

"Yes Mr Standish?"

"Shut up and kiss me!" I did.

You hear about all the love crap of angel's singing and flowers blooming when a man first takes his bride, and I had to admit making love in my back garden with not a care in the world was one of the most beautiful, most exceptional experiences I had encountered in my entire twenty-two years on the planet. The sun mirrored the heat of our lips, the wind assisting us in the gentle flow of our bodies. Lying there naked with him, as one, fulfilled me as I had never been fulfilled before. We were man and wife, and possibly the simple knowledge of this 'piece of paper' society ridicule made all the difference. I'd never loved him more; had never been more aroused and attracted to him, as I was now.

Lying there, catching our breath, and soaking up the solitude and desirous atmosphere were all that encompassed both of us. I smiled down at my lover nestled into me, drawing his hands slowly over my body, revelling in the afterglow together. "We should make a move," Lorien sighed against me, neither of us in any hurry. We knew they'd all be waiting for us for as long as it took to get back to his place. "I could lie here all day Baby," he mumbled, teasing at my breasts again.

"If you keep doing that, I may not give you a choice," I laughed softly.

"Hmmm," he growled, working his mouth more intensely against me. "There is no other choice…"

"So, you consider yourself to be a boob man?" I teased. He moved slowly down my body, raising my legs into the air.

"It's these long, shapely legs that do it for me most," he said, running his hands over my calves. "Not that every inch of your body doesn't do it for me Baby…" Moving in between my knees, he positioned my feet onto his shoulders, running his hands again from calves to thighs, caressing with his light touches. "What I wouldn't give for you in a pair of white ankle socks and pig-tails," he purred and entered me again. Holding my ankles tightly, he rocked against me.

My eyes feasted on his hard body, watching the muscles ripple and strain through his movements. When I met his gaze, he was smiling lazily at me, watching me watching him. I opened my arms to him, wanting him against me and he lowered himself to me, not breaking his stride. His lips were urgent against mine as our breathing escalated. "You are so incredibly hot Lorien. You get sexier every day…" I exhaled.

"I'm hot for *you* Baby," he crooned and quickened his pace, bringing us together into the soaring heights as I lightly scratched my nails over his warm, broad back, mindful of the white shirt he would have to put back on. I didn't want to mark him as I had when at the Bay a few years ago. Our small party-in-waiting would immediately realise there had never been a photographer.

Finally spent, we reluctantly started to pull ourselves together, slowly dressing each other. "You're so beautiful Ashlyn. I love you with all of my heart." I smiled at him widely and drew in for another kiss, working my hands under his shirt and across his hard pecs, purring in appreciation. I loved the feel of the intoxicating combination of soft skin over hard muscle. He drew back and laughed, "You're insatiable."

"So are you," I said.

"Yes, it's unfortunate for both of us isn't it?" he said, waggling his eyebrows at me.

He carried me back to the car after draping the rug across the chair where he'd found it and ensuring the gate was properly secured. "Time to go Mrs Standish," he smiled at me. I flicked the mirror open on the back of the windscreen visor and checked my reflection, hoping that my hair and makeup wasn't 'whored' all over the place. Everything seemed to be in order, but I noticed an addition to my neck jewellery. A small, faint hickie was nestled at my throat.

"Lorien," I admonished slightly.

"It wasn't intentional Baby," he smiled. "I just got a little carried away. I couldn't help it; your neck is like ambrosia..."

"Sure it is," I tsked and sidled over to him.

He dragged me against him and held me tightly with his left arm and I started to move my lips across his throat, feathering them up to trace around his ear. "Hmmm," he sighed, "I won't be responsible if we have an accident, but what a way to go." I drew back and laughed.

"You're so silly sometimes Lorien." His response was another wide grin.

"Can you imagine the faces of the rescue team? You pantiless; your dress hoicked up past your waist."

"You with a glorious hard-on..." This made him laugh.

"Glorious?"

"Truly Baby," I purred and was at his throat again, sucking lightly.

"Ashlyn..."

"Hmmm?"

"What are you doing?"

"Nothing..." He flicked down the mirror on his visor and checked his throat. I hadn't given him a hickie, but I certainly wanted him to think I had.

"You're a tease," he smiled, and turned off the ignition. We were home.

"Am I getting dressed?" I asked.

"No, this is our reception," he smiled at me.

"Wonderful!" I was ecstatic. He'd made all the right choices to make me so happy. "I have a wedding present for you. Do you want it now?"

"Do you want yours *right* now?" he countered.

"Here?"

"Yes, you're sitting in it." It took me a second to understand his point.

"The car?"

"Happy wedding Baby." He leant over and kissed me briefly, drawing back to take in my reaction.

"I love it Lorien, what a wonderful surprise."

"It's a family car," he winked at me, "just the right size for three at the moment, plus room to move." I laughed and kissed him in thanks.

I went to climb out of the car, and he stopped me once again. "I love you," I whispered into his ear as he lifted me into his arms. His dark eyes flashed at me, wanting to turn the emotion into the physical sense of the word, but we both knew it would now have to wait until much later. Where the anticipation used to make me insane, it now drove me. When we'd eventually reform our union later tonight, it would be like the first time again, and again, and again.

He stopped at the door and kissed me before we joined our family and friends inside. "You've made me so happy Ash," he sighed and looked at me so tenderly my heart skipped a beat. It was amazing that after five years he still had this effect on me, would apparently always have this effect on me; nothing had changed since we first got together...

The applause started before he even had the door halfway open. The revellers were scattered around the lounge room, drinks in their hands, grins on their faces. Lorien looked at me and smiled, which I returned with a brief kiss. "Awww," they crooned, and I blushed. I blushed again when I realised if he hadn't caught the back of my dress against his forearm I would be smiling at the crowd in a whole new way. I quickly ran my hand over the back of my thigh and sighed in relief when I noted the fabric was not hanging loose but was flush against my body.

"It's OK," he whispered, "I thought of that." He smiled at me devilishly.

"You can put her down now Lori, you're over the threshold." Nick said.

"No, one more," he answered. They laughed and watched our procession as Lorien trotted up the stairs with me still in his arms.

"Don't be all day!" Michael called out as I opened our door for him, already initiating the next kiss.

He leant against the door to close it and let my feet slowly find the ground. "Oh Baby, do we have time?" he moaned into my mouth. I shook my head slightly and drew away from him.

"No, I need to readjust myself and get some more underwear on!"

"Not even five minutes?" he asked.

"Our parents are downstairs," I reminded him.

"Like that's ever made a difference," he laughed, but let me go. I saw the bed.

"Oh Lorien!" It was covered in rose petals, with a trail leading from the doorway to its centre, forming a heart.

"I didn't do this," he said, noticing what I was looking at. "Must have been Bree or Michael," he mused.

"Are you sure this isn't your handiwork?"

"Nope. I would certainly take credit for it if it was. Now get in there and 'readjust' yourself. I want a few more minutes of passion at the very least before we go downstairs." I smiled and went into the bathroom.

He was sitting on the edge of the bed when I came back out. His eyes glinted at me and drew me to him like magnets as I crawled onto his lap for one last, deep kiss before we had to join the others. He ran his hand slowly over his chest when we finally separated. "It hurts so much…" he sighed.

"What does?" I asked in concern.

"How much I love you."

"I love you more," I said, kissing him again lightly.

"I love you mostest," he replied through the kiss.

"I love you plus one always," I murmured.

"I love you…" he exhaled, and lay me back on the bed. I struggled to sit up.

"Lorien…" I said, my brow drawn. He laughed.

"Come on hottie, let's go." He took me by the hand and led me out of our room to join our eager guests on the lower level, the level below paradise.

More applause greeted us as we descended the stairs together, hand in hand. All of our friends were there - Simon and Bree, Michael and Glen, Cyndi and Frankie. I took the kisses and hugs in turn then went to my parents and my new mother and father-in-law, spreading the love. Everyone had a camera or mobile, and more shots were candidly snapped, as they had been at the baths when we married. They would be wonderful memories and I was joyous in the fact that Lorien had indeed seemed to have thought of everything.

Cara and Mum busied themselves in the kitchen with the food whilst Nick and Dad started on pouring the champagne. We all went outside onto the verandah. Someone had thought to pull the wicker sun lounges from the northern side to ensure there was enough seating, and Lorien lay in one, opening his arms for me to join him. Elijah sat on the other and winked at me; he knew what was also around on the northern side of the house. "Present time," Michael said, and went into the house to retrieve two large boxes, one of which he handed to me. I felt a little guilty as I had arranged the present list and I knew that in each of these boxes we would find matching black motorbike helmets, kitted out with earpieces and Bluetooth receivers for ease of communication. Lorien laughed when he opened it and said,

"Looks like I'll have to get myself a bike!" He was unaware that he already had one. It was my present to him. "Thanks everyone," he said and dragged it onto his head. He tried to kiss me, which was impossible considering the circumstances, but it got an appreciative laugh. He pulled it off and put it carefully back in the box.

Elijah had bought us boots, and when our parents joined us on the verandah, they handed us their combined presents, Draggin jeans, bike jackets and gloves, all fully fitted with protective armour. Lorien's set was blue and black, mine matching but in red. It was pretty cool, I had to admit. "This is all so great guys, but I don't have a bike." I stood and held my hand out for Lorien to take. He rose and looked at me curiously.

"Come with me Mr Standish."

"Right O," answered Nick, smiling. I kept forgetting there was already a Mr Standish and I laughed with him before walking Lorien around to the northern verandah.

Sitting in the garden was a red Honda VFR 800, second hand but still in great condition, complete with side bags and a top box. Dad had found it for an excellent price too. "Happy wedding Lorien," I said as I watched him goggle at the bike.

"Oh Baby, I love it!" he exclaimed, picking me up and swinging me around in his arms. "How did you pay for it?" He knew that if I'd used our bank account, he would have seen the debit, so realised there had been other forces in play.

"Haven't you noticed my car has been missing for several days?"

"You told me Dom was working on it."

"Yes, that's what I told you…" It dawned on him that I hadn't been telling the truth. "Our parents helped with the rest of it as part of our wedding gift, especially as there was no major outlay for wedding costs. This is from them too."

Lorien sized it up and straddled it, turning over the key and hitting the ignition button. The engine roared into life. He gave me a broad smile and was off. "Wait!" I called after him. "You don't have a licence, you're going to kill yourself!"

"It's OK sis," Elijah pacified me, slipping his arm over my shoulders. "We had dirt bikes in Sydney, he can already ride. He'll be OK, I'm sure he's just checking it out." I looked at him dubiously and thought that maybe a motorbike wasn't the best idea as a gift after all. I would no doubt spend every waking moment worrying when he was on it. "Trust me Ash, but I don't want to see *you* on it until after the birth." He delivered this last line quietly, knowing my parents were unaware of this fact yet. I smiled at him weakly and waited for my groom to return.

Sure enough, a few minutes later I could hear the engine as he neared, and suddenly a bright red flash whipped back into the garden, silencing the dragon's roar. "Sweet!" he exclaimed and dismounted. "Eli, you have *got* to try it." And, of course, he did.

"You could have at least put a helmet and shoes on!" I chastised as he came to me for kisses.

"I didn't go far Honey, it's OK."

"I know. Elijah told me you can both ride, but we'll have to establish a few ground rules with that contraption, or I will never be able to relax when you're on it."

"Contraption?" he queried with a smile. "And don't you mean when *we're* on it?"

"Elijah said not until after the birth," I told him quietly.

"Good point," he whispered and leant down to kiss me. I stopped him so I could add,

"And you aren't to ride it without L-Plates, and I insist you get your licence as soon as possible."

"Yeah, give it to him bride," encouraged Michael. "See twin, your life is no longer your own!" I was the only one to hear Lorien's reply as Elijah roared back into the garden,

"It's been hers for the longest time." This time I let him kiss me.

"Anyone else?" Elijah asked as he went to turn off the ignition. I was surprised to see Glen approaching.

"It's OK Ash, I have my bike licence," he told me before climbing on. Michael stood beside me and put his arm around my waist, hugging me to him as his man took off, putting it onto the back wheel.

"Well, that's just showing off!" I snorted and Michael laughed loudly. "You know the twins will want to try that now!" I told him, frowning, but this did not dampen his mirth. "You are not getting back on that thing today Lorien," I informed my husband, standing on the other side of me.

"Thing?" he laughed, but promised he would not ride again until he had his learner's permit, and I inwardly sighed in relief.

When Glen returned, neither Frankie nor Simon wanted a go, they had not ridden before, but it didn't stop Dad and Nick; each saddling up and roaring off up Bridge Street in turn. Finally, when all the little boys had had their fun, the mothers called us back to the verandah. The food was ready, and I was starving.

God love Mum and Cara, they had done wonders. The aperitifs and finger foods looked like something from a cooking magazine. I couldn't get enough of the bruschetta and deep-fried camembert with cranberry sauce. This was to become Lorien's lament over the next several weeks as they became the top two on my cravings list, not to mention the prunes wrapped in prosciutto.

The prawns made me want to gag so I left the chilli skewers to the other revellers and concentrated on the bruschetta, dipping my hand repeatedly into the salsa with mini toast. "Jeez Ash, are you eating for two or what?" Michael laughed. I looked at Lorien guiltily, we hadn't told our friends yet. It was only the Standish's that were aware of the upcoming surprise in December, and I felt bad that it was being kept from the others that we loved, including Mum and Dad. I looked at Lorien with my brows drawn and he patted his lap for me to come and sit with him.

"You want to tell them?" he asked.

"I think so. I just had a massive guilt rush, and I don't want to feel that way. Can you do it though Lorien?"

"Of course Baby." He cleared his throat and said, "Can I please have your attention, we have an announcement to make."

"God, don't tell me you're pregnant!" Michael added. Lorien rolled his eyes at him before continuing.

"Now this has nothing to do with the wedding being brought forward, but we officially found out recently that we're pregnant." I couldn't help but laugh when I saw the look on Michael's face. He had no idea how accurate he'd been with his jibing.

I looked around for Mum and Dad and saw them on the other side of the table. Mum had tears in her eyes, and I wasn't sure if they were full of joy or sorrow. Seconds later, she was standing in front of me, and I stood so I could hug her. She howled on my shoulder. "Are you OK Mum?" She sniffed and nodded.

"Congratulations Honey," she said. "When are you due?"

"The tenth of December." I kept waiting for it, but it didn't come. It appeared she *was* OK with this. Dad hugged me too and told us both congratulations. I stood at the end of the receiving line for the second time that day and Lorien and I were hugged and kissed by our friends and family.

"So, you've obviously been having sex then," Simon laughed with his arms around me. Bree pulled him off me for her hug, saying,

"Where have you been for the past five years Simon? Living in a cave?" She knew he was kidding, as did we; if nothing, our friends were well aware of our sexual liaisons when in their company. Simon was happy though, he had made me blush which was no doubt his intention.

After Mum had calmed down, Cara went into the house, bringing out the wedding cake. Lorien disappeared for a second into the garden, returning with a rose tucked into one of his buttonholes. "I thought you may want me a little more formal for the more formal photos."

"I think you look sexy as you are and I can't wait to get to bed," I whispered to him. We got lost in another kiss, and when it started to get a little heated, Nick tapped him on the shoulder, handing him a knife with a ribbon secured around the handle. I blushed again.

I was happy to say that it was not your average 'gak' wedding cake made out of heavy fruitcake and horrendous white, almond icing. My morning sickness, which reared its ugly head at any time of the day, could not be trusted sometimes, and I did not want to vomit up my wedding cake. It would seem a little sacrilegious at the least.

It was instead two interlaced hearts made of chocolate sponge with pink icing, and I eyed it hungrily, waiting on the command to cut it. Lorien offered me the knife and then wrapped his hand over mine and we sliced it together.

He dragged his finger through the icing and looked at me with a knowing smile and I knew what was about to unfold. As with their birthday cakes, the twins had always dragged their iced fingers down the cheeks of their respective others, and I knew I was about to cop it with the wedding cake too. I grimaced at him but ran my finger through the icing also, each wiping our fingers down each other's cheeks and then proceeded to lick it off. Lorien artfully managed to collect it off my face in one long sweep, he'd had lots of practice over the years, but I made a mess of him. It took me several goes to get it, and then all the smears I'd managed to spread over him like peanut butter. He laughed and kissed me when I was finally finished, taking care of the portion still on my lips.

Dad wanted to make a toast, as did Nick and they ensured everyone had a charged glass, also handing one to me. "Can I drink this?" I turned and sought out Elijah.

"You can have a couple but don't go crazy." I had not intended to do so, but was secretly glad I was able to toast properly on my wedding day.

Dad made a speech, Nick made a speech, Elijah made a speech. Lorien said the reply of thanks and then Michael made a speech, and what a speech. Although all quite above board, the innuendos and connotations were hard to ignore. When he mentioned the chains and

manacles of the bond of marriage, I knew he was referring to our Easter
Holidays at the Bay when Lorien and I had visited the sex shop, coming
home with various cuffs, body paint and blindfolds. Our friends laughed
harder than our parents, who I hoped were still in the dark about that little
adventure.

When I heard the opening intro' to 'Ashlyn's Song', a song written
by both twins many years ago for me, Lorien offered me his arm and led
me back into the garden. "May I have this dance?" he asked, taking me
into his arms. I smiled at him and lay my head against his chest, soaking
up the love that threatened to burst my rapidly beating heart. I loved him
so very much and I had never been happier in my life.

When I came out of my daze, he was smiling at me so tenderly
and leant down to kiss me, invoking another 'Awww' from the rest of the
crowd. I noticed the rose in his buttonhole again and asked if he had
found out who left the petals scattered on our bed. His simple answer
amazed me - it was Elijah. I was fortunate to have such a wonderful and
caring new family and I looked around to find him, noting Dad was waiting
to cut in.

I danced with Dad then Nick. Nick smiled widely when I also
called him Dad, and then Elijah was waiting to take me from him. "You did
the roses?" I asked quietly, not sure if anyone else was meant to know
about it.

"It was supposed to be a surprise for later, but I should have
known Lorien wouldn't be able to keep out of your room until then. Do you
like them?"

"I love them Elijah, thank you for thinking of it." I leant up to kiss
both of his cheeks softly and then applied one to his lips. It felt strange to

be kissing him after so many years. Although certainly not the kind of kiss we had exchanged in the past, my lips had not touched his since, and it was a weird sensation. He didn't seem to mind though and he held me to him in a warm embrace after, finally separated by my anxious groom, wanting his bride back.

"OK, that's enough, my lips are getting cold," he said, and Elijah laughed as he stepped back to let his brother reclaim me.

Everyone had gone by 10.00 pm and Lorien and I made our excuses to turn in, citing it had been a long day. I knew his family was not that stupid, but I still had reservations about being too open in front of them regarding our sexual conquests of each other. "Thanks for everything today Mum," I said to Cara, a little sheepishly.

"That sounds lovely, thank you Ashlyn. I like being called Mum by my new daughter."

"Night Mum!" Lorien added and stooped down to kiss her cheek. She tsked him and said,

"He's all yours Ashlyn." Lorien just grinned at me.

"Thanks Dad," I said to Nick and kissed him on the cheek.

"You're welcome kids," he said and returned my shy smile with a grin. "We love you both."

"Night Dad!" Lorien said and Nick rolled his eyes at him. Elijah had been sitting at the dining room table; textbooks already open in front of him. He hugged his twin then came to me and kissed me on the cheek before grappling me in a bear hug.

"Just remember that I sleep in the room next to you please," he whispered, then laughed when he saw my blush.

"Wear ear plugs," Lorien said quietly, standing behind me.

"Wait, before you go, I have something for my new sister." He reached into his pocket and pulled out a velvet box, handing it to me. Inside was a replica of the wedding cake. Two interlaced hearts made from silver on a fine-spun chain. I grabbed him to me and held him closely, not able to speak for fear of bursting into tears. "You're welcome," he said and swung me lightly, tightening his embrace. I looked up into his eyes through my blurred vision and he smiled warmly. "I think Lorien is waiting for you," he said softly and let me go when I turned to find my groom, waiting near the stairs with a small smile playing at his lips.

Lorien carried me up the stairs and broke the kiss only to sit me gently on the bed. "Stay there, I'll be right back." I started to undress, and he stopped me. "Stay *right* there," he repeated, "and don't move!" I laughed and he darted out the door, returning a minute later with a bottle of champagne and some strawberries.

"I don't think I should drink anymore, I've already had two glasses today. I don't want to get 'Bump' drunk on our wedding night."

"This is for me," he winked, then said, "Bump?" I pointed at my still flat stomach, but there was going to be one hell of a bump there at some stage in the not too distant future. He laughed and came to me, caressing my stomach. Not only did this area contain our tiny little peanut at present, it was also one of my strongest erogenous zones, and being pregnant infused, not diffused these sensations.

He interlaced his fingers with my own and I stood with him, kissing each other slowly. His hands worked at the zip of my dress and it pooled around my feet on the floor. He crouched down to assist me in stepping out of it, and then carefully laid it over the desk chair, out of harm's way. He got to his knees and looked up at me, his dark eyes intense as he wended his hands up my calves, over my thighs and across the contours of my rear, purring as he slid my French knickers back down the lusty trail.

He stood with me again and unfastened my bra, leaving me standing totally naked in front of him. "You are seriously overdressed," I told him, but he shook his head and lowered me to the bed, the heat of the next kiss already in full fervour.

He teased my body for some time with his hot breath, his searching fingers, his eager mouth. When he sat up slightly, I could see his calicos were straining under the force of him. "Is that for me?" I asked demurely and he smiled, reaching for the champagne.

"Roll over Baby," he instructed, and I moved onto my stomach, jumping a little when the cork popped.

I was surprised to feel the fizzy foam cascading down between my shoulder blades, running over my bum and between my thighs. I clamped my legs together and it pooled at the back of my knees, captured in a long channel. He pressed a strawberry lightly between the junction of my thighs and rear, then moved back down to my knees, sucking up the excess liquid before slowly dragging his tongue up the crevasse leading him to the strawberry. He shifted position and moved to my shoulder blades, tracing his mouth once again down the trail of champagne, suckling my lower back and working down the line of my bum until he once again encountered the waiting strawberry. This time he took it into his mouth and ate it before nuzzling his face into me from behind. He lightly tugged at my clamped thighs and legs and I relaxed them immediately, not wanting to interrupt his explorations.

He ate four or five strawberries in this fashion and then asked me to roll over. I was hoping he was now ready to 'copulate' as I most certainly was. He'd brought me to the brink and held me there and I was ready to explode, but he was not finished with his ministrations. Biting the end off a strawberry, he dipped it into his glass of champagne, rubbing it slowly around my nipples before lowering his head to me. "Hmmm, I love strawberries but you're my favourite fruit," he moaned, lightly probing another between my thighs again. I wasn't sure how long I could stand this as I was aching for him now.

One final drizzle of champagne over my body, he put the bottle down and worked his way from my breasts to the strawberry waiting for him at my altar. He devoured it with the intensity to finally bring me soaring into the heights he had teased me to for over half an hour. "I love you so much Ashlyn," he whispered against my thigh. I sat up, wanting him naked, wanting him. He removed his shirttails from his pants, his eyes ablaze. I knelt beside him, running my hands over his firm pecs, across his shoulders and sweeping his shirt off as I trailed my hands down his arms. I flicked open the button on his pants and gently eased down the zipper; I didn't want to catch any part of him in it, which may have happened in a more urgent ripping motion. Mr Winky sprung out before I even had them down to his hips.

"Someone is really happy to see me," I said, and he chuckled deeply, kicking off his pants and rolling onto his back. He motioned to me with his finger, and I went to him eagerly, lowering myself slowly over the length of him. I sighed as he rocked gently, savouring every inch.

"Oh Baby," he groaned, "Oh Sweetheart..." His hands found my hips and he held me to him tightly as he started to move me faster. I beat him to it however, and threw my head back, my bottom lip between my teeth. He was not as gracious as I, with his moans becoming louder and louder as he neared his climax, and finally let out a bellowing, "Oh God, Oh Ash," as the orgasm seared through him.

"Shhh!" I whispered through a fit of giggles.

"We're married now, what does it matter?" he puffed, then pulled me down to him, entwining himself around me and finding my lips with his.

"It's called courtesy to the other people in the house," I mumbled through the kiss. He chuckled and kissed me deeper, making it impossible to talk.

Round two we took care of in the shower, I was all sticky, and in more ways, than one. When finally in bed, ready for sleep, I took his hand and placed it over my heart. He nuzzled into my side and played light kisses to my face, looking so intently into my eyes. "Forever Mrs Standish."

"I'm yours Lorien."

A BRIEF WORD FROM LORIEN

Fear

"And no amount of knowledge can alleviate the pain."

L Standish, 'Panic Stations'

MUM AND DAD WERE LEAVING on their twelve-month romp around Australia this afternoon and Ashlyn, Eli and I were doing what we could to assist, but also keep out of their way. Keeping out of their way was not an exceptionally hard thing to do considering I'd been a married man for just on a week now, and I entered our bedroom with one thing currently on my mind – Ashlyn Standish. "Hey Baby, what are you doing?" I asked, taking her into my arms.

"I am *trying* to strip our bed, what do you think *you're* doing?" she said, a little exasperated. Ash was just over six weeks pregnant and although the mood swings were becoming easier to read, she was more easily aroused than she'd ever been. I intended to take full advantage of my beautiful, brunette wife struggling futilely in my arms. "Lorien, let... me... go...," she said, and I allowed her to wrestle free, for the moment. "You were the one who wanted to move into your parent's room, the least you can do is help me and not hinder."

"Hinder?" I asked and her warm smile reflected the lack of anger that had been at the forefront, quickly dissolving.

"I'm sorry Lorien," she said, coming to me and taking me back in her arms. "I don't know what comes over me at times."

"You're pregnant Baby girl. It's all part of the territory." I leant down and brushed my lips over hers, absorbing their moist flavour, their softness and her natural perfume. "Ash, I love you so much," I murmured, taking her face in my hands and looking into her eyes. Her response was to align against me, kissing me intensely, and I gladly matched her pace.

"Boys! Ashlyn!" Mum called up the stairs, "We're leaving." I groaned and pulled away. She laughed and patted my cheek,

"We have all the time in the world, lover," she cooed, which did not help in deflating me. I went to the door and called down,

"Be right there," then sat on the bed waiting until I was able to present myself in front of my parents without the need to salute them farewell. Ash waited with me, a playful smile on her knowing lips.

As their Range Rover backed out of the driveway, we stood and waved; a small leaving party of three to see them off into their future. They had debated on buying a Winnebago but decided against it, instead trading in their much beloved Mercedes for the ever-practical four-wheel drive.

Mum was crying when we said our goodbyes and I could tell by the tissue at her eyes that she still was. Thankfully, Dad was driving the first shift, taking them as far as Sydney tonight. They intended on a few days of luxury at the Shangri-La before embarking on the next stage of their semi unplanned trip.

It was hard to keep it together when Dad said goodbye. His eyes were damp, his chin trembling a little as he drew in to hug me. I loved my parents so much and although they were authoritarian in some ways, were foremost loving and caring people, let alone as parents. I was going to miss them a great deal, but they would be coming home for the birth and I was glad of this.

We waved until they were out of sight and my Ashlyn was sobbing loudly, letting out the true emotions that no doubt Eli felt, as did I. "It's OK Ash," I soothed, "we'll speak to them on Sunday, every Sunday."

"I know, I'm just being emotional. You'd think they were my parents."

"Well, they are now Baby," I smiled down at her.

"I'm just so tired…" she sighed and laid her head against my chest.

"Eli, can Ash take a nap in your room?"

"Sure, I'm about to take off myself; help yourself Ash," Eli told her.

"Why can't I use our bed?"

"You were in the process of stripping it, remember?"

"Oh yeah," she said and smiled. We both knew that her memory was also a little off these days.

I led her upstairs to Eli's room and kissed her gently as she made herself comfortable on his bed. "Do you want me to let you sleep through or wake you at some stage?"

"Let me sleep Lorien, thanks. I love you."

"Not as much as I love you," I told her before sliding both sides of our interconnecting bathroom doors closed.

I had a lot I wanted to achieve whilst she was asleep. I started by stripping ours then Mum and Dad's beds, putting fresh linen on both. I emptied out the walk-in wardrobe and put all the clothes they hadn't taken with them in a pile on our bed. I repeated this with the contents of their tallboy and bedside tables, truly claiming their whole room. With all the storage areas now empty, it was a simple process to take all of our belongings in, filling the vacant spaces quickly.

When I'd repacked our room with Mum and Dad's clothes, I put on a load of washing, grabbed some steak from the freezer for dinner and went back to our new room to write. I plugged my headphones into my keyboard so I wouldn't disturb her in case I lost myself in the music, as I was wont to do at times.

I must have been there for hours; time always slipped by so quickly when I was in the midst of an avid composition. I felt her light touch on my shoulders and stopped, pulling off the headphones and swinging in the chair to face her. "Have a good sleep Baby?" I asked, guiding her onto my lap. She put her hand to her mouth and yawned widely before saying,

"I only just woke up; it must be nearly 6.00 pm." I checked my watch, and she was right, it was five past. "I won't be able to sleep tonight," she said which I doubted; her body was craving this sleep now and I knew she would have yet another deep slumber when we retired. "What do you want for dinner?" she asked.

"You!" I said and drew her face down to mine. A few minutes later I could feel her smile and I pulled back to look at her, to see what was so amusing.

"We're in your parent's room Lorien," she said.

"It's our room now," I told her. "Look in the drawers and wardrobe," which she did.

"Did you do all this whilst I was sleeping?" she asked, sitting on the bed. I nodded. "I don't know if I can do this in here." I laughed,

"Pretend we're in a hotel."

"I'll certainly try!"

I laid her across the bed and kissed her tenderly, moving my hand down to gather the fabric of the floor-length, white, cotton shift she had taken to wearing of late, drawing it up to her thighs. A few days ago, she had also stopped wearing panties much to my delight, claiming them to be too constrictive and annoying.

This reminded me of the surprise I had for her under the bed. Ever since she wore the French knickers on our wedding day, I had thought of little else on her sexy body. I'd bought several pairs of lingerie for her, comfortable but still very spicy; matching satin camisole tops and of course, French knickers, all one size too big to give her room to move and grow. I was glad she enjoyed wearing beautiful and sensual sleepwear, otherwise I'd have to admit that I bought them for myself, as stupid as I would have looked in them. I laughed at the thought and she questioned my amusement. I shook my head and reached under the bed to grab the box of surprises. "For me?" she asked kittenishly.

"For both of us." She opened the box and pulled out the turquoise set, her eyes wide.

"These are beautiful Lorien, I love them!" She stripped off immediately and put them on. The sides of the knickers rode high up her thighs, drawing my eyes directly to her smooth, creamy skin and I found myself lowering my lips to them involuntarily. "Can I see the rest first, Mr Eager," she chided, and I sat back, smiling up at her.

She worked her way through the six other pairs, ranging in cut and colour. She put the red set aside from the others, saying that these were her favourites. They were mine too, however the pair she had on right now were also sublime. "They're so comfortable. I could wear these all day when Elijah isn't home."

"Looks like I won't get anything done ever again then, hey?"

"No, it would appear not," she said, taking in my tented jeans. She dropped the box to the floor and sidled over to me on the bed, leaning down to kiss me. I soon felt her hands tugging at my shirt and I sat up to pull it over my head, my little kitten about to morph into a lion.

I rolled her onto her back and worked my way down her body, gradually drawing the knickers down to slowly reveal herself to me. First, the small patch of brown curls, then the glistening, velvet folds surrounding her delicate aperture. I gazed at her for a few moments, planning my route.

I knew even now she still had her shy moments, but I couldn't understand this. We'd been together for so many years and on so *many* occasions; it baffled me how she could continue to blush over the simple acts involved with our lovemaking. However, it heightened me greatly when she did react this way, always revelling in her bashful moments. She didn't surprise me this time either. "Lorien stop *looking* at me!" This was not the first time I'd heard this, and I chuckled lowly, waiting on her to speak again. "Lor -" As soon as her mouth was open in protest, I lowered my lips to her, working to her centre. She had no more to say, although she soon found her voice again when my fingers sought to explore deeper than my tongue would allow.

All five of my senses were occupied in experiencing her, her touch, her sounds, her delicate scent, her flavour and of course her beauty; it was as if the rest of the world no longer existed. I lightened the ministrations to allow her to descend from her peak before I drilled her again, touching, tasting, nuzzling and infiltrating. Moments later, her whimpers turned again into a moan, escalating to a deep growl punctuated only by her erratic breathing.

I could seriously lie there all day pleasing her; she had no idea of how much arousal I also gained from it. Instead, I let her calm, wrapping my hands around her thighs from underneath and nuzzled into her gently, letting her know it was to soothe, not to incite. "Oh Lorien, you're amazing."

"And you love it."

"And I love it," she agreed, tracing her fingers across my hands as she waived off the ebb. "And *you* love it!"

"Yes Baby, I *adore* it! I love *you...*"

"And how do you show you love me?" I grinned and eased back between her thighs, knowing full well she was referring to fucking. She sat up a little and laughed, seeing me poised there gazing up at her.

"Just give me the word Baby."

"Fine then, I'll have to help myself!" She pushed me away and crawled over me, pressing at my side, wanting me to roll over. I couldn't disappoint the lady, could I? This was a position that we were going to have to use more and more throughout the course of the pregnancy, and Ash never had a problem with who was on top. It was a place we liked to share.

As her honey vice swallowed me, I sighed and lay back, lacing my fingers together under my head, letting her use and abuse me at her will. She'd let me know when she was ready for me to finish off, and until then, I was happy to settle from the ensuing urgencies by thinking of Arnold

Schwarzenegger comedies - to hell with running through the standard sport statistics.

"Lower me a tasty boob Baby," I whispered, and she lay forward to grant my wish. "Hmmm" I mumbled, "these are getting bigger by the day." The softness merging with her hardness turned me on no end and I couldn't wait until the day I could suckle her properly, when her milk started to flow. I found it difficult to believe that I would be the only father to have ever tried this. In fact, I would call the majority of others who would deny it barefaced liars.

When I was nearing the point of no return - I was no tantric master, I held my hips up firmly, knowing this would take her over the edge, which she did, right on cue. Allowing her to subside for a few moments I then lowered her back slightly and sat up, driving into her horizontally, one of *my* favourite positions. "Oh God Ash," I moaned, feeling the tingle alerting me to the inevitable out-rush. "Oh Baby..." I lightly swept my thumb over her clit a few times and she joined me in the final act, soaring together.

I loved that she could pop out three or four in one session, not that it had changed since she fell pregnant. She called me a great lover, but I thought it was more akin to the fact we were so suited to each other. She was even now as hot for me as I was for her, which is why we still went at it like teenagers. There was no such thing as enough.

I also loved to beg and plead to her. It gave her a power in our relationship she didn't ask for, and most likely didn't want. Every area of our combined lives was fifty-fifty, but when it came to our sex life, I was happy for her to be the predator, and I her willing sacrificial lamb. It didn't happen often, but when it did it really turned me on, and helped her sexual confidence, as well as my cock.

We lay together for some time, not speaking, occasionally seeking out each other's faces with our hands and lips. I loved her so much and wanted to make her as happy as I was, being with her. My 'slip up' as I now referred to it, was inexcusable. The thought of her ever being with another man was enough to drive me insane, including all those who came before me, that specifically my brother. I knew this was an insane thought; like I could be jealous of anyone when I had no right to be. However, from the moment I met this lady, I was enamoured with her. This sounded flaky coming from what I considered myself to be as a blokey-bloke, but it was nothing but the simple truth.

Ash was also unaware that I had insecurities, although she believed me to be the most confident man in the world. Did she love me as much as I hoped? Did I have it in my power to be able to make her as happy as she deserved? Was I good enough for her? I was certain that the answer to all these questions was yes, but we all like to give ourselves a good mental bashing at times. It proves we're human I suppose. Many men run or work-out when faced with the need to think things over, and I imagine, often about a woman they loved. Thankfully, I had my music. It allowed me to express through the lyrics and the notes how I felt inside, how I *always* felt inside. I wore my heart on my sleeve, or more aptly, within the magic of those five horizontal stave lines.

I sighed deeply and she asked what I was thinking. It upset her when I tormented myself with these thoughts, the ones she knew about and the ones she didn't. So, I lied, telling her it was a contented sigh.

"Lorien," she said sheepishly. I grinned, knowing she was ready for round two.

"Yes?" She surprised me with her response,

"I'm hungry, can we make dinner now?" I laughed, saying,

"Of course we can Sweetheart, is steak OK?" She nodded and climbed off the bed, grabbing her knickers and heading for the bathroom. I pulled my boxers from the insides of my jeans and joined her.

She busied herself at the island bench making a salad as I fired up the barbeque. "Is Elijah going to be home for dinner?" she asked through the open kitchen window.

"He didn't say, but I'm cooking enough in case he's hungry when he gets home." I watched her through the window whilst I waited for the coals to heat: chopping lettuce, slicing tomatoes, scooping out an avocado among other things, and finally tearing some crusty bread apart.

"Do you want to cook the onion, or shall I put it in the salad?" she called out, breaking my trance. She'd caught me staring though, and smiled serenely at me before shaking her head, waiting on my response. I hadn't even started the steaks and put hers on immediately, she liked it medium-well.

"I'll cook it." I watched again as she sliced the onion, small tears forming at her lids. She looked so cute. A grimace shot across her face and I saw her bend slightly forward. My brow furrowed and as I went to ask if she was OK, she straightened up and went back to work. I assumed it was from the onion vapours and gave a little note of thanks to whoever watched over us.

She brought the onion out as I turned her steak and put mine and Eli's on, handing me a beer. "Thanks Baby," I said and leant to kiss her. She took a seat and sighed. "Tired?" I asked.

"No, I'm just thinking about Mum and Dad."

"Yours or mine?"

"Ours," she laughed, then realised this gave me no more information than before. "Yours," she said. "I'm going to miss them."

"Me too Ash, but I'll tell you what. If either of us gets to where we need to see them, we can find out where they are and fly there. How does that sound?"

"Relieving," she said and came in behind me, wrapping her arms around me from behind. "I love being part of your family." I flipped the steaks and put the tongs down, turning to face her, to kiss her. A few minutes later I could hear a key in the front door. Eli was home after all.

"Hi guys, what's for dinner?"

"Steak and salad," Ash told him.

"Nearly ready?"

"Close enough. You've got time for a quick shower if you want," I said.

"Great, I'll be back."

"You did that deliberately didn't you?" Ash asked when Eli had taken to the stairs and I took her back in my arms.

"I would never do that," I murmured and drew her to me to continue our kiss. She laughed into my mouth and I moved slightly back, smiling at her.

"Cook the onions please Lorien," she said heading back into the kitchen, giving her bum a little shake. I grabbed the tea towel and managed to crack a pretty good one across her saucy rump before she got through the door. "Cheeky!" she called and darted inside, coming to the window to poke her tongue out at me. I chuckled and threw the onions onto the hotplate, pouring beer over them to assist in their flavour and texture.

I awoke early the next morning, not sure why. I realised immediately that my bride was not lying against me, and as usual, was attuned to when she was no longer there. I drew back the covers to slide out when I stopped abruptly. There was blood on the sheets. I jumped out of bed at the same time she came out of the bathroom, a look of horror on her face. "Lorien, I'm bleeding."

"Sit down Ash, lay down, I'll go get Eli."

When I reached his door, I knocked once and entered, not concerned if he was in the middle of a wank or deeply asleep.

"Wha?" he grumbled as I shook him.

"It's Ash, she's bleeding." His eyes flew open and he grabbed his bag, following me quickly to our room.

I was amazed at how calm Ash now was, considering the current situation. She was lying back on the bed, her feet propped up on a pillow and her arms folded lightly across her stomach. "How are you feeling?" Eli asked her.

"Fine, but I did have some light cramping yesterday evening. It went as quickly as it came though." And here I was thinking it was from cutting the onions. He took her blood pressure and then checked her pulse.

"Everything seems normal," he said.

"I read spotting is common for some women in their first trimester. Is that right?"

"It sure is," he told her, and I loved him for the light tone he kept in his voice. I, however, was ready to start climbing the walls.

I sat near her feet to keep out of Eli's way and rubbed her shins gently, protectively. He pressed lightly against her stomach with his fingers, checking her reaction for pain. She didn't seem to be in any. "I doubt there's anything to worry about, but we can take you to emergency if you like, or you can wait to see the doctor today. What would you prefer?"

"Emergency," I said.

"Wait," she said, at the same time. Eli looked at me, knowing that one decision and one alone would have to be reached.

"Lorien, it's already 7.00 am. I'm sure Doctor Wood will let me in as a preferred patient as soon as the surgery opens," Ash said.

"Eli?" I asked him.

"You could be waiting longer in emergency than what it takes for you to see the Doctor."

"OK, but I'm ringing Anna to let her know you're coming in first thing." They were both in agreement on this.

Recent Developments

"You don't know what's missing, until your kissing, produces wishing.
Hang that sign 'Gone Fishin'."

L Standish, 'Shallow Water'

DOCTOR WOOD TOOK ASHLYN IN as the first patient; I don't think I would have given him a choice if it came down to it. No one wanted me to accompany Ash in, but nothing was keeping me away from her. However, after a routine examination, he was giving us some good news. "Everything is fine," he said.

"So it was random spotting?" Ash asked.

"Not exactly. Your cervix is inflamed which can be a fairly common occurrence. It happens most often as an outcome from intercourse. The cervix is quite tender when you're pregnant and the penis striking against it can make it rupture, causing it to bleed lightly. From the amount of blood you described, I believe this to be the case. We will certainly run some further tests whilst you're here though."

"You mean this is something I've done to her?" I asked, taking her hand.

"I would hardly be placing blame on yourself Lorien," Doctor Wood said. "People have intercourse right through their pregnancies. I see no reason why you should stop unless the tests show otherwise." Ash looked relieved. I did not feel the same.

"We have a lot to talk about Ash," I said. She pulled a face at me and put her arm out, waiting to have blood taken.

"We can do that at home," she said.

Eli met us at the door on our return and laughed when I told him what the doctor thought the problem was. "How can you laugh?" I asked incredulously.

"I was hardly going to tell you that earlier this morning, was I? I suspected it may have been the case, but I was happy for Doctor Wood to be the one to have *that* conversation with you."

"So, what does it mean Eli?"

"Nothing critical. I assume he took blood though."

"Yes, he's going to run some tests."

"Just keep your eye on it and if it happens again before the results come back, we'll take Ash straight to emergency, OK?" I wasn't happy with the calm that had encompassed everyone. I wanted to know right now what was going on inside the most treasured person in the world to me, and to the precious cargo she was carrying.

"So, Bump should be OK?" Ash asked him. Eli nodded and smiled.

"Don't get too overworked Ash, there are a lot of common issues that freak first-time mothers out."

"Mothers?" she asked flippantly, turning her gaze to me.

"Well, fathers too," he corrected and they both grinned at me. I started to ease a little, knowing that my best friend and my beloved were settled over this; there was no point in my spinning out.

"Can we still have sex?" she asked coyly.

"Yes," Eli said and chuckled.

"No!" I said. "Not at least until the results come back!" Ash stood and came to me, taking my hands in hers, putting my arms around her so I could draw her against me.

"Lorien, it's going to be alright. I feel it, I can feel a lot more than I ever could, and my body is telling me everything is OK."

"For now," was all I would give her. She sighed and hugged me; this was a conversation we would no doubt revisit when alone. I was prepared to let it drop for the moment. Eli flicked on the kettle and pulled some bacon and eggs from the fridge.

"Want some breakfast guys?"

"Sure, thanks," I said, but not my Baby girl.

"I want bruschetta," she told him, making Eli laugh.

"I believe speciality dishes are your area Lori," he told me. I wondered whether she'd asked for this deliberately, knowing it would make me smile. She had some wondrous cravings, which also included deep-fried camembert and prunes wrapped in prosciutto. She had also taken to eating ice cream with barbeque sauce, which was one I couldn't fathom. Fortunately, I now kept the kitchen stocked with the ingredients to make 'any time of the day' food demands and I kissed her lightly before going to dice the tomatoes.

When she smelled the bacon frying, she looked at me and smiled, her eyebrows raised. I knew there was about to be a change in the menu.

"Prunes in prosciutto?" I asked and she nodded. I covered the bruschetta and put it in the fridge for later, knowing she would want it eventually. I grabbed the prosciutto and tossed it to Eli who added it to the pan with the bacon.

Ash excused herself to go to the bathroom. Her bladder was anything but her best friend. I took this opportunity to tackle Eli over the current issue again. "Before you open your mouth Lori," he already knew what was coming, regardless of being my twin, "you won't hurt her. You need to also understand that pregnant women are irrational and by you not having sex with her, it could hurt her feelings."

"How is that possible?" I asked.

"She'll think you don't find her attractive, that she isn't arousing or wanted by you anymore. That kind of thing."

"Like that would ever happen."

"You try telling that to a pregnant woman who wants sex." I saw his point... a little. When she returned from the bathroom, she was smiling lightly.

"No more bleeding," she said. Both Eli looked, and I felt, relieved. We settled in to enjoy our breakfast.

I loved to watch her eat these days. The prunes would still have been piping hot, but she grabbed the first one and bit into it gingerly, scalding her tongue in the process. She seemed to have lost the desire to use utensils and I got up to get her a glass of milk as she fanned her hand over her open mouth, rolling the prune around her tongue to cool it. "Are you sure you don't want any eggs Ash?" I asked, wishing now I hadn't. She had some aversions to food as well as cravings. She couldn't eat eggs unless they were scrambled, seafood would have her running for the bathroom at the sight of it, not that she was the greatest lover of it before she was pregnant, and if I were to run a mango under her nose, she would no doubt vomit directly on me. She'd managed not to lose it at my suggestion, but did move to the island bench to finish her breakfast, not wanting to take in the fried eggs that Eli and I were still tucking into vigorously. There was nothing wrong with my appetite and there never was. I had always been voracious when it came to food... and her.

I rinsed our plates off before stacking them in the dishwasher, not wanting to leave even a scrap of yolk or egg white sticking to them. She cuddled in beside me and handed me her plate to rinse, smiling widely. She had polished off all twelve of the sweet and savoury mixture, and no doubt the prunes would also work through her system quickly, having to run to the bathroom to 'keep the mail moving'. I found her pregnancy to be a myriad of emotions for me: comical, arousing, entertaining and fascinating; some of which she did not enjoy.

We stretched out at the dining room table enjoying a coffee, and Eli broached an interesting subject. "I was thinking of asking a few of my Uni friends over on Saturday, have a few drinks and whatnot." I looked at Ash and she smiled, saying,

"Let's invite our friends too! Oh, of course if you would rather it's just your Uni friends Elijah, I'll understand."

"May as well make a party of it," Eli said, grabbing his mobile and sending out the texts of invitation.

"So, tell me more about these Uni friends?" Ash asked.

"I've asked five of them to come, two guys and three girls. Two of them are a couple – Trudy and Patrick. There's also Jared who is pretty keen on Faith, and Melayne."

"And is Melayne a set-up for you?" I asked, eyebrows raised. I knew my twin was not getting it as often as he should be.

"I told you, I'm not interested in any relationships until I'm finished my degree."

"Sex doesn't *have* to involve a relationship," I winked at him.

"Lorien Thomas Standish!" Ashlyn chastised me.

"God, you sound like Mum," I laughed.

"I *am* going to be one!"

"You haven't answered my question Eli," I prompted.

"Melayne is very sweet, but I would no more run her up to my room than I would Michael." That visual made us all laugh.

"It's been a while since you went on a date," Ash added.

"Are you two going to make this difficult for me? I can always cancel you know."

"We'll be on our best behaviour, won't we Lorien!" Ash promised. I could only try. I wanted to see my brother happy, but would not dream of deliberately hurting him any more than I would Ash. I was keen to meet his new friends though and promised to behave.

"Are they all in your classes?" Ash asked.

"Trudy and Faith are the only ones who aren't. I know Trudy through Patrick, she's a hairdresser, and Faith runs the coffee cart at Uni."

"So Melayne must be a very smart girl?" Eli looked at her sternly, letting her know to drop this subject once and for all. Ash laughed and said, "Well it sounds like Trudy and Bree will hit it off anyway." They no doubt would.

Ash told me that Bree's parents were upset when she decided to be a hairdresser and beautician. She'd been an A student at school, and they held higher hopes for her choice of career. However, Bree had always loved sculpting hair, nails and being creative with makeup and was extremely happy with her chosen vocation. A top of the line hair and nail artist could also earn the big bucks! She would often pop in for a visit on her own when Simon was at work and would do Ash's hair or nails, making her feel beautiful. I didn't think Bree could improve on what was already perfect; Ashlyn would then call me silly.

Cyndi and Frankie were unable to make it on such short notice, but Bree, Simon, Michael and Glen were confirmed. Glen was even taking the night off from Snipers to join us. Two of them could have our old room and two would have to sleep on the sofa bed downstairs; we decided they could flip a coin to determine who slept where. "You don't have a problem with the boys sleeping in our bed?" Ash asked.

"They're not welcome to join us in our bed, Baby," I said, waggling my eyebrows at her.

"I mean our old bed silly," she said and laughed.

"Why would I?"

"They might have sex…" she hinted.

"There's nothing that comes out of them that doesn't come out of me." She blushed slightly and I caught her in my arms, swinging her lightly from side to side. "You never got back to me about the anal sex either Baby," I teased, my gorgeous girl now a lovely shade of crimson. God, I wanted her again right then and there. "Come with me, I want to try something." I said, leading her upstairs to our room.

"It better not be anal sex Lorien!" she cautioned. I chuckled but didn't answer her.

Eli had obviously stripped and changed our bed whilst we were at the Doctor's and I made a mental note to thank him later. "Sit down Baby," I told her and went to the desk to get some music. I wanted our little Bump to hear some of her Daddy's music. I pressed the earphones to either side of Ash's stomach, and then looked at her in confusion. "Where is she, I mean where's Bump's head?" I asked.

"Where you have them positioned is fine Sweetheart," she told me and smiled down at me warmly, crouched on the floor in front of her. Shortly after, I heard Eli's burst of laughter from our doorway.

"You're wasting your time Lori, the foetus can't hear yet. Wait until the twenty-second week and then go for it."

"Will you stop referring to the baby as a foetus; she has a name - Bump."

"Well, 'Bump' is currently deaf." Eli smiled at Ash and she smiled back, both knowing that I would take this under my own advisement, and I was currently choosing to ignore Eli's comments.

"You won't know the sex until the eighteenth week either."

"I refuse to call her 'it' until then."

He came and sat next to Ash on the bed and asked us about any names we'd considered. "If it's a girl Lorien likes Mercy, the middle name will be Cara-Anne regardless. If it's a boy we've agreed on Thomas Elijah." She knew her words would be profound, and Eli smiled widely at her and then at me. I lowered my cheek onto Ash's knee and smiled back at him. Like there would have been any other choice for the middle name of our son. *Thanks for changing the bed*, I mouthed to him and he winked back in recognition. Ash didn't notice our interchange, as she had often missed in the past.

"What girl's names do you like Ash?" Eli asked.

"I haven't really thought of any and I like Mercy too. It's unusual and dramatic, just like her father." She looked down at me and that very look had my cock twitching. I felt the familiar stirring as I started to harden. I drew her other leg toward me, running my hand under the cotton shift, drawing it up to her thigh. Eli coughed a little and excused himself, closing the door behind him. He was used to dealing with the sudden onslaught of passion that had plagued us now for so many years. I stood; Ash took my hands in hers, drawing me onto the bed over her. I moved to the side slightly, so my body weight was not on her, and our mouths fused, feasting lustily on each other.

I worked my fingers at her buttons and my lips followed the trail in hot pursuit. She stopped me and crooned softly, "No Baby, I want you *inside* me first," her fingers threading into my hair.

"No Ash, not until the results come back. There's plenty of other things we can do…," I said and continued to lower myself across her stomach, circling and lapping at her navel. She sat up and pushed me away, scowling.

"Why are you always cutting me off?"

"What?" I asked in disbelief, she had taken me by surprise with this one.

"You arsed around taking my virginity and then when *you* played up on *me* you held me at arm's distance for weeks. Maybe I should just go and fuck your brother!" She was *way* out of line. I sat up and moved off the bed.

"Go ahead!" I told her and walked into the bathroom, closing the door behind me.

I sat on the toilet seat, my face in my hands. I had to get a grip. Although what she'd said was the most hurtful thing she'd *ever* said to me, I knew it was the hormones talking, not that this understanding made me feel any less wounded. The door opened and she stood there, tears streaming down her face. "Oh Lorien," she cried, coming to me and working her way onto my lap, "I am *so* sorry Sweetheart, and I'm sorry I have to keep saying I'm sorry. Just because I'm hormonal doesn't give me the right to treat you like crap. I just hurt you so terribly and I don't know how to take it back. You know I love you with all of my heart and didn't mean any of those nasty things I just said to you." She was instantly forgiven of course, but sometimes it was best for her to get it out of her system, and I held her to me, letting her cry.

She cried for the longest time; her sobs finally subsiding into sharp breathy intakes. I ran my hand soothingly across her shuddering back. She rested her head against my chest and a few minutes later, I heard her breathing deepen – she had cried herself to sleep on my lap. I stood as smoothly as possible and carried her back into the bedroom, laying her down gently. She didn't stir. I sat and watched her for a while, moving the hair from her face when it tickled her nose, touching the crease on her forehead lightly to dampen the unpleasant dream; just loving her. I eventually plugged the headphones back into my keyboard to write some more, waiting for her to wake up.

A Few New Faces

"It's not that they're not welcome or we don't need their point of view,
But Baby, no one compares to you. There's only you."

L Standish, 'Reflection'

ELI'S UNI MATES were the first to arrive and we were introduced one by one. I took an instant liking to Patrick and Trudy and we led them outside whilst the others joined Eli in the kitchen, sorting out their drinks. I wasn't surprised that I liked these people, it wasn't often that Eli and I didn't have the same preference for friends, let alone women.

We had an esky on the verandah to leave more room for the guest's drinks and I dug into it, passing Ash lemonade and taking a beer for myself. My bride was sitting on the chair next to me, which was totally unacceptable, and I opened my arms to her, wanting her on my lap. She came to me and kissed me openly in front of the now six people in our presence. It was hard to believe that her public affection issue had finally gone. I realised how wrong I was when I saw her blush, pulling away from our intimacy. She'd been unaware everyone had joined us outside. Jared sat next to us with Faith and Melayne on either side of Eli. It was obvious both of these girls were interested in him, Faith being a lot more forward than the seemingly shy Melayne. They were both attractive girls, so he had his work cut out for him. I couldn't help feel a little sorry for Jared who Eli had said was chasing Faith. It didn't appear he was going to get anywhere tonight.

I saw the splash of headlights in the driveway, and Ash and I went to welcome our friends. They'd brought their own esky and followed us outside to the verandah. Eli took care of the introductions and I asked him to move around so we could all sit together, with me and Ash next to Melayne. I thought they'd hit it off and I was right. They connected immediately and I was pretty sure the initial reason for this was Ash wanted to set Eli up with her. I was going to have to have another word to my little Angel before the evening was over. She needed to let him make these choices; her shoving them together wasn't going to work. I knew that from going out with Keren.

Bree was next to Trudy and they were also getting on well, sharing their vocation and similar personalities. It was always great catching up with our friends. I laughed with Simon and Glen for some time, before realising my Baby girl had gone very quiet. She got up under the pretence of preparing food and I followed her, Michael right behind me. She started banging platters around on the island bench, upending crackers and chips onto them. "What a bitch," Michael said. I'd obviously missed something. "Are you OK Ash?" he asked, putting his arm around her. Her eyes were misty and she was trying not to cry.

"What happened?" I asked him. How had he seen it when I had not?

"She said to Ash 'so you're the knocked-up sister-in-law we always hear so much about. I must say, I'm a little disappointed'."

"Melayne?" I asked, not able to believe those words could come from such an unassuming girl.

"Faith!" Ash whispered with venom.

"I thought you'd been talking to Melayne," I said, confused.

"I was and then Elijah joined our conversation and apparently Faith wasn't happy in having his attention averted."

"Do you want me to take care of her?" Michael asked, a shrewd look on his face.

"No, she's Elijah's friend. I don't want to make this any more difficult for him than need be," Ash told him. Eli came into the kitchen then.

"Sorry about that Ash," he said, giving her a hug. "I've never seen her like that before."

"You have to stop talking about me to people Elijah," she told him. "All it ever does is get me into trouble. Remember the problems we had with Keren over all this crap?" She was really ticked off and I didn't blame her. She didn't need to be treated like that in her own home let alone anywhere else by someone in my brother's company.

"Do you want me to speak to her?" I asked, taking her into my arms. She shook her head and hugged me to her, happy just to stand like this with me for the moment.

"I'm OK, but everything seems to want me to become a drama queen these days," she laughed.

"Excellent Ash, you can be in the 11.00 pm floor show next weekend," Michael laughed.

"Need any help?" Faith came in and sidled up to Eli at the island bench.

"Well, that's my cue," Michael said and went back outside. She had done permanent damage there it would seem. Faith had obviously worked out that she'd crossed a line, as she touched Ash lightly on the arm and apologised.

"I'm sorry if that came out the wrong way Ashlyn, it's just that Eli talks about you so much it feels as if we already know you. I meant it as a joke." I didn't believe one word of it and neither did Ash.

"Don't worry about it," Ash said graciously and led me back outside.

As she went to sit on my knee, Michael interjected, patting his leg, "Come to me sexy boxers," he said. The crowd appreciated it and laughed with her, lightening her mood considerably. He grimaced playfully as she sat on his lap and said to me, "Christ twin, you must have thighs of steel. How much weight have you put on Ash?" She punched him lightly on the arm and told him to knock it off. He grinned at her before pressing his lips against her cheek in a loud 'Mwuah'.

"Hey, I haven't had one of those yet," Glen said and gave Ash his own application.

"Your lips are really soft Glen," she told him, and he gave her another one on her lips.

"I rub baby oil into them every night," he told her, and she looked at me smiling.

"No Baby, no baby oil for Lorien."

"You know how they get baby oil don't you?" Michael asked. Ash shook her head. "They squeeze babies." She smacked him on the arm again and snuggled into him. She was always exuberant when in the company of our friends.

"Can I have her back now?" I asked.

"Not yet twin, I'm not done driving her crazy." Ash smiled at me and I grimaced, motioning her over, but Michael wouldn't let her go. I sighed and grabbed another beer, turning my attention to Melayne.

Eli was doing his best to keep both girls occupied but was struggling a little. I stood and tapped him on the shoulder, asking to see him inside for a second. "You have your hands full," I joked.

"More than you know, bro," he said and laughed.

"I thought Jared was after Faith?" We started to walk to the bathroom, not wanting anyone coming in to 'assist' us before I could find out what was happening with my twin.

"She doesn't look very interested in him tonight have you noticed?" I had.

"How's Jared taking it?" I hadn't really spoken to him much so was unsure what his reaction was to it.

"They're not a couple so I assume he's taking it all in his stride. He does keep trying to get her attention though. The worst part of it is I'm not interested in either of these girls, well certainly not right now." We finished peeing and I said,

"Hang in there bro." He rolled his eyes at me and flushed the toilet. Whilst washing our hands, Eli asked,

"Is that the best advice you've got for me?"

"Yep." I clapped him on the back, and we made our way back to the verandah.

Several more beers and other drinks later, the party was starting to take hold. Everyone, including myself, was getting pretty full with the exception of Ash and Melayne; Melayne was driving. I always got extra horny when I'd been drinking, and Ash didn't stop me when I started to lightly stroke the side of her breast with my fingers, nuzzling my face into her ear. I chuckled when I felt her squirm a little on my lap and I looked up to see her already smiling softly at me. "I'm horny," I breathed into her ear, using enough force to make her shudder. I was so glad I *could* be horny again, having the results back, giving us the green light for continued sex.

"You'll have to wait lover," she whispered back. I lowered her face down to mine and kissed her. It was dark where we were sitting so she didn't seem overly inhibited. She drew back, saying, "Poo! What's that stink?" Glen had sparked up a joint and was in the process of passing it around. Everyone took a hit except Melayne, even Eli, but when it came around to me, I knew better. Drugs had put me in a problematic position with Ash once before and I was not about to do it again. "It's OK Lorien, take it; it's the chemicals I don't want you near again. I have to go for a second though as it's making me nauseous." She climbed off my lap and went around to the other verandah. I took a quick hit and passed it to Michael before going in search of her.

I'd never smoked pot before and had heard the first time didn't do anything. However, lying on the sun lounge with my Baby in my arms, I realised that I was buzzing nicely. Adding it to the several beers I had probably didn't help either. "How do you feel Lorien?" Ash asked.

"Good, floaty, weird."

"That's quite a combination of words," she laughed, then kissed me. "You taste sweet and musky," she said, twisting her face up a little. I hadn't brought my beer with me so couldn't wash it away. Fortunately, the smell of beer was not one of her aversions.

"Let's go back to the others. We can come out here the next time Glen sends one around."

"Won't you want some more?" she asked.

"I'll remember to bring my beer with me," I winked.

The mood was completely different when we returned, and I couldn't help but notice Eli holding Faith's hand. Well, not exactly holding it, she had hers on his upper thigh and he had his hand over hers. I wasn't sure whether he was stopping her from going any further or whether it was a sincere intimate gesture. Interesting…

Someone had cranked the music up and they were all singing to Crowded House. I joined in with the harmony and Faith looked at me before saying, "Looks like there's a *big* talent in this family." Eli was *certainly* going to have his hands full. I was curious as to whether Faith had already had a handful of him, as her comment bawdily suggested.

I didn't realise that Bree and Simon were missing until they came out from the kitchen with plates of heated party food. The pot had taken its toll, and everyone hooked into it, warding off the munchies. "No rhyming foods tonight, Bree?" I asked, remembering back a few years to the game Ash, Bree and Michael had when presenting items on display.

"We've outgrown it," she smiled at me.

"And no party games from you either tonight Michael? That's a switch."

"The night is still young," he said and winked. Ash looked at me and made a face, knowing that she'd be his victim, once again. I hugged her and laughed, opting to then snack on my favourite party food, her lips.

My erection popped up to say hello not long after and she smiled down at me, tracing her finger across my jaw. "Go and slip your panties off," I whispered which made her laugh.

"You know I don't wear them anymore," she said at my ear and I licked my lips and purred at her. I had forgotten. I dropped my hand to the edge of her long skirt and moved it slowly up her silky leg. She stopped me when I reached her knee, telling me it was far enough. Every time she moved, or I did, I inched my hand further upwards. She eventually worked it out and frowned at me, so I went for broke, sidling my hand up to quickly tease her for a millisecond before she had the chance to intervene. It had not gone unnoticed however, and I saw Michael grinning and Faith watching us intently.

"Lorien!" she whispered, and I laughed, wrapping both arms around her again securely, melding my lips to her throat. I growled into her ear and started lightly stroking her breast again. My other arm managed to block this view from the others.

"I will take her back from you twin if you can't keep your hands to yourself!" Michael interjected. "How long have you been together?" He knew the answer, but I still responded,

"Nearly five and a half years."

"Are you ever going to get sick of each other?" I looked at Ash and she returned my smile as we answered together,

"Never."

"I think it's sweet," Melayne said, and Faith scoffed. Apparently, I missed many interactions that night. Melayne rose and said, "I'm going. Anyone who wants a lift, now is the time to decide." Patrick and Trudy rose, as eventually did Jared, looking at Faith forlornly. It didn't seem she was going anywhere and had sunk even further into Eli's side.

Ash and I stood to see them to the door and when it appeared Eli wasn't, I gave him a light smack to the back of his head. "What?" he said. He was pretty drunk, or stoned, or both.

"Some of your guests are leaving."

"Be right back," he said to Faith and joined us at the door to see them off. Melayne and Ash even had a little hug. They had bonded well tonight.

When back at the table, there was complete silence; no one had obviously said a word in our absence. I was hoping if Eli was going to nail this girl, he would just get on with it and take her to his room. He was enjoying himself though and was in no rush. "I really liked your friends that just left," Michael said pointedly. He was not keen on the one that was still here.

"Trudy's a riot," Bree added. "We exchanged numbers and we're going to stay in touch." It looked like we would be adding Patrick and Trudy to our circle of friends.

"Is everyone ready for a game?" Michael asked. We were. I noticed Simon had been very quiet and when I looked at him, realised he was smashed.

"Hop up for a second Baby. I want to pull the sofa bed out in case Simon needs to crash."

"Are you OK Simon?" she asked.

"Hell yeah, I'm rockin' on in my own head here." Ash laughed and followed me into the lounge room. I took the pillows off the sofa and she started tugging on the flap to extend the frame out.

"What are you doing Baby?" I chastised her. "Let me do that." She smiled and stepped away, allowing me to pull the bed out. The best thing about this sofa bed was there was no middle support. The trampoline base under the mattress would provide a good sleep to whoever ended up on it. Not that anyone in this crowd would care by the time they went to bed.

When back outside, Glen was passing around another joint and I took a hit, taking my beer with me this time and following Ash to the northern verandah. "Come here," I said and pulled her to me, kissing her as deeply as our mouths would allow. I smiled at her and dropped to my knees, ducking under her dress. "Oh Baby, I have waited all night for this," and I teased her softly, savouring the sweetness. After a few minutes, I could feel her legs trembling and she said,

"Stop Lorien, I'm going to fall over."

"But you haven't…"

"Later Baby," she said and flicked her dress back from over me.

"That's a promise!" She smiled and pulled me up to her, nuzzling her lips at my throat.

"It's your turn first tonight."

"If you keep doing that, it will be over right now." She laughed and kissed me again before leading me back to the sodden messes that awaited us.

Eli was getting right into it now; he and Faith were locked at the lips and the rest of them were watching in silent amusement. I grabbed another beer and lemonade from the esky before sitting down. "How long has this been going on?" I asked, tilting my head toward the hungry couple.

"Long enough. It reminds me of you two," Michael said, laughing.

"You think so?" Ash asked sarcastically.

"Well maybe not the lead actress, but the play they're performing seems familiar." We all laughed loudly at this image and Michael was right. "Ready to play now?" he asked with a hint of inference to Eli and Faith. We were. "OK, it's called 'I Twitter, therefore I am'. All you need to do is write a better time waster than being on bloody Twitter, for example, count the individual hairs on each of your arms. Got some paper Ash?" She hopped up, grabbed a pad off the fridge, and passed it to Michael along with a handful of pens. At least this game of Michael's couldn't take constant shots at her as many of his other games usually did. I was sure she was happy about this too, although Michael was a character when it came down to embarrassing my wife.

She climbed back onto my knee and took the paper from Michael, handing a sheet to me before pursing her beautiful mouth up in thought. I wrote down the first thing that came to my mind, 'learn the ancient art of mummification' and handed it back to Michael. When all the sheets were in, he read them out, numbering them to make it easier to remember.

"OK, here are your choices people and I will read through them a few times so you can pick who wrote each one. Faith and Eli did not participate.

1. Sort your record albums by hue.
2. Bookmark every page on the internet.
3. Build a car out of used tissues.
4. Film an amateur porn video.
5. Learn the ancient art of mummification.
6. Further impregnate Ashlyn.

We laughed all the way through the list, with Ash throwing a well-deserved glare at Michael when he reached number six. "Don't you think I've tried," I laughed and she smacked me lightly. "In fact, the sex is so good the surrounding wildlife has a cigarette when we're finished." She smacked me again but laughed with the rest of us.

"If you smoke after sex, you're doing it wrong," Glen said, and we laughed again.

"Yes is the answer, sex is the question." Simon said quietly, smiling, his eyes closed. He had been quiet for so long and we all looked at him in initial silence before bursting into peals of laughter. God, it was all so funny.

We handed our paper back to Michael and he shuffled through them, this time marking them for us. Ash got all six; I had four. Michael's was obvious as was Glen's, him being the only one actually to still have enough record albums to need to sort. Simon's was the porn video, you could always rely on him to bring it to the gutter, but I had Ash and Bree's reversed. Bree wanted to build the car out of used tissues.

Eli and Faith found their feet, the hilarity being a mood breaker. They muttered their goodnights before heading for the stairs. We played a few more rounds and then Ash yawned widely, trying to conceal it with her hand. "Time for bed Gorgeous," I said.

"No, not yet, I'm having a great time. I'll sleep in tomorrow."

"OK," I told her "but put your pyjamas on at least." She nodded and I led her upstairs to change.

"I can do this on my own Lorien. You didn't have to come with me."

"I love coming with you," I said, making my point obvious by pressing against her at the hip.

"You're a sex maniac," she said, knowing she was just as guilty.

Neither of us was expecting the sight that welcomed us in the upstairs hallway. Eli and Faith were bonking right there with Faith backed up against the wall, her skirt around her waist. "You want to take that into your room Eli?" I said and quickly herded Ash into our room. She wasn't a happy camper and started fuming at me. "Hold on Ash, just remember that Eli caught us at it on the dining room chair once."

"And he was really pissed off about it too!" He had been.

"Are you going to let that spoil your night?"

"No," she said, "I guess not, but I can't *stand* that woman!"

"She was standing OK in the hallway," I joked. She smiled at me then changed into her pyjamas, covering them with a robe, all done whilst muttering under her breath. The hallway was vacated when we left our room.

Simon was asleep on the sofa bed when we came back down, snoring lightly. I was feeling pretty ripped myself. "Do you want a tea Ash?" I asked as she went to join the others outside.

"Can I have a hot milo?" she asked.

"Of course Baby, I'll bring it out to you." She gave me a kiss and went outside.

Ash got off the chair to let me on first and I handed her the milo. They were in the midst of discussing Snipers, and Glen was telling them about the floorshows. "Since you didn't have a buck's night or doe show, I think you should come in and have a joint belated one," Glen suggested. "You'll have a great time and will of course be my special guests for the evening."

"I've had enough joints for tonight," I said and laughed. It was agreed that we would go within the next few weekends and the girls were excited, discussing what to wear. Bree and Simon would come here and get dressed and we would leave together. Ash was happy to drive so Bree and Simon would then stay the night.

Bree snuck off to bed shortly after. I was surprised she'd lasted as long as she had. Usually, it was Simon putting Bree to bed first. My bride was going on the nod, so I told the guys to make themselves at home and to lock up when they were done. Michael knew his way around and where to find my old room. I lifted Ash into my arms and said goodnight; they both smiled at me and whispered goodnight to Ash too. She was out to it though and I was glad I'd asked her to put her pyjamas on earlier.

I opened the door and switched on the light in the guest bedroom so Michael and Glen could see when they made their way to bed. All was quiet from Eli's room. I eased Ash into bed and stripped off, nuzzling into her from behind. I seriously thought about waking my Baby girl when she settled further against me, her little bum wriggling to maximise her comfort. I eyed her hungrily and let my hands run softly from her shoulders down to lightly squeeze her firm rear and she sighed and edged closer until she was aligned fully to me. I thought this might get me into more trouble than needed at this time of the morning so instead fell into the easy slumber of a pissed stoner, my arms holding her against me. This would be ample until we both woke.

Fireworks

"Let her cuss, let her scream – drive me wild Baby, be mean.
Your ire's like fire,
Take me down, be obscene."

L Standish, 'Underworld'

MY BABY GIRL MIRACULOUSLY WOKE BEFORE I DID and chose a *truly* exceptional way to bring me from my dreams. Her supple little mouth was working me diligently under the covers and I was about to thank her inappropriately by blowing the back of her head off. "Baby, come to me," I whispered in half sleep, not wanting this to be over just yet.

"Nuh uh," she mumbled, "this one's all yours." I groaned, nearly there, and tried to lift her exquisite mouth from me. At the very least, I didn't want her ingesting it.

"Ashlyn, stop," I said urgently, but it was too late, and I erupted, working my fingers through her soft hair until she had indeed drained me. She gave Mr Winky a final kiss and moved up beside me.

"You're naughty," she said, an impish grin playing on her lips. There was no greater way to thank the woman who had just brought you off orally than to kiss her deeply in appreciation. I pulled her to me, my breath still coursing as I sealed my lips to hers, already in full twitch for round two.

"Why am *I* naughty?" I asked through the kiss. This would be interesting. She just laughed softly into my mouth as her answer. She would give me no more than that, not that I expected her to. "Let's be naughty together," I suggested and started to move down her body, stopping to torment at those wonderful boobs on the way past.

"No Lorien, we have guests. We can't stay here all morning."

"What time is it?" I asked, sitting up slightly to view the clock on the nightstand.

"Nearly 10.00 am." Wow, I hadn't realised it was so late. I didn't see how it mattered though and captured her gaze as I worked my hand past the elastic of her pyjama knickers, gliding my fingers through her slick arousal. She must have enjoyed her method in waking me, as much as I had. Sighing lightly, she lay back, not stopping me, and after only a few minutes, I evened the score. My twitching erection was now fully awake as I watched her writhe and squirm next to me, trying to move away from the hand that was invoking so much pleasure, subsequently putting hers over mine to keep it there. Her face was flushed and when she finally opened her beautiful blue eyes, she smiled at me kittenishly, making my heart lurch. God, I loved this woman.

I worked her pyjama knickers off and lazed her camisole up, moving in behind her. I took one breast in my hand as I entered her, loving the tight slickness of her grasp. "I love morning sex," I purred into her ear, driving her crazy.

"You love sex, full stop," she said, laughing quietly. The quiet laugh became a soft groan as I pushed into her harder and deeper, changing the erotic game of making love into pure unadulterated fucking. She arched her back slightly, giving me more room to move and I soon took us both to the orgasmic frenzy that governed our little world.

We lay together, still connected, the slight smile on my face welcoming the new day, and what a way to start the day. I chuckled lowly against her back and kissed her softly, tracing a line from shoulder to shoulder before nuzzling into her neck. "I love you so much Lorien," she sighed and rolled slightly toward me, breaking our seal, muttering a disappointed, "Oh." I smiled down at her, taking her delicate face in my hands and brushing my lips over hers.

"I love you Ashlyn Diane Standish and I love that I get to prove it to you over and over and over and..." She cut me off, laughing, then drew me to her to finish our act with the soulful, open-mouthed kisses we both loved to share. God, I *loved* this woman.

She eventually sighed and sat up, looking at me with a wry smile. "Time to get up?" I asked and she climbed over me to get out of bed. I gave her cheeky bum a light smack on the way past, and she scowled at me, trying not to laugh.

"Come on Lorien, get up," she said and tugged on my arm futilely.

"Make me." She grabbed Mr Winky and led me out of bed. I didn't want it coming off in her hand, and the force she dragged me with, made me believe she would do just that. "OK, OK," I laughed and scooted to the edge of the bed and sat there for a few minutes, rubbing my hands over my face and raking my fingers through my hair.

"Do you have a hang-over?" she asked, pulling clothes from the wardrobe. Her chosen long shift for the day was blue, which matched her cerulean eyes so perfectly. I lost myself a little in them, forgetting she'd asked me a question. "Lorien?" she prompted, curious as to why I hadn't answered. She smiled, having caught my expression, knowing I'd been elsewhere for the moment.

"Huh? What?"

"Do you have a hang-over?" She came and sat next to me.

"No, but I feel a little groggy, which I assume is from the pot."

"Are you coming to shower with me?" she asked. This was a question she didn't need to ask twice.

We made our way downstairs, noticing the other two bedroom doors were closed. Bree and Simon were awake, but still lying in bed; Simon looked a little worse for wear.

The sight that met me in the kitchen took me by surprise and I knew Ash would have seen it too. Faith was rummaging through the fridge dressed only in one of Eli's T-shirts and nothing else. She was bent at the waist and her entire landscape was on display. I had forgotten she was even here.

Michael and Glen came down the stairs at that moment and I heard Ash suck in her breath. Faith turned around and smiled sarcastically before throwing out a 'good morning'. "Would you *mind* putting some clothes on Faith, we have guests. And, two of those guests are gay men who do *not* want to see your tonsils from behind!"

"Sorry Ashlyn, I didn't know anyone else was up."

"Where's Elijah?"

"Still in bed. In fact, I think we'll be there for most of the day," she responded with a wink.

"Well, I suggest you go back to him and get the hell out of my kitchen until you can dress yourself properly." Faith smirked at her but went back to Eli's room.

I was stunned. I'd never heard my little one get stuck into anyone before, well, other than me. When she turned to me with a pissed-off look on her face, I was smiling widely and I took her into my arms, laughing. This broke the silence and our friends joined me, laughing hysterically. "Go get her Ash!" Simon said. "Not that I wasn't enjoying the view."

"How do you put up with him Bree?" Ash asked, rolling her eyes at Simon. I gave her a quick kiss on the forehead and released her so I could put on the coffee, chuckling and shaking my head as I went into the kitchen. I couldn't help myself and pulled my boxers to under my butt-cheeks, bending deeply and reaching into the fridge, waggling my bum at them.

"That looks a hell of a lot better than the badly packed kebab we were just visually raped with," Michael laughed, and this set us all off again.

We made ourselves comfortable on the side verandah; it was a beautiful day. "What do you want to do today?" Michael asked. No one was in any hurry nor had any momentous plans in the hopper, so we decided to hang out at our place. No doubt, most of them were waiting on the second instalment of the Faith versus Ashlyn challenge and I felt a little sorry for Faith, knowing that she couldn't win this one in our home.

I grabbed some tomatoes, mushrooms, bacon and eggs and lit the barbeque. My stomach was growling, and I assumed everyone else would be hungry too. "What do you want for breakfast Sweetheart?" I asked Ash, and today's menu selection was to be a bacon sandwich, which was a new one. It wasn't as simple as it sounded though. The bread was to be un-toasted with just a teaspoon of barbecue sauce, a light spread of maple syrup and real butter, not margarine. "Not a problem Baby," I said and pulled her back to me for a kiss before she sat down, keeping our seat warm.

With my brother in mind, not Faith, I cooked enough for eight and put theirs in the oven to keep warm. The eggs would be like poison by the time they got around to eating them but that was not my concern. I handed out the plates and grabbed the juice from the fridge, the cutlery and sauce, salt and pepper. Eli and Faith were on the way downstairs. This time she'd managed to put on a pair of his boxers, and I was relieved; I didn't want her working Ash into a pointless frenzy. "That smells so good, is there enough for us?" Eli asked.

"It's in the oven. I just put them in there so they should still be hot." Ash got up so I could sit down, circling her with my arms to get to my plate. She pouted at me. "What?" I asked through a mouthful of bacon.

"You didn't cut the crusts off," she said playfully, and I smiled at her and proceeded to do so.

"Pregnant women are *really* high maintenance hey?" Faith said as she took a seat. A foreboding silence fell over us. Michael's mouth was twitching. I knew he wanted to answer on Ash's behalf, but he wasn't given the chance.

"Don't start Faith," Eli said to her.

"It's OK Elijah," Ash said to him. "I assume you've taken your beer goggles off now though? It must be pretty hard to see through them in the clear light of day." She took a bite of her sandwich and smiled at Faith sweetly. Faith wasn't an ugly girl by any stretch of the imagination, but this comment seemed to have hit the target nicely.

"What's your problem with me Ashlyn?" Faith asked innocently. Ash scoffed before answering.

"The first words out of your mouth to me last night, in *my* home, were an insult and then every word after that was a constant dig. And then, to top it off, you go flashing your gash all over the place this morning. You need to remember I'm hormonal Faith, and I would get away with first degree murder on a sympathy or temporary insanity plea at the moment, so don't push it!" She delivered the last three words with a poke to Faith's chest. She slapped Ash's hand away, and suddenly everyone was standing, including me.

"Eli, if you don't do something about this *right now* I will, and I don't think you'll like my resolution." I stood Ash behind me protectively and when I looked across the table, Bree and Michael were fuming.

"Let me at her," Bree said. "I can hit a girl where Michael can't."

"Can't I?" he said and slipped Faith a sneer.

"This is a jealousy thing isn't it?" Faith asked. "You're just pissed because Elijah cares for me."

"Are you sure you don't have that the wrong way around Faith?" Ash responded.

"Why would he? You're just a fat, old, pregnant woman with nothing to give the world except some bastard kid."

"Says she who runs a coffee cart!"

"I'm a barista, thank you very much."

"No, you're just a bitch!" Michael added.

"Right, that's it. Faith, get your stuff, you're out of here." I said.

"Hang on, everyone just calm down!" Eli said and took Faith under his arm, rubbing her shoulder lightly. She smirked at me and then at Ashlyn and Michael, thinking she had won. Glen took Michael by the hand and led him to the other verandah in an attempt to cool him down.

"Eli, if you don't get her moving I will go to your room and personally throw her stuff out the window. It's your choice bro!"

"Come on Faith, we'll go back upstairs. I'm guessing you'll want to have a shower and freshen up before I take you home."

"Definitely Elijah," she crooned as he led her through the dining room. "After all the great sex we had last night I can hardly sit down," she called over her shoulder and Eli picked up the pace.

"What a fucking bitch!" Bree said. "You should have let me smack her one Lorien!"

"Yeah, great idea Bree, and then you'd be on charges for assault."

"It would have been worth it," Simon grumbled and took Bree onto his lap. I turned to my Baby and silent tears were streaming down her face.

"I didn't mean for anyone to get this upset, especially causing friction between you and Elijah," she sobbed, and buried her face into my chest.

"No Honey, Faith had no right, and Eli should have stopped her before it went that far. No one is blaming you..." I held her for a while and ran my hand over her back, "Shhh Baby, shhh."

"Is she OK?" I heard Michael ask behind me, having returned a little more level-headed.

"I *am* high maintenance!" Ash said and Bree handed her a tissue to wipe her nose.

"No Baby girl, you're pregnant."

"With some bastard kid," she said and started to cry hard again.

"We're married Sweetheart. Bump won't be a bastard. Faith was just trying to get a rise out of you. And besides, the term is a little outdated now, don't you think?" She smiled through her tears and nodded.

"If I *ever* see that slag again..." Michael muttered under his breath.

Eli came back down with Faith about twenty minutes later and they both walked straight through to the front door, leaving without a word. I knew Eli and I would be revisiting this conversation when he got home, and rightly so, he had some explaining to do. How could he let Ashlyn be treated so abhorrently? He loved her nearly as much as I did, and she was his sister, *and* about to make him an uncle.

After they'd been gone about an hour, the mood lightened again, Glen assisting by bringing out another joint. I didn't have any this time, choosing to be in the same frame of mind as my Baby girl, but we revelled in the rest of their hilarity. We ended up pulling 80s Trivial Pursuit out and were still playing aggressively when Eli came home. "Let me up Baby," I said when he came through the door. There was no point putting this off or evading it until everyone had gone; they were all witness to the scene, the same as I had been.

"It's OK Lori," he said and came to Ash. "I'm sorry Ash, so very sorry. It should never have happened, and I should have put a stop to it before it started." At least he was seeing reason and was dutifully taking the blame, as he should have been. "I promise I'll never bring her here again and I hope you can forgive me." She took him into her embrace and hugged him tightly.

"I love you Elijah, I don't want to see *you* hurt."

"I know," he muttered into her hair and held her for a long time. I still wanted to have a go at him, but the reason had now passed. They'd managed to get through it between them. However, I was going to have a pre-warning word to him later about anyone else he ever brings home, going through the same situation again.

"Awww, that's sweet," Michael chimed. "Looks like the twin sandwiches are back on the menu again hey Ash?" The four of them cracked up and Eli looked at them, smiling.

"You guys are all stoned, aren't you?"

"Want some?" Glen offered.

"May as well," Eli conceded, and they all went out onto the verandah to pass another one around.

My lips were on hers the moment the door slid shut and I kissed her, holding her to me as tightly as I could. "I love you Ashlyn, I'm sorry you've had to go through this."

"Lorien, just hold me," she whispered, and I did until she tilted her head back and sought my lips again. By the time the rest of them came back in, I was hard against her and she looked down, smiling at me warmly. God, I loved this *woman*.

It was a wonderful lazy day we spent together. Even Eli stayed with us, not holing himself up in his room for a change, swatting over the ever-thickening textbooks. I imagine he'd missed the social interactions with our friends and was making up for last night and this morning. I saw him cast a few wistful glances at Ash over the course of the afternoon, the pot possibly making him consider the events more deeply than necessary, now it was done. She saw him looking at one stage and smiled at him, causing his slight smile to break into a grin.

No one was fit to drive as the day went on and it was decided they would stay tonight and leave for work from here tomorrow morning.

Simon was the only one it really affected, as Michael and Glen were free to work at their leisure and Bree was part-time.

Simon and Eli went out and started the barbeque and Glen followed them. "Don't you want to join the other men?" Michael asked, relating himself to being one of the women.

"Nope." I was quite happy sitting with my Baby on the sofa, listening to her yak it up with Bree and Michael. I was however watching the guys outside and saw Glen light another joint. Simon tapped on the glass and waved it at the rest of us, Ash saying to me,

"Go on, have some Lorien." She smiled at me as I got off the sofa, throwing her a dazzling smile. Why not? She watched us through the glass door, laughing as we laughed, enjoying the stupidity that was happening on the verandah. At one stage Bree collapsed on the ground in a braying hilarious gasp, and I left Simon to rearrange her, grabbing a beer on my way back through.

"They're a bunch of characters," I told her.

"I'm sure you had nothing to do with any of it."

"Of course not Baby, I can't be carrying on like that. I'm about to be a father." I crawled back onto the sofa, laying my head in her lap. She snorted and leant down to kiss me.

Bree and Michael joined us inside and I was only partially aware of the conversation going on around me. Ash jostled me every now and then with her tummy as she laughed. I ended up rolling to face her and placed my hands on her stomach and lay there content, just holding her. She curled her fingers into my hair, and I looked up at her. *You're smashed*, she mouthed to me. I leant up and kissed her. *I know!*

The three guys ended up back in the lounge room with us and I wondered briefly who was cooking the meat. I felt Ash's stomach move and it had such an effect on me I jumped and ended up rolling onto the floor. They laughed hysterically at me and I couldn't get my words out. "Bump just kicked!"

"Wake up to yourself Lorien," Eli said, "it's impossible." I got onto my knees and put my hands back onto Ash,

"I'm *telling* you, I felt something." I waited for it to happen again.

"Ash?" Eli asked.

"I didn't feel anything," she said.

"Are you sure Baby?" I asked and lay my head against her, trying to hear something.

"It won't be blowing a horn in there you know," Michael said.

"I'm sure Sweetheart," she told me, and I relaxed a little, still thinking in the back of my mind I'd felt something. She was trying not to laugh with the rest of them, but her smile was wide. *I love you*, she mouthed, and I laughed too, realising I was just stoned. Then I started to panic.

"What if she needs to go to hospital and we're all stoned!" Some responsible father I turned out to be.

"We'll call an ambulance Lorien," she said, calm as ever. I looked around the room, my eyes wide, still feeling a little unconvinced, and Eli nodded.

"It's OK Lorien, you're just freaking out because you're stoned." I knew this, but it was still a possibility that something could happen.

"Please Lorien, calm down, everything's OK." My Baby girl took my hands in hers and I helped her stand. She hugged me and whispered to me again the words of comfort. I was happy just to hold her, circled by our little group of friends.

"Ah Elijah," she started, looking over my shoulder onto the verandah, "what's on the barbeque?" Glen, Eli and Simon all looked at each other and burst out laughing.

"Nothing!" they blurted out before the laughter took them off again.

"Sorry," Eli said, getting to his feet. "We got side-tracked and only lit it." He went to make his way outside and I stopped him, taking Ash with me. I was happy to tend the food as long as she was happy to sit with me whilst I did so. They could look after the side dishes.

Over an hour later, we all finally pulled it together to actually eat.

BACK TO ASHLYN

Clubbing

> "*Rat a tat tat, make your feet do that*
> *And match the beat of my heart*
> *Take my lead, hit the mat.*"
>
> L Standish, '1, 2, 3, 4 - On the Floor'

MY EYES WERE ASSAULTED with a spray of activity and colour as we reached the top of the staircase that led us to the entrance of Snipers. Glen directed us straight in, not forming part of the paying line that was waiting to get through the door, nodding to the girl in the box taking money from the waiting entrants. She nodded back and then smiled at our small group, mouthing something we couldn't hear over the thumping music. "She said she's been looking forward to meeting you all," Michael said at my ear, understanding her unheard voice. He was obviously used to reading lips in this environment, as did they all. I smiled at her, and Glen moved us onwards, directing us to a vacant front row table on a raised area on the left-hand side of the room. From here, I could take in the whole venue and I was fascinated.

Disco balls and flashing lights held and moved the dancers on the lit up 70s style dancefloor. This drew my gaze for the longest time and Lorien finally had to take my face in his hands to get my attention. *Do you want a drink?* he mouthed at me. I nodded and he leant down and gave me a quick kiss before heading to the bar with Michael, Glen and Simon.

"Full on!" Elijah said at my ear and I grinned at him, enjoying myself immensely.

"Don't tell me you've been to a gay bar before!" I yelled back, not able to swing fully around to get to his ear.

"No!" he laughed. "But I assumed it would be something like this!"

"Not worried you might be propositioned!?" He squinted his eyes at me and tilted his head, shaking it. He hadn't heard me. I pointed to him and yelled '*propositioned*!' and this time he understood, laughing and leaning over to say,

"It wouldn't be the first time!" I laughed with him, and then looked deeper into the room.

There was a myriad of people here, and we weren't the only 'straights', or 'breeders' present. The handsome women confused me at first as I wasn't sure whether they were men, but noticing breasts swelling under some of those T-Shirts, I realised they were girls. And, speaking of girls, there were some beautiful women here; some were on the dancefloor and others were chatting at the bar, just looking fabulous. One group of men was dressed all in leather with their chests, and in some instances their bum-cheeks, prominently on display. Another genre of men included more effeminate types who danced merrily on the dancefloor, spinning and laughing amongst their peers. My eyes couldn't process all that this club contained in one sweep of the room.

I saw Kylie standing at the bar amongst some of the fabulous looking girls and nearly choked. I knew many celebrities were icons in the gay community, but I never expected to see such a famous Australian artist in a Castlebrook club. Lorien came back with the drinks and I stood quickly, speaking at his ear. "It's Kylie!" I squealed and pointed her out in the crowd. Lorien laughed and pulled me close,

"She's a drag queen Baby." All I could say was *what* a drag queen. She looked as much like Kylie as Kylie did herself; even her diminutive stature signalled in every way that she was the real thing. I realised that a lot of effort and possibly money went into looking that superb.

The guys handed around our drinks as Michael said something to Lorien who then guided me to the chair against the wall. "Michael doesn't want us 'rooting around all over the place', so he's asked us to take a less obvious spot," Lorien explained as I settled onto his lap.

"I don't think I'll have time," I told him, and he laughed, nuzzling into my neck as my hungry eyes once again scoured the room.

Glen excused himself shortly thereafter and a few minutes later, I heard his voice over the microphone. "Welcome patrons of Snipers!" he called. "It's nearly time for our 11.00 o'clock floorshow but first I want to introduce you to some friends of Michael's and mine and I expect you to make them all welcome." A spotlight hit our table and we all cringed from the brightness of it. I felt like a deer in the headlights and was not expecting this kind of attention, didn't want it to be honest. I was happy sitting back and letting it all happen around me. "Bree, Simon, Ash, Lorien and Elijah. Wave to the crowd guys," he said, and I lifted my hand in salutation, as did the rest of us. Michael sat there grinning at me, and I wondered whether he had something to do with this. It certainly smelt like Michael's work. I poked my tongue out at him and he poked his out right back at me and laughed. "And without further delay, please welcome Irma Gerd and Geoffrey." Applause rang out and a beautiful dark woman and one of the most handsome men I had ever seen had a curtain opened on them, in full starting pose. The music blared out.

They mimed to the George Michael version of 'Secret Love', and I became entranced in their web of dance, not realising I was jigging on Lorien's lap until he started to bounce me lightly on his knee. I turned to him, smiling; I was having *the best* time. I continued to check out Geoffrey. I was surprised the application of makeup to a man, when he was meant to *be* a man, could enhance so enticingly. He was very hot, scorching hot, and I was a little envious of Michael. What a smorgasbord surrounded him, but he loved Glen and I loved him even more for it. "I'm going to put makeup on you tomorrow!" I leant in and said to Lorien.

"No, you are not!" he said back, laughing. I smiled at him and returned to the floorshow, clapping loudly when the number ended.

"Is that it?" I asked Michael when the dance music started again, expecting there to be more.

"Only one song for the 11.00 pm show, there will be more shows." I couldn't wait.

Glen re-joined us a few minutes later. They were obviously a couple to be reckoned with. Many people stopped by our table, including the girl on the door, Leisa, to say hi to Glen and Michael, and also to us. They were such a group of unassuming people and I felt very welcomed. A few of them even touched my blossoming tummy after asking permission and I allowed their hands on me warmly. "I hope they don't rub your stomach with the same effect I get from you!" Lorien said at my ear. Turning me to face him, he grazed his lips over mine playfully.

"I want to dance!" I said and I got up off Lorien's lap, holding my hand out to him.

"I have to pee first!" he said. "I'll be right back!" I nodded and stood behind Elijah, tapping him on the shoulder.

"I want to dance!" He laughed and shook his head at me. "Come on!" I said and dragged him to his feet. There is no way I would have got him standing unless he allowed it, so he had resigned himself to his fate. He spun me around and drew me to him, leading me in our dance right next to the table. Simon and Bree joined us and soon after so did Glen and Michael. I had never had such a wonderful evening and I couldn't keep the smile off my face.

I felt myself being spun out, and found myself in Michael's arms.

"Having a good time!?" he asked.

"The best. This is great Michael!" He grinned and dipped me backwards, and I noticed upside down that Bree was now dancing with Glen. It didn't seem that the men were as desperate to dance as the ladies. Perhaps Michael and Glen hadn't given them a choice either.

Lorien came back to the table laughing, moving in behind me to speak to Michael. I couldn't hear what they were saying but I saw Michael nod and they both laughed loudly.

The next song was a slow one, well slow in comparison to the others, and Michael Jackson's 'You Are Not Alone' mixed into the current track, but in an upbeat dance version. Michael passed me to a waiting Lorien, and he held me close, slow dancing to the effervescent ballad. I lowered my head to his shoulder and let him lead me, floating in time to the music surrounding us. His hand moved to the back of my neck and he held me to him, lightly rubbing my nape as his other hand tightened around my hips, leisurely tracing down over my curves and back to my waist. I sighed and settled into his warm embrace.

We eventually took our seats and Glen headed off to get ready for the 12.30 am show. I couldn't believe we had been there for nearly two hours. I looked through the strobe lighting to find Glen at the back of the room and saw Kylie making her way in our direction. She was dressed in a Little Bo Peep type outfit with a parasol over her shoulder and she stopped at our table to talk to Michael. I was over-awed that this was *not* Kylie, and looked at her like a dumbstruck fan. I was sure if I had a piece of paper and a pen on me, I would have asked for her autograph.

Michael introduced her to us, and I stood and said in her ear, "You look wonderful!" I managed to refrain from asking for a selfie with her.

"Thanks," she said, "gotta go earn a living!" and headed for the entrance of the kitchen which would no doubt take her through to the back of the stage. I assumed we were to see Kylie perform in the next show, and she did, to 'I Should Be So Lucky'. She skipped and danced around the stage miming to perfection in a semi erotic performance, her parasol used successfully as a prop in this endeavour. When she whipped off the stage at the end, I couldn't believe she was redressed and back for the next number, containing another drag queen and the hot Geoffrey.

We were then entertained by an act from 'Cabaret' – 'Two Ladies' and it was humorous and enlightening, and I was lifted by the wit of the show. It was sexy, beguiling, engaging and honest, with comedy as the main affair, yet brimming with sexuality and inference. Kylie and Taffy Apples were dressed in the famous Liza costume, of whom Taffy resembled a great deal. They had matching black chokers and bowler hats, teemed with the short black halter bodysuit and thigh-high stockings. They were true artists and performers, professional and just... amazing! I leant over to Michael and said, "I'm hooked!"

"Kylie's birth name was Ray!" Michael said; it was still impossible to believe.

At the end of the show, I once again clapped loudly, and the guys whistled through their teeth. Glen introduced the four performers who bowed deeply when each of their names was called. The final drag queen in the show's name was Lotta Bagina and I admired their cleverness in selecting their names. I saw Lorien speaking to Elijah and Simon, then came to me and let me know we were about to go. "But I want to see the last show!" I complained.

"It'll be after 3.30 am before we get home if we stay for that. I think you've had a late enough night as it is!" I didn't argue with him but would have loved to see the rest. He caught my expression, leaning back to me and saying, "Another night Baby, this club isn't going anywhere!" I accepted that and thought what a time I would have next time I came here. I'd be able to drink, and dress in non-maternity clothes. I was really looking forward to it.

We said our goodbyes to Michael and waited for Glen to come back to the table. I hugged him fiercely and told him what a wonderful time I'd had. They escorted us downstairs to the car and I was surprised to see Elijah climb into the driver's seat. It was supposed to be me. "I only had a few drinks Ash, I'll drive," he told me, his voice having to compete with the ringing in my ears. Bree and Simon sat up front with him to allow me to stretch out across the back seat, but I was too excited to relax or nap, as possibly Lorien had in mind for me. He ended up sitting in the middle seat belt so I could lean into him instead.

For the first fifteen minutes, I didn't shut up, gushing and replaying the highlights of the evening. I then remembered to ask Lorien what he and Michael had been laughing about when he came back from the toilet. "They have a glory hole in there."

"Is that what it was?" Simon asked. "Lucky I didn't go looking through it, I might have got a poke in the eye." They all laughed, but I had no idea what one was. Lorien ended up telling me its purpose as tactfully as he could, explaining it was for anonymous oral sex encounters and I looked at him with my mouth open and eyes wide. Nothing about that club would cease to amaze or shock me; it was like a completely new awakening for me.

"We should get one installed at home," Lorien said, and Elijah piped up,

"I'll vote for that!" and the front seat inhabitants laughed in appreciation, continuing the conversation.

Lorien drew my head to his shoulder and played his fingers through my hair, his intention to get me sleepy no doubt. I was too wired though and didn't even have to fight off a dreamy half sleep. I was wide awake. "If you aren't going to sleep Baby, I'll take some of this instead," he mumbled and tilted my face up to his. He kissed me gently, slowly and then attacked my face, moaning, "Oh Kylie!" I broke away from him laughing, joining in with the trio up front. "Sorry Baby, I forgot where I was," he apologised and laughed, coming back to kiss me again. A few minutes later when the kisses deepened, he moaned, "Oh Geoffrey, Geoffrey!" and I sat back, laughing again.

"You are a worry Lorien," I said and shook my head.

"You thought he was hot, didn't you Baby? Did he get you all wet between the legs?" he asked, and sidled his hand up my thigh.

"Damn right!" I answered in stereo with Bree from the front seat, and we both laughed loudly with each other. The guys thought we were a little weird.

"Are you going to leave me for a male dancer?" Lorien teased, his hand riding higher until he found what he was looking for. "Hmmm?" he prompted when I didn't answer.

"I don't think I have the right appendages," I whispered.

"Oh Baby," he sighed, "yes you do…" I kissed him, trying to move his hand back into view but it was a struggle I couldn't win. I told him to stop though when it was getting a little out of control. He chuckled lowly and ceased his teasing, content to kiss me for the rest of the trip, not that his wandering hands didn't find other areas to keep themselves busy.

We made love twice when we got home and all within half an hour. I nuzzled into Lorien, still lying on his back catching his breath and I started to laugh. "What's so funny Baby?" he asked and tightened his arm around my shoulders.

"I must admire your form tonight Lorien, that was an impressive bout. What do you think brought that extra special horniness to the table? All those sexy drag queens and gay men?" I asked playfully. He rolled his eyes at me and sat up slightly.

"I think it was the make-out session in the car on the way home; nothing better than knowing you could be caught!" His eyes flashed as he smiled down at me. "I want to try it on the train sometime," he confided, making me laugh. "I'm serious Ash," he purred into my ear and I could tell he was, already half erect again.

"You're abnormal," I said.

"Why?"

"No man can get as many working erections as often as you do, surely." He laughed softly and reached between my legs.

"It's your fault Gorgeous. I just can't help myself, you drive me *insane*." He moved his hand slightly and started to massage my perineum, not knowing how sensitive the small patch of skin between my vagina and bum would be when he introduced this new activity a few days ago. He'd been Googling apparently, and it was *supposed* to decrease the chance of tearing during childbirth. It was only when an extremely embarrassed Elijah confirmed this that I took him seriously. Knowing Lorien, it could solely have been for his pleasure... and mine...

He dipped a finger into me and slid his now slick digit back again, this time not stopping until I felt him lightly circling against the entrance to my virgin orifice. I gasped. "Relax Baby," he chuckled, "I'm not going to go sticking anything in there."

"Then what are you doing?"

"It's something I came across in the Kama Sutra Michael gave me and Google is good for more than just pregnancy tips." He hadn't stopped and not that it was uncomfortable, it was making *me* feel uncomfortable. This was a new area for me, and I wasn't sure how I felt about it. "Relax Baby," he whispered, "it's supposed to feel good... Does it feel good?"

"I don't... know... I don't think so," I answered. I was anything but relaxed, so it wasn't doing what it was supposed to anyway.

"Do you want me to stop?"

"Yes." He chuckled and gave me a few last final prods, moving back to my perineum, stroking lightly.

"Fancy a tongue-lashing Baby?" he asked playfully. My face was hot and if the lights were on he would have been able to see my scarlet face, blushing furiously.

"No." I could feel him moving slightly under my touch and I knew he was laughing quietly. "Why do you put me through this Lorien?" I asked.

"Nothing wrong with pushing the boundaries is there? How would you know you don't like it until you've tried?"

"Is this something you would want me to do for you?"

"Not really Baby."

"But men have a prostate."

"So?"

"Isn't that why men like it more?"

"That's something I can't answer, I wouldn't know." I was fully aware of this, but wondered if he was curious. I wasn't sure I could help him anyway. "Want to ask Eli tomorrow?" he laughed.

"No! Definitely not!" He rolled to face me and held me to him, pressing his soft lips against mine.

"I love it when you get flustered," he whispered and worked his lips slowly around my jaw.

"I know you do, and I'm still waiting for the day you get sick of it." I felt him smile against my throat.

"That's never going to happen, unless you ever manage to get past the flustered stage. I don't see that happening either, well I hope not..."

He played the soft kisses to my face and lips for several minutes, then sighed breathily and sat up. "Roll onto your side Ash and scoot down the bed." I was a little nervous when he had me in whatever position he was contemplating, laying across the bed on my side with my back to him. He raised my top leg, and I was surprised to find him upside down to me, leering up at me over my pubic mound. I understood his intentions and he brought his mouth down and watched me through my V splayed legs, working his magic. I could feel him pressing hard into my upper back and the variant to the angle he fed on me from heightened me quickly, loving the new sensations. As I ebbed from my climax, he moved down my body, drawing my legs out straight in front of me, bending me at the waist to form a 90-degree angle to myself and he held my ankles in front of him as he drove in slowly, creating a T intersection.

"Oh God Lorien," I moaned, this was *so* incredible. "Oh…" He flicked his tongue over the soles of my feet and I burst alive, reeling with the force. "Don't stop Baby…" I implored, and he bent my upper leg to prise my curled foot open, licking the crease at the back of my toes. "Oh fuck," I cried, and he was relentless. I felt like I was falling through a deep ravine and wondered briefly when I would actually bottom out, when he would no longer be able to hold on. "Come on Baby, give it up for me," I urged, and he sucked the pad of my foot for one more blissful moment before tucking my calves between his shoulders and neck, locking me against him. Grasping my thighs firmly, he thrust harder, speeding up and finally moaned loudly, grinding himself into me with a final force, moving my whole body across the bed.

"Oh God, Ash," he cried, and followed with two more equally final and compelling hard thrusts, his back shining with perspiration. I smiled down at him and he blew the hair off his forehead with a quick upward exhalation. "That's a great position for your G-spot Baby," he said and smiled, bringing his legs up against my back, turning us into a whole-body V.

"From Google or the Kama Sutra?"

"Neither," he said, playing his toes into my hair as he lovingly stroked my thighs, "that was off the cuff."

"Wow!"

"I reckon," he laughed. "God I love you," he said and moved up to kiss me. I kissed him back and wondered whether anyone had ever died from being so much in love with another person?

Surprise Visitors

"When you least expect it, expect it!
When you know you don't want it,
It will be there, so take it."

L Standish, 'Who's at my Door?'

WE CAME BACK from our eighteen-week ultrasound in the same high spirits as we had from our twelfth. On the former visit, we were assured that our baby was healthy and not afflicted with any developmental problems; on the latter, we not only got to see Bump, it was now confirmed she was a girl. Our pleasure was obvious. We sat smugly toasting to our success on the sofa, me with juice and Lorien with a beer, when there was a knock at the door. "Hey Mr O," Lorien said to our high school music teacher when he opened the door.

"Hello Lorien, you're looking well," Mr O'Dowd said as Lorien showed him into the house. "Hello Ashlyn, you're positively glowing."

"Thank you, Mr O'Dowd," I said, climbing off the sofa to come and greet him with a kiss to his ruddy cheek.

"Please, call me Alan. We're all well and truly adults now." He smiled and I offered him a seat at the table, going to put on some tea.

"What brings you here Sir...? Alan..." Lorien asked, joining him at the table.

"That sounds like I'm part of King Arthur's court," Alan said, and we laughed with him. "A couple of things actually. I heard through your mother before she left that you were expecting. I must say Ashlyn, it's very becoming on you." I smiled a little shyly and brought the mugs to the table. Lorien moved around so I could climb onto his lap, as seemed to be our preferred seating arrangement these days. Mr O'Dowd... Alan... smiled warmly at our natural positioning. We were barely aware of it anymore as our bodies compelled us to be constantly touching. We were pregnant weirdos.

"We had some good news today Sir," I started.

"Alan," he reminded me.

"Sorry, it's hard to get used to." He nodded, waiting for me to continue.

"It's a girl," we said in unison. Lorien's hand lovingly caressed my stomach, smiling up at me warmly. Alan eventually broke our intent gaze with a slight clearing of his throat, and I felt my face warm.

"It's wonderful to see you both so happy, not that it wasn't a burden to me when you were in my care six periods a week." We laughed with him; never a truer word had been spoken. "Have you heard from your parents? How are they going on the road?"

"We speak to them every Sunday night. They're currently in Lightning Ridge; Dad's even had Mum out fossicking," Lorien laughed.

"Yes, hard to imagine," Alan agreed with a smile.

"When are you due Ashlyn?" he asked. As pleasant as this unexpected visit was, I felt that he was beating around the bush.

"The tenth of December," I said, clambering off Lorien's lap.

"Where are you going Ash?" he asked, much to Alan's enjoyment.

"To get some biscuits for our guest, Sweetheart." I gave him a light kiss and headed for the kitchen, grabbing the chip jar and other opals off the top of the fridge that Mum and Dad had sent through the week. Alan grabbed a biscuit and dunked it in his tea, much to *our* enjoyment, before putting on his glasses to inspect the opals.

"This one is unusual," he commented before passing the black opal to Lorien.

"I'm going to have it made into a ring for Ash when Mercy comes, but I suspect Mum and Dad bought it." I agreed with him, it was perfect - rounded and smooth and the size of my thumb.

"I think you may be right by the look of it. It would have cost them a pretty penny too I imagine." He put all the opals back into the bag and then looked at us both, smiling. "There's something else I wanted to talk to you about today; your future plans."

"I'm still composing Sir, Alan... sorry."

"And you're selling them?"

"Yes, it's financing us very well."

"I always knew you would be a major success Lorien," he said. "And you Ashlyn? Still thinking of teaching one day?"

"It's certainly my intention when Bump, I mean Mercy, is old enough." I smiled down at Lorien and he laughed, kissing me softly. I felt embarrassed at this level of intimacy in front of our beloved music teacher and drew away, blushing. Lorien chuckled softly. "Lorien is going to be the stay at home Dad."

"I assume Bump was a nick-name before you knew the gender?" I nodded and he laughed. "Very cute. Now," he said, coming back to his initial point, "I'm going on leave for two weeks at the end of August and I was wondering if either of you were interested in taking up my position as a casual?" Neither of us saw this coming and we looked at each other in surprise.

"Don't we need to be in the government to be able to work at the school?" Lorien asked.

"For you to become permanent you would need to go for a formal interview, but anyone with the credentials can be put on for up to six months without major formalities, along with my recommendation for the position, and the required qualifications, which you have. You'll need to undergo a criminal record and working with children check, but I don't imagine there will be a problem with either of those requirements." Lorien looked at me, obviously considering me for the role.

"I don't know Alan. We'll certainly help you out, but I think Lorien would be better suited for it than me."

"And why is that Ashlyn?" he asked.

"Yeah, why?" Lorien parroted.

"My memory isn't the best at the moment. Lord knows what it will be like by then." Alan laughed and shook his head.

"A lesson plan is all it takes to get through the day, I assure you. I've been teaching for nearly forty years, and quite successfully I believe." We smiled at him in recognition, knowing that his two favourite students had done very well, especially Lorien.

"Can we think about it?" I asked, "Just for a day or two?"

"Certainly Ashlyn, here's my phone number. Give me a call when you make up your minds. I will obviously handover to you properly before I go on leave too."

"Thanks Alan, I'll get back to you by the end of the week; well one of us will." I pulled a face at Lorien to let him know he wasn't off the hook yet either, it may be him going back to our old school. Wouldn't the young girls have a field day over Mr Standish! Hearts would rupture and melt... "Would you like to stay for dinner Sir?" He frowned at me playfully and I corrected myself yet again. "Alan."

"If it's no trouble, thank you Ashlyn. May I use the phone? I need to call my wife and I left mine in the car."

I pulled the chicken from the fridge, set it to bake in the oven, and started peeling some vegetables whilst Lorien challenged Alan to a game of chess. Elijah walked in fifteen minutes later. "Hey Mr O!" he said and came over to shake his hand. "I haven't seen you since our first gig."

"Alan," Lorien and I chorused together, and 'Mr O' laughed. Elijah had no problem in picking up the new name; he hadn't taken Music and therefore calling him Sir or Mr O'Dowd was not as ingrained. He sat with them at the table, and I brought in three beers, including a glass for Alan in case he was not a 'straight from the neck' kind of guy.

Elijah started driving Lorien insane, tut-tutting his choice of moves and calling him crazy at times. In final frustration, Lorien ordered him away from the table and he came to join me in the kitchen. "Hmmm, that smells good Ash, what are we having?"

"Baked chicken and vegetables. Can you pull it out of the oven for me Eli; I need to turn it over." He stared at me and I saw Lorien turn his head toward me. "What?" I asked.

"You called me Eli," Elijah said.

"No, I didn't."

"Yes, you did. Didn't she Lori?"

"You did Baby girl. Wow your guard is really down at the moment." He grinned at me and I saw the confusion on Alan's face.

Lorien explained it to him. "She's never called us anything but Elijah and Lorien, has never shortened our names. That's why it sounded so weird to hear her say it for the first time. You don't use a lot of pet names at all, do you Baby?"

"No 'Lori', I don't," I said, stressing his abbreviated name. I frowned at him slightly and he laughed, returning to the game. I could see the smart-arsed grin on 'Eli's' face as he put the vegetables around the chicken before putting it back in the oven. I nudged him playfully and he nudged me right back. Twins!

It was a wonderful meal, and when Elijah opened a bottle of wine, even I had a small glass. Conversation was effortless and many an old anecdote was told about Lorien and me in Music classes. It seemed so long ago to think back on it now. We also told Elijah about the temporary teaching position and that he was going to be an Uncle to a little girl. He was thrilled, and not only because there would now be a girl in his immediate family other than his mother, but this was what we wanted.

True to form of late, I ruined it all. When taking the apple pie from the oven I stumbled and dropped it all over the floor, bursting into tears. Lorien was instantly by my side, holding me to him. "Shhh Baby, it's OK." As he led me back to the table, Elijah cleaned up the mess.

"I'm just such a klutz these days, I can't do anything right. We had such a perfect day and evening, and now I've spoilt everything!"

"Now, now, Ashlyn, it's only a pie. And, if you remember back to your Year 7 maths class, you'll recall pi is 3.14. We don't have the .14 of a person to eat it anyway." I laughed into the wad of tissues Lorien had grabbed and looked at him through my tear-swollen eyes. His smile was warm and sincere.

"Do you have a family Alan?" I sniffed, pulling myself together. We'd never really been very personal with him prior to this.

"Yes, six children. I'm an old hand at dealing with an upset pregnant wife."

"Would you like to move in Alan?" Lorien asked, still rubbing his hand soothingly over my back. I dug him in the ribs with my elbow and he smiled cheekily at me.

"Everyone for coffee?" Elijah asked from the kitchen.

"Just a small one for me and then I need to be off, thanks Elijah," Alan said.

"None for Ash, give her a whiskey," Lorien added and received another jab to his ribs. I was feeling a lot better, however. I leant my cheek against his forehead and sunk further into his arms. "Are you OK now Sweetheart?" he asked lowly, and I nodded and kissed him lightly on the forehead. "Your aim is a little off," he said and kissed me properly.

"It's OK Alan," Elijah said, bringing in three coffees and a green tea for me, "you'll get used to it in time." Alan smiled and said,

"What you have is very special Ashlyn, Lorien, and you will make wonderful parents." We smiled at each other and then at Alan. We were certain of this too.

When he left, the twins shook his hand and I gave him another kiss. He hugged me, which was hard for him to do with Lorien's arm around my waist, but he managed. I felt embarrassed all over again at my tirade earlier. "Are you sure you still want me for your position Alan, after what you witnessed earlier? I can be rather erratic at times."

"You'll be fine Ashlyn. I certainly hope you'll consider it."

"I will," I told him. "I'll speak to you soon."

He waved as he pulled out of the driveway and I was still smiling when Lorien closed the door. He led me to the sofa and drew me onto his knee. Elijah was watching some crime show and we settled in to watch it with him.

Minutes later, I could see Elijah moving slightly in my peripheral vision and soon after, got the same quaking from under me. They were both laughing at something I'd been left out of, and I turned to Lorien for the explanation. Damn their unseen twin interactions. "What?" he asked. I raised my eyebrows at him, knowing he would relent sooner or later.

"It's because you called me Eli," Elijah said, aiding his twin with the answer.

"I didn't mean to. Lorien's the only person who I hear say your name and I guess it slipped out."

"You *can* call me Eli, Ash. It's not a problem you know."

"Hey, how come you shortened his name but have never had that problem with me? Surely your husband is the one it should have happened to first." I checked him before answering, not sure if he was serious. He was grinning at me and I rolled my eyes at him.

"I say *your* name about one hundred times a day; therefore, I'm immune."

"I love how you say my name," he said and took my face in his hands, lowering me to him and kissing me deeply. I forgot where we were and sunk into the kiss, allowing it to build and inflame.

"Are you going to bed, or shall I?" Elijah asked eventually.

"We'll go," Lorien answered quickly and darted up the stairs with me in his arms.

It was certainly a week for unexpected visitors. Lorien and I had just finished lunch the next day when there was another knock at the door. "Alan is eager for an answer," Lorien said as he went to open it. Of all people, it was Keren.

"Hi Lorien!" she said excitedly and hugged him.

"Hey Keren," he said and looked at me over her shoulder with his eyebrows raised.

"Ash, I heard. How are you going?" She hugged me with equal enthusiasm and rubbed her hand gingerly over my belly.

"Great Keren, it's really good to see you." She looked around the open-planned room, taking in any changes since she had last been here.

"Something hot or cold to drink?" Lorien asked from the kitchen. We both opted for cold and followed him out onto the verandah when the drinks were poured.

She caught up on a lot of gossip, letting her know how Bree and Simon were going, very proud that he was doing Accounting and how favourable that was for us at tax time. She knew Bree was hairdressing as she had made an appointment with her last month. I was surprised that Bree hadn't mentioned it. She asked about Michael and we told her that he'd finally met someone earlier this year, giving her the background on Glen and what a wonderful guy he was. She was surprised that they were living together, and that Bree and Simon had moved in. I was confused as to why she didn't already know all of this if she had seen Bree. "What's Michael doing these days?" she asked.

"He's a web page designer, working part time from home for a prominent Sydney based company and also free-lancing when the mood strikes him."

"I can't imagine he's changed very much?" I looked at Lorien and we laughed,

"No, not very much," I confirmed. "Glen is very suited to him too." She smiled and nodded, then mentioned the Honda and the new Lexus in the driveway.

"They were our wedding gifts to each other, not that I've been on the bike yet, but Lorien has his P-Plates now. You'd better have your full licence by the time Mercy comes along Mister," I told him. "I'm busting to get on it." Keren laughed and didn't mention her non-invitation to attend the wedding. I felt like I should explain it to her; it wasn't like we ended up on bad terms, although her constant jealousy grew very thin by the end. But, we had been friends for a long time before the Standish's rode into town. "It was a lovely wedding, wasn't it Sweetheart?" I said to Lorien.

"The best Baby."

"He organised the whole thing you know. It was very small and simple, just our parents and Cyndi, Frankie, Bree, Simon, Michael and Glen."

"What about Elijah?" she blurted out. I had been waiting for her to bring him up. "Of course he was there too. In fact, he formed the only part of the bridal party as Lorien's best man. I didn't have a bridesmaid; I couldn't choose between Michael and Bree."

"Got any photos?" she asked and Lorien went inside to get the albums.

She flicked through them slowly and Lorien caught my eye, both of us still curious as to the purpose of this visit. Not that there needed to be a reason, but I assumed there was. "So how is Elijah?" she asked finally, after staring at one particular photo for a length of time. It was the three of us standing at the end of the baths, the twins forming bookends on either side of me.

"He's great, second last year at Uni," Lorien said.

"Is he seeing anyone?" Keren asked, almost timidly.

"No, not since you broke up," I said. She smiled widely and then buried it, assuming that there had been no one 'special' enough to compare. I shot this down in flames quickly. "He swore off women until he's finished his degree although he does date every now and then. There's a lovely girl called Melayne in his classes at Uni." Lorien shot me a warning glance.

"Oh." She couldn't hide her disappointment. "Is he here?"

"No, at Uni." She didn't ask any further and I didn't offer. He'd be home in about an hour though and I thought I should warn him that Keren was visiting in case she was still here when he got home. I excused myself to use the bathroom and texted him whilst I was in there.

On my return, Lorien was apologising to Keren and I was curious as to why. "Keren asked for a ride on the bike, but I told her that the first pillion ride was saved for you." He leant over and kissed me but didn't linger. I wasn't on his lap for once and realised it was silly not to be in my usual position. There was no need to be formal just because Keren was here. If we didn't worry about it in front of Alan, why should we care with Keren? Lorien patted his knee and I smiled at him and climbed on. He could read my mind.

"I should have never let you go Lorien," she sighed. "It looks like you two have what it takes to make it forever." My considerate and tactful man didn't go into the details to explain that he and Keren wouldn't have lasted anyway, but answered her last statement with,

"Yes, it will be forever," and he kissed me again.

"I had my doubts after you played up on her that time." Neither of us acknowledged her comment, and I changed the subject.

"Are you seeing anyone Keren?"

"I was for a while in Sydney, but nothing too heavy. I got into the post office not long after Eli and I broke up and my first assignment was in a Sydney location. It's really hard to get a rural placement, but I finally got a transfer and have been at Castlebrook for a few months now."

"Where are you living?"

"Not far from Cyndi and Frankie. I've run into them a few times." So, she would have known a lot more about our current lives than she let on, it would seem.

She was in no hurry to leave and we eventually ran out of things to talk about. She sat there fidgeting for a while. There was something else obviously on her mind. I knew what it was as soon as I heard Elijah's key in the door. Her face brightened. "We're out here Eli!" Lorien called as he came through the door.

"Keren!" Elijah said when he saw her, possibly expecting her to have gone by now.

"Hi Eli," she said and stood, kissing him softly on the mouth.

"Ahhh, what brings you back to Sommersett?" he asked, taking a seat next to us. How did he know that she no longer lived here? Lorien and I excused ourselves and went to start dinner. It was only 5.00 pm, but thought we should make ourselves scarce.

It was another twenty minutes before Keren finally said her goodbyes, hugging Lorien and I again, saving the last goodbye for Elijah at the door; another soft kiss. Lorien was onto him the second he'd closed the door behind her.

"What was *that* all about?" he asked.

"I only have myself to blame," Elijah said, shaking his head. Lorien and I looked at each other, and then turned our gaze back to Elijah. He sighed and sat down, knowing we wanted the story. "I ran into her in Castlebrook one Friday night after Uni. I was at the Duke Hotel with Trudy and Patrick and I ended up going back to her place." Lorien laughed. It seemed Elijah was getting more action than either of us was aware. "It's not funny Lori, and I should have known better, but you know how it is when you've had a few and you start walking down memory lane."

I was pissed off. She hadn't come for a visit to see Lorien and me, she had come to further her liaison with Elijah. At least I didn't need to feel guilty about not having been in touch with her for so long. It didn't seem Keren had changed much over the years, any more than Michael had. "What are you going to do about it?" Lorien asked.

"She's taking me out for dinner on the weekend."

"Are you crazy?" I asked. The twins both looked at me in surprise.

"Ash, this is none of our business," Lorien said.

"Well don't bring her back here!"

"What's wrong Baby? Why the sudden anti-Keren sentiments?"

"She came here under the pretence of visiting us and it was all a scam to get into the house, waiting for Elijah. This means she's no better than she was the last time I saw her. And, if she's going to end up being a permanent fixture around here again, I think I'm entitled to my opinion."

"Come on Ash, it's not that bad," Lorien said.

"Oh Lorien!" I sing-songed to him. "I should have never let you go! Take me for a ride on your hot, throbbing, red bike! What the hell was that all about if she came here on the hunt for Elijah?"

"You're exaggerating just the merest smidge there Baby."

"Don't worry about it Ash, she isn't going to be a fixture around here, I'm not interested in her," Elijah told me.

"Going through the motions to get to the pot of gold?" Lorien asked. I ignored him and added my own comment,

"Then you're no better than she is if you're leading her on Elijah."

"I'm going to straighten it out on the weekend."

"You could have done that this afternoon."

"She didn't give me a chance, just kept insisting on taking me out for dinner."

"And that won't happen again of course. She'll accept what you have to say this time?"

"Ash, leave him be. He's big enough and ugly enough to work this out for himself," Lorien said.

"You have a knack of picking the most unsuitable women for yourself," I said to Elijah, once again ignoring Lorien.

"That trend started when I first came to Sommersett," Elijah said, laughing. Lorien joined him. I screwed my face up at Elijah; I had been his first girlfriend when they moved here. "It'll be fine Ash, don't stress over it." I couldn't help but stress over it though. I didn't want to see Elijah hurt or caught up in a 'basic instinct' type situation.

"You need to listen to me Elijah," I said. "You may not be aware of this, but you are an extremely attractive, single man who is about to become a doctor. You can do much better than Keren, or Faith!" Elijah laughed.

"Extremely attractive?" Lorien scoffed.

"Extremely attractive," Elijah confirmed. I ignored them both. "You didn't like Faith at all did you?"

"No, she was rude and selfish. Please tell me you haven't slept with *her* again at least." Lorien stood and took my hand, dragging me upright.

"Come on Baby girl, time for a shower."

"Lorien, I'm not finished!"

"Yes, you are. This is not our business. Eli is single and he's free to root, shoot and electrocute anyone he wants." The twins laughed loudly at this, but I was still seething. Elijah looked at me and smiled and I knew Lorien was right. It was still a hard thing to let go of; I had become so protective of my little family and I didn't want to see anyone getting hurt or mistreated.

"Are you going to get in with me?"

"Of course Baby." With those three words, he managed to sweep my foul mood away.

"Good, I have an itch that needs scratching."

"And you have the hide to make comment on *my* love life," Elijah said to me, smiling.

"Please be careful Elijah."

"I always am Ash," he said and winked at me. But, I couldn't shake my concern. It didn't take long to evaporate once the steam in the bathroom took my mind to other places, and I wasn't talking about the hot water vapours.

Decisions, Decisions

"If you want to play this game with me, you better know there are no rules,
I call the shots, I make the plays, I oversee this fool."

L Standish, 'Toss of the Dice'

WE HADN'T SPOKEN about Alan's offer any further and I tackled Lorien the next day. "I think you should do it Lorien."

"Why Ash? You're just as capable as I am. We *both* got our Bachelors of Music if you recall."

"I know Lorien, but I don't think I'm up to it. I'll be nearly two-thirds of the way through the pregnancy by then and I'm erratic enough as it is without adding a completely new job to consider. I don't want to let Alan down either, so I think you should do it."

"I don't want to be away from you though Baby." I looked at him, waiting for him to realise what he'd said. He just looked back, smiling.

"If I take the job Lorien, *I'll* be away from *you*." He laughed,

"Of course, I didn't think of that."

"Don't you agree it would be better for you to take this on?"

"I suppose so…" he mused, but didn't seem too keen about it. He was more interested in opening the buttons at the front of my dress.

"Sweetheart, can you focus for a second?"

"Hmmm?" he said absentmindedly, gazing down at the breast he'd managed to wrangle free. He cupped me, squeezing gently as he ran his thumb over my nipple, watching it respond to his touch.

"Lorien?"

"What?" he said, finally looking up.

"Alan's position?"

"I prefer Lorien's position," he said, taking me into his mouth. I drew his head back and kissed him lightly before redoing the buttons.

"We have to talk about this Lorien." He sighed, saying,

"Then can I have my way with you?"

"Yes Baby," I said laughing.

"OK, I'll do it." He captured my hand and went to lead me upstairs, but I stopped him and handed him the phone.

"Business first!"

He rang Alan, saying he'd be taking up the offer. I couldn't hear the conversation from the other end, but assumed from Lorien's expression that Alan was delighted. When he got off the phone he said Alan would come over in a few weeks to run over the lessons and answer any questions we may have. I think Lorien was going to enjoy this a great deal. He was wonderful with people - patient, resourceful and sincere with his interest. "Come with me Baby, you owe me one!" he said, his eyes dark and full of lust.

He took my hand to lead me upstairs and this time I brooked no interference. "Look at how huge they're getting! It's like it happened overnight!" Lorien fondled my breasts, taking great delight in the changes my body was going through. Where his large hand in the past could not quite cup my entire breast fully, he was now unable to fit even half of it into his hand. "They're like the size of my head!"

"Will you shut up Lorien," I said, smiling down at him. He took my advice, silencing his chatter by slowly drawing a nipple into his mouth.

"It will be hard sharing these with Bump," he mumbled, looking into my eyes as he tormented me with his tongue. He always aroused me so easily, and now it was getting ridiculous. I felt like my thermostat was constantly set to 'smoulder'. "God, these are even better than the size of your boobs!" I couldn't help but laugh, and he appreciatively watched my breasts jiggling with the movement of my laughter. "Oh Baby," he grinned at me lecherously, "I do hope you're ready to make love." Of course I was and so was he. Nothing was ever going to change that, we always were, pregnant or not.

Several minutes later when we were still *not* making love, I asked him what was wrong. "I feel weird."

"Why Sweetheart? You won't hurt her or me."

"I know that, I'm just a little concerned about denting her head or spraying her with what could be her brother or sister in another pregnancy." I laughed loudly at this analogy. "I know it's not an issue either way, but... you know..."

"Haven't you spoken to Elijah?"

"I didn't know if it was still appropriate to ask him."

"I have. In fact, I've barraged him with questions. I also expect him to be there during the delivery."

"Yeah, that's a good point, I never thought of it."

"You've been in a fog since I told you we were pregnant." He grinned up at me, and relaxed, moving his hand down to caress slowly between my thighs.

"Daddy's waving to you princess," he said against my stomach.

"Lorien don't, seriously." He looked confused. "It's a mood killer, OK?" He smiled, promising me he would not talk to Bump at any stage during current or future sexual interludes. He continued to work his lips around my stomach and moved down, so painfully slow. A few minutes later, he said to me,

"You taste so different."

"Good or bad?"

"Neither, just different... you're still better than chocolate Baby," he looked up at me and slowly licked my entire length before easing back up my body. "I can't get enough of these massive boobs though!" I laughed again, he watched them jiggle again, and then he fed... again. "I love you Baby girl," he moaned as he moved across me, impaling me.

His previous apprehension had disappeared, now reclaiming his tenure within me, his force ruthless and powerful as he coaxed my nipples to their full extent again with his lips. My groans became whimpers as my orgasm raced through my body, his eyes capturing mine to intake my enjoyment of him as he built his speed, climaxing with me. "Now *that* was a baby maker," he exhaled as he came to lie next to me, cradling me in his arms. I laughed and leant up to kiss him,

"You're silly,"

"I know," he said and smiled down at me, his eyes glinting. He moved down, raining playful kisses over my face, and then got up, "I have to pee."

I sat up on the edge of the bed and caught myself in the full-length mirror, not liking the reflection I saw cast back at me. I usually kept away from the mirrors. The changes in my body were so rapid I didn't want to watch myself mutate into someone else; a sadder, less attractive person than I had been before. And sitting there, staring at myself, I could feel the blues coming on. I stood, turning sideways and lacing my fingers under my ever-growing bulge; looking higher to see the alien, twin globes balancing above it. My legs and hands had started to swell, and I likened myself to a troll-like creature, missing solely the green shading to my skin and a few layers of scales. I burst into tears. Faith was right, I was a fat, old, grotesque hag and I reached onto the bed to grab my dress, covering the monstrosity immediately.

Lorien came out of the bathroom and smiled at me, turning it into a pout when he saw I was fully dressed again. "I wasn't done with you yet Baby," he crooned as he sidled up next to me on the bed. He ran his lips across my cheek, pulling back when he tasted the salty tears. "You're crying?" I turned to him and he took my face into his hands, searching my eyes for the problem.

"Oh Lorien," I cried as my face crumpled into a fresh outburst, flinging my arms around his neck, howling into his chest.

"Sweetheart, what is it? What happened in the few minutes I was out of the room to have upset you so?" I didn't answer immediately, and he let me cry. Aware of my hair-trigger changing moods, he ran his hand soothingly over my back, waiting until I was ready to speak. "Baby, surely it can't be that bad?"

"Look at me!" I said, standing and pulling my dress in under my stomach, pronouncing my swelling midsection. "Faith was right. I'm becoming more hideous every day." He laughed quietly and pulled me onto his lap, embracing me tightly.

"I never thought I would hear you agreeing with Faith," he said.

"I don't have much of a choice, and I'm still only halfway through! What am I going to look like in another three months, let alone four?"

"You'll be as beautiful then as you are now."

"You have to say that."

"No, I don't. You'd know if I was bullshitting you. Now has this got anything to do with the fact that you're turning twenty-three on Wednesday and this marks your halfway point?"

"I don't think so, I hadn't really thought of it that way."

"So, you're just emotional?"

"No, I'm just hideous."

"Ashlyn Diane Standish, every time I look at you, I want to hold you and never let you go. I think how lucky I am that we still get to spend every day together. I don't know how I would manage if it were any other way, as I assume it will be, one day."

"Like when you go back to school."

"That's only for two weeks. I think I'll cope with that one, just." He smiled down at me and I smiled back. It was hard not to, when met with such a handsome face. "You're carrying my baby, Baby. Seeing you blossom and grow makes my heart race; I can't keep my eyes off you moreso than before we were pregnant. You're breathtaking, whether you believe it or not. You mean the world to me Ash and you're *my* world, my total world."

"I love you Lorien, you always make me feel so much better when I hit my lows. I just hope it stops when Bump comes. I don't think I can take this much longer."

"I'll always be here for you Baby, anytime you need anything, OK?" I nodded and smiled at him again, leaning up to kiss him. "I had some plans for your birthday, but I think a few last-minute changes are necessary," he mused, and I wondered what on earth he'd been planning and was now about to change. He had always made my birthday special, and I knew this year would be no different. I let the excitement build a little, starting to look forward to Wednesday.

Standing in the co-joined shower on Sunday night, on my own, which was so very rare, I felt Bump kick for the first time. This time it was the real thing, not just a product of Lorien's pot visions. "Lo-ree-en!" I screamed out, hoping he was near enough to hear me. I heard Elijah at his side of the door.

"What Ash! What is it?" he sounded panicked.

"Get Lorien!" I heard him try to open the door and he appeared ten seconds later at our side of the bathroom door, bursting in - Lorien right behind him. I suddenly didn't have enough hands to cover my nudity and went bright red. Lorien threw me a towel, which caught Elijah partially on the back of his head as I went to catch it; he was on his knees in front of me. Once I was covered, I started to laugh. I shouldn't have, but it was impossible to hold it in.

"What Ash! Tell Eli what's wrong!"

"The baby kicked," I managed, bursting out another trickle of laughter as I looked at their strained faces.

"Christ, you could have said something," Elijah said as he got to his feet. "Sorry for bursting in on you Ash, I thought there was something wrong." Lorien started to strip off, obviously about to join me in the shower; the towel he had thrown at me now soaking wet. "Bloody hell Lori, let me get out of here first will you!" And with that, he was gone.

"Quick, put your hands on me," I told him, "no, here." I guided him to where I'd felt the kick, and a few seconds later, there was another. We looked at each other with open mouths and wide eyes. We had been waiting for this little miracle to unfold ever since he had sensed the phantom kicks several weeks earlier. He dropped to his knees and wrapped his arms around me, pressing his cheek into my tummy. There was another one.

"Got me right in the face this time," Lorien looked up at me and laughed. "This is great Ash!" He faced my stomach again and got his mouth as close as he could before yelling, "I'm your Daddy!" The acoustics in the bathroom made his voice amplify so much more, and I tapped him on the head, making him look up.

"Don't do that again!" I chastised. "You nearly sent me deaf," I added with a laugh. He was so excited. He stood up then knelt down again, pressed his face into me then stood again. He didn't know what to do next. I turned off the taps and led him out of the recess. He dragged a towel over himself quickly, not really capturing much of the excess water, then dabbed me off an inch at a time. "I'm not going to break open Sweetheart," I told him, smiling at his attentive care. His response was just to smile, and he continued his work.

The best part of being well into my second trimester was that the morning sickness had gone, my constant tired state had also departed and mostly, my cravings. I still had a little whim every now and then, but I was back onto normal food again. I think Lorien missed the weird and wonderful concoctions he made for a lot of my first trimester. I was still very partial to the deep-fried camembert with cranberry sauce, however. Who wasn't?

As Wednesday neared, I pulled out one of our bags to make a start on packing when Lorien came through the bedroom door. "What are you doing Baby?" he asked, taking it from me.

"Packing for Wednesday."

"I've already packed everything we need and we're going tomorrow evening, not the day after." I didn't know what to say, I wasn't expecting to be leaving a day early.

"Are you sure you have everything?"

"Most definitely," he said, and ran his hands down my thighs, lifting my dress up and over my head. "However, I just need to check I've packed the right size." He cupped my breasts into his hands. "Yes, I'm sure they'll still fit by tomorrow," he purred, and lowered his head to me. I was oblivious at the time how apt this fit-out session was to be. "Hmmm," he murmured and started to chuckle, which sent the most amazing tingle through my super-sensitive nipples, turning them into granite. "Oh, great reaction," he said, looking at me with fire in his eyes. He knelt and pulled me toward him, slowly lazing his tongue from the top of my pubic mound to my navel, leaning back to blow gently over the invisible liquid trail. It turned my flesh into goose bumps, and I shivered. "Cold Baby or was that in anticipation?" He laughed softly when I didn't answer him. I was going to have to stop him though as I suddenly needed to pee.

"Lorien, I have to go to the loo," I told him.

"I thought your bladder had gone back to near-normal again?" he asked, still working his tongue over me, now dropping it further, grazing it lightly between my thighs.

"Oh..." I moaned, wondering if I could hold on. He looked up at me, his eyes dark,

"Necessity gone now?"

"No," I breathed, "I still need to pee." He chuckled and drew back, sitting on the bed to wait for me to finish my business.

When I came out, he was leaning up on one elbow, sprawled across the bed without a stitch on. As I crawled onto the bed, he got me onto my hands and knees and came in from behind. Once he had entered me, I felt his hands on my shoulders and he gently tilted my upper body backwards and held me up. This was a new one and it was intense. They were always intense, but I loved it when he introduced me to new positions and with it, new sensations. Such *incredible* sensations.

Lying there after I asked him about the new style. "It's another from the Kama Sutra, but I thought I'd leave some of them until they would work for us in pregnancy sex. Did you like?"

"Hmmm, I liked!" He kissed me so softly, my face in his hands.

"Want to go again?" he whispered in my ear.

"Hmmm! I like!" He laughed and started to ease back down my body, readying me for the next round.

In the Eye of the Beholder

"The fire and flames consume me, rip through me.
You've no idea of your power, I cower
And embrace my destiny… you and me…"

L Standish, 'Blinding Vision'

HE OPENED THE DOOR to a beautiful wooden cabin. "Where on earth did you get onto this?" I asked.

"I rang Dad. One of his workmates owns it and it's all ours for the next few days. Do you like it?" I loved it! There was a huge open fireplace with the biggest merino fleece on the floor in front of it. I could imagine what we'd be doing on that rug in many varying positions over the next few days. It was one large room encompassing the lounge and dining areas with the kitchen tucked away at the rear. I opened the fridge to find it already stocked.

"This is where you slipped off to yesterday, I'm guessing," I asked.

"You guess correctly my lady," he grinned at me and led me to the only doorway in the room, the bedroom.

It had a king-sized bed with a warm, thick doona and two fat chairs sitting either side of a massive window. It was too dark to see out of now, and I would keep that wonderment as a surprise for tomorrow. There was another doorway off the bedroom, which led into the bathroom. It had a shower over the large bath, not that I could wallow in it all day anymore, but half an hour at a time could easily be spent in that tub.

Lorien put the bag on the bed, and I went to help him unpack. "I thought you said you'd packed for me?"

"I did."

"But there's hardly any clothes in here, Sweetheart."

"I know." I looked at him curiously and went to the wardrobe, seeing if he'd brought our things with him when he came to stock the fridge yesterday. Nope, nothing there.

"Lorien?"

"Yes Baby?"

"Where are my clothes?"

"Wait there for a minute whilst I get the fire going."

"Can I have my clothes first please?"

"Just wait there." He disappeared into the other room and I sat on the bed, going through what items were actually in the bag. Both of our personal bits and pieces were there, the usual toothbrushes and such, a cryptic crossword book – his, and the latest novel I was reading, but in the clothes department, it was sadly lacking. I pulled two aprons from the meagre offerings and pondered them briefly before searching further. There was a small, wrapped package and a few pairs of socks. Other than that, there was one pair of trackie pants and a hoodie each, and that was it.

He came back through the door and took the bag from me, taking the aprons and socks out. "Strip off Baby," he instructed, and I did as he requested. He removed everything else from the bag with exception to the warm clothes, and then stripped off also. After the clothes on our backs were back in the bag, he zipped it up and put it on top of the high dresser, out of my reach. He came and sat with me on the bed and took my hand in his, smiling.

"What are you up to?" I asked and sidled in under his arm, I was starting to get a little cold.

"Since you're up the duff, we're doing this trip in the buff." He smiled again and laughed when he saw my bemused expression. "You still don't get it do you?" I shook my head and waited for him to continue. "We're going completely in the 'all-together' this mini-break, no clothes whatsoever."

"I can't Lorien. It's just not my thing."

"I brought this in case you felt that way and can't get past it. Open it." He handed me the small package and I ripped the paper away, revealing a full length, totally sheer, chiffon robe. Robe didn't really do it justice though; it was more like what was called a peignoir back in the 1950s. It was a beautiful crimson colour and I put it on, loving its soft texture. It certainly didn't leave much to the imagination. "Now I only brought that *in case* you needed to feel covered at some stage, not the entire time we're here. The warm change of clothes is to ward off the possibility of freezing, but you don't get those unless you need them. Socks are optional." He grinned at me. "I did bring your slippers too, they're in the car. Slippers are OK I suppose."

"But why Lorien? Not that being naked around you is a booby prize, if you'll excuse the pun, but I don't understand your logic behind it." I should have known better; he didn't need a reason to do something like this.

"It's to remind you of how beautiful you are. I love your body and adore you looking so round and full of arms and legs. By the time we get home you'll never think of yourself as anything but the gorgeous creature I see before me every day, and *will* do for the rest of my life." I lowered my face and was astonished to find I was crying. "Baby, don't cry, this is supposed to make you feel wonderful, not make you sad."

"I'm not crying because I'm upset, I'm crying because I can't believe what a special person you are. Bump and I are lucky to have you."

"You have that back to front Ashlyn. I love you with all of my heart and have felt that way since I first lay eyes on you. It may have grown since our tender ages when we met, but it has developed into the adult love that we share in our hearts, let alone several times a day."

"I see why you write your own lyrics," I laughed. "You certainly do have a way with words. Did you get the fire going?"

"Yes. Ready to go and stretch out?"

"Let's go."

"Are you going to leave this in here for the moment?" he asked, fingering the robe. I sighed and took it off, laying it over the end of the bed. He smiled and took my hand, leading me back into the warmth of the living room.

I spread out over the thick, soft fleece, loving the feel of it against my naked skin. Lorien busied himself in the kitchen for a few minutes, putting together a tray of snacks. I was lying on my back with my hands behind my head, watching him. It was impossible not to watch him. His lithe muscular frame drew my eyes to him unbidden and they crept over his flesh in a visual indulgence.

"I just need to get my daily exercise in first," he said when he joined me; climbing over me so we were horizontally aligned. He moved his feet in between mine and held his weight off me with his strong arms. I laughed when he started doing push-ups, ending each downward motion with a kiss. After several repetitions of this, I got the giggles.

"You're silly Lorien," I laughed. He lowered himself one last time and kissed me more intensely; thrusting his feet apart and taking mine out with him. He had me spread-eagled below him and there was nothing I could do about it.

"You're trapped little one, at my mercy."

"I love being at your mercy, Sweetheart." He waggled his eyebrows at me and leant down to continue the kiss, eventually moving to my side so he could lie with me, wrapping himself around me. I felt like I was in a womb, so shrouded by the soft fleece and the strength of his love. The fire crackled and emitted its soft warmth and we fooled around again like teenagers for the longest time.

My trusty bladder woke me in the wee hours of the morning, the bedside clock telling me it was 2.30 am. As I went to climb out of bed, I noticed the weird position we were lying in. Lorien was cradled in behind me, nothing unusual about that, but he was *inside* me, which made me re-question what happened before we went to sleep. Fair enough, he *was* flaccid, but how did he get there? I didn't remember making love. My curiosity became even more aroused after I'd used the toilet, there was no residue and I wondered why on earth he would have used a condom.

I crept back into the bedroom, trying not to wake him, and lifted the covers to see what had become of the elusive condom. In the moonlight he was beautiful, and the pale blue light seeping in through the open curtains made him glow in the near-dark. I sat and just looked at him for a few minutes, glorying in the love that I had for this man and how lucky I was to have him with me every day and every night.

I remembered my reasoning for stripping back the covers and went in search of the condom; he was certainly not wearing it and I started to worry that it may have still been inside me. I sat contemplating what to do when he stirred. "What are you doing awake?" he whispered as he rolled onto his back and stretched out.

"I had to use the loo." He smiled at me so warmly and patted the bed, wanting me back against him.

"You look a little confused. What's on your mind?"

"Did we have sex earlier tonight?"

"What makes you ask that?" he said and smiled knowingly. I felt like a bit of an idiot replaying my thought processes and chose to ignore him. The missing condom, if there was one, could wait until morning. He cuddled me into his warm side and started to chuckle.

"What's funny?" I asked.

"You don't remember, do you?" I looked up at him.

"No, I don't. Are you going to draw this out or tell me?"

"I can't wait to tell you…" he muttered and kissed me softly. "You were asleep, very deeply asleep I assume, and lying on your side, facing away from me. I was watching you sleep…"

"You do that a lot, don't you?" I asked, laughing quietly.

"I'm going to do it a lot more too," he said.

"Well, come on," I prompted.

"Anyway, I was leaning up on my elbow, just watching you, and you started to giggle a little. I assumed you were dreaming again, dreaming about me."

"And what makes you think it was about you, stud?"

"I'm getting to that," he said. "You started to nuzzle your cheek into the pillow and arch yourself back into me, slowly grinding your hips back and forth."

"I could've been riding a horse and simply enjoying the feel of my face against its soft mane," I suggested.

"You remember the dream then do you?" I didn't, but he didn't need to think he was my only waking and sleeping thought, even though he was, damn it, and he knew it! It wasn't the first time this had happened. I shook my head and he continued. "I didn't want to wake you, you seemed to be having such a wonderful time. But then you moaned my name a few times and told me to make love to you, and then giggled again."

"I did not!"

"You did Baby."

"So, what did you do?" I had a pretty good idea by now.

"I took full advantage of course," he said and grinned at me. I smiled back; of course he did. "I started fondling those incredible boobs and they were very responsive I must say, and then you rolled toward me slightly with your upper body and flung your arm up so I could get better access."

"I did not!" He laughed, louder this time.

"You *did* Baby, and you managed to whack me in the face with it on the way through to the pillow." He rubbed his nose lightly to emphasise his point.

"I'm sorry," I said and leant up to kiss him.

"It's OK, believe me, it was *seriously* OK." I laughed with him this time. "I nuzzled into your armpit gently, once again not wanting to wake you. You got more aggressive then, and were calling out 'Oh God Lorien, Oh God...' I thought you were actually awake at that stage." He started to laugh again, and I gave him a light smack on the chest.

"Stop it!"

"I'm only relaying to you what happened; it's all true, every single word."

"And then what?"

"You told me again to make love to you."

"And?"

"I made love to you Baby," he whispered to me.

"You did not!"

"I did so." He was enjoying this immensely, but I wasn't sure that he was being truthful, well not completely. "You were getting right into it, moving against me, working with me."

"How come there's nothing to prove this little romp?" I asked.

"Neither of us came."

"What?" I asked, definitely not believing him now.

"You have a habit of waking when you orgasm, and I didn't want to rouse you from your illicit wet dream."

"Girls don't have wet dreams!"

"You certainly do. It was like sliding into butter; you were *so ready* for me Baby." I lowered my face a little, knowing by its heat I was blushing. He wouldn't be able to see that in the dim light, but he would have known from my reaction what was going on.

"So how did you manage to restrain yourself?"

"I made love to you until you eventually fell back into a deep sleep and I cuddled in behind you and went to sleep too."

"Wow."

"Indeed!" he said and pulled me across his chest, nuzzling his chin into my forehead.

"We haven't made love since we got here. How weird is that?"

"Yes, we have, you were just unconscious, but you *were* at least dreaming about it." I grinned up at him, knowing he had been the centre of my dreams before, bringing me to him from another life that hadn't involved him; bringing us together. "Are you still horny Baby?" I yawned,

"No, I'm sleepy."

"Well go back to sleep." He kissed me slowly and settled me back into him, aligning behind me again. As I was drifting off, I heard him chuckle through the haze, "Sweet dreams Baby…"

When I woke the next morning, I wasn't sure whether I had dreamt the early morning conversation. I felt really addled and confused, but it didn't last long. He came through the door a few seconds later with two mugs and smiled at me widely, saying, "Happy birthday Ashlyn." He leant over and kissed me.

"Thank you, Sweetheart."

"No more erotic dreams?" he asked, confirming it had been real. I shook my head slightly and let my eyes devour his naked body, moving over to let him climb back into bed, wanting my birthday present. He noticed my gaze and laughed before putting the mugs on the bedside table, reaching for the bag of clothes. "I need to get some wood out of the car first, the fire needs stoking."

"It's stoked," I hinted.

"That's not helping Ash." He dragged his trackie pants on and pulled the hoodie over his head. "Be right back."

I made my way into the lounge room to sit in front of the fire until he was finished. He walked in with a load of wood as I settled onto the sofa. A gust of freezing air followed him, and I started to shiver. He dropped the wood to the floor and stripped off his hoodie, handing it to me. "Although the sight of your erect nipples takes me to places you don't even know about," he chuckled, "I don't want you cold. It'll only take a minute to warm up." He went into the bedroom and brought the bag out with him, leaving it on the table, letting me know I would have to give it back shortly.

"You're still clothed," I reminded him, and he looked down at his trackies and shoes, laughing. He pulled off his shoes, dragged his trackies down, and kicked them off his feet and I whistled appreciatively. He threw them into the bag and pulled out one of the aprons, putting it over him before he went to the fire to refuel the logs. It looked strange with him dressed only in socks and an apron and I laughed.

"I don't want any straying embers; we don't need a bush fire in our little cottage, do we?" The thought of him racing around with his pubes on fire made me laugh aloud and he smirked at me, no doubt understanding my little visual.

When done, he stood in front of me and took off the apron, holding his hand out for the hoodie. I sighed and stripped it off, tossing it to him. Everything stored safely away, he came and sat with me on the sofa, handing me an envelope. "Happy birthday Baby," he said and kissed me.

"I thought this trip was my birthday present?"

"Part of it, open it." The envelope had a simple heart drawn on it with my name inside. I turned it over and tore it open, pulling out the card. There was a photo in it, which I put aside to read what he'd written first.

"Thank you, Sweetheart, your words are always so beautiful," I said and nestled into his side. I picked up the photo and looked at it, not sure exactly where this photo had been taken. It looked like a store. When I took in the focal items in the display a little more closely, I noticed it was all nursery items: a crib, bassinet, drawers and various stuffed toys.

"It's for Bump's room," he said.

"I know," I whispered. "It's beautiful Lorien, I love it! When are we getting it?"

"It'll be there when we get home. I asked Bree and Simon to come and stay so she could let them in when they arrive today, just in case Eli couldn't be there. The painters are coming too..."

"What do you mean?" I asked in confusion.

"I think the blocks of black, red and white might be a little much for a nursery, don't you?"

"Oh Lorien no!" I said in dismay. "I don't want the room painted. I fell in love with you in that room. We should have talked about this." What we *had* talked about was the room would still need to serve a purpose as a guest bedroom. Other than putting all the furniture into storage, we would still need a bed for when Cara and Nick came to stay with us and for us to move back into when they came home. We had agreed to move the bedroom area into one side of the room and make the nursery into the other. We could worry about further renovations once Mercy was older and needed her own space, not that we intended on living with his parents forever. When she came out of hospital, she would be in our room anyway, including when we had guests.

"Just wait until you've seen it Ash. If you hate it, we can always paint it back the way it was."

"I'm sure I'll love it Lorien, it's just come as a shock. I don't want to sound ungrateful either. I love all the nursery furniture. Thank you, Sweetheart." Sitting there naked, talking about such serious issues made me smile.

"Funny?" he asked. I shook my head. "Come on Baby, tell Lorien what's so funny." He started to tickle me, and so much of myself enjoyed it when I shook in tickle aversion these days. Once again transfixed by my jiggling bosom, his teasing slowed, and he grinned at me before laying his head at the apex of where my stomach and breasts met. He moved his face to the side, laying lightly on my tummy, and brought his hand up to fondle me gently. My nipple sprang straight to attention and I heard him laugh lowly. He stuck out his thumb and put it next to my nipple in comparison and I said,

"Don't say a word Lorien!" He chuckled and said nothing, drawing me into his mouth. A few minutes later, he bit me, too hard. "Ouch!" I said and drew his face away. Either he was getting carried away or my ever-increasing sensitive nipples were unable to cope.

"Sorry Ash, it was no harder than I've done before."

"It's OK Lorien." I smiled down at him, my breast still in his hand.

"Maybe I'm hungry," he smiled and went to get up.

"Are you going to take that with you?" I asked. Lorien looked at the treasure he still had in his hand, then took the other and stayed put for a few minutes longer - weighing them, moulding his hands to them, teasing them. "You're really crazy about my boobs lately, hey?"

"Always Baby, but at the moment especially. They're like wow!" I laughed. "Just a bit longer and then I'll make breakfast," he sighed and sunk down into them again, feasting prematurely.

When he finally made his way into the kitchen, apron jauntily attired, he threw the puzzle book onto the sofa and handed me my novel, assuming I would want to read to pass the time. "No, I'll help you," I said, and he smiled, going in to get the other apron. No sooner did I have it on, Lorien's mobile rang. I couldn't make much out from our end and he walked into the bedroom. I followed him.

"Doesn't look like I can get away at the moment. Do you want to talk to her? OK, but don't *tell* her anything." He handed me the phone, smiling.

"Happy birthday Ash!" I heard Bree and Simon call.

"Thanks guys. I hear you're staying at our place?"

"Yes, we are, and what a lot has been going on." It was Bree.

"Care to tell me about it?" I asked.

"No," she said and laughed, "I'm under strict orders."

"Say goodbye Bree," Lorien called out behind me.

"Goodbye Bree!" she said and hung up, laughing.

"Are you going to censor all my calls today?"

"Just when you start to get inquisitive, so it's up to you really." He shot me a sweet smile and I pulled a face at him.

All was quiet for many hours and after lunch, we ended up sitting in the two chairs facing the huge bedroom window. I had my novel and Lorien was working on his cryptics when his phone rang again. This time it was Elijah. At first I thought he had rung to speak to Lorien solely, but after a few minutes, he handed me the phone. He was obviously aware of Lorien's intentions for this holiday, relating to the forced nudity, as his opening statement to me was, "Hey Ash, how's the rough upholstery working on your bum?" He finished with a laugh.

"Is that all you have to say?" I asked.

"No, happy birthday sis."

"That's better," I said. "What's happening at home?"

"Do you think I'm that stupid?"

"Yes!" He laughed again.

"Are you having a good time?"

"I'd be having a better time if I knew what was going on at home."

"You'll see soon enough." We chatted for a few more minutes and I passed the phone back to Lorien, his hand already outstretched to receive it, prompting me. Once again, I had no idea what was happening from our end of the conversation. I would have to make do with the information I had, and my imagination.

Absorbed back in my book, I felt Lorien's hand tracing the curves of my breast. When I looked at him, he was still concentrating on his puzzles, his hand seeming to have a mind of its own. He kneaded, cupped and tickled for several minutes before I marked my page and put the book down. "What?" he asked, totally innocent.

"Do you know how hard it is to focus whilst you're doing that?"

"It hasn't affected me," he said, eyebrows raised and a slight smile on his lips. He was a liar though, as his eyebrows weren't the only things raised. I snatched the book from him and studied his answers. Random letters, numbers and squiggles were entered into each of the boxes, and I knew damn well that he'd not been paying attention to what he'd been doing either. When I looked up at him, he was grinning.

"You're silly Lorien," I said and laughed.

"I know." He leant over and kissed me, slowly at first then standing and drawing me up to him. For not having made love in over the past thirty-six hours or so, or that I was aware of, he did remarkably well, taking all of fifteen seconds before his arousal was even more apparent. I was ready too.

He led me to the bed, and just as we were getting comfortable, locked at the lips, my phone rang. "Ignore it," he mumbled through the kiss.

"It'll be Michael," I said, breaking away and reaching for the phone.

"Let him leave a message!" he implored, trying to coax me back to him.

"I'll be just a second. Hello?" It was Mum. Talk about a passion killer.

"Happy birthday Honey!" she and Dad cried in unison, and then Mum proceeded to give me a rundown of the anything-but-special events of the week. I eventually fobbed her off by telling her that Lorien had made afternoon tea and it was getting cold. When she asked me what we were having, I stumbled verbally for a few seconds, and then blurted out,

"Scones." Lorien made a face at me and raised an eyebrow, having no idea what I was talking about. I smiled and shook my head at him. When I finally hung up, he didn't even bother to ask, he just dragged me back to him, making me laugh.

Our slow tender ministrations went on and on, lasting from go to whoa for nearly two hours. He built me slowly, taking his time, revelling in every inch of my flaming body, yearning for him. It was a mutual involvement and we both soared many, many times.

When my phone rang about halfway through the marathon, I made a move to answer it and Lorien interrupted his oral magic and moved up, grabbing both of my hands and pinning me down. "Not this time Baby," he said. "You can answer this handset if you *must*." Mr Winky was prodding into my thigh, desperately wanting to be answered, so I took his call – it turned out to be an obscene one.

I was excited pulling into the driveway, excited, but still a little nervous. I couldn't wait to see the new room, but I was terrified it would have removed all of my memories of fooling around and falling in love with Lorien in there. Bree and Simon met us at the door and Bree helped me out of the car. "You're going to love it Ash," she said as she led me inside.

"Well, they'll be back if I don't," I answered and looked to Lorien. He smiled at me and took the virtually empty bag from the back seat. We were both fully clothed again of course, and I was surprised to find that I missed my mini-break of clothing abstinence. Lorien placed his hands over my eyes as Simon opened the door, moving me forward into the centre of the room, diverting me around furniture where necessary. He whistled between his teeth when he took in the new surroundings and I remembered that he hadn't seen it either, but surely had left instructions on what he wanted done.

"Come on Lorien, let me see."

"You *are* going to love it Baby," he said and removed his hands from my face.

I was stunned, absolutely gob-smacked. The ceiling and top two-thirds of the walls were painted in elongated vertical diamonds of mauve and light pink with a strip of wallpaper at its bottom edge. This also ran the full outlaying circumference of the four walls, covered in the alphabet repeated eternally in letters about twelve centimetres high. The bottom section of the wall colour was a light citrus green and one area near the bathroom door had a chalkboard as its entire coverage. On the other side of the bathroom door frame was a beautiful mural of a little girl having a tea party in the woods with her dolls. "Who did this?" I asked, tears starting to brim at my lashes. Lorien came over and slipped his arms around me, realising my emotion. He too was still looking around and absorbing it all, a smile on his lips.

"Glen," Bree said.

"What? I didn't know he could paint."

"Not bad hey?" she said. I ran my finger lightly over the darling scene and noticed all the baby accessories now had a place to live. Where the wardrobe used to be, everything was tucked into an open cupboard arrangement with various niches and holes to store the bassinet, stroller, her drawers and toys. A small table and two wicker chairs were in the corner and a few colourful prints were artfully positioned on the walls.

"Lorien, where's your pappadum chair?" I asked, noting how the adult area of this room now worked into the colour scheme for Mercy.

"It's at our place for the moment," Simon said, "until you want it back." The double bed and nightstands aligned next to it were now under the window at the rear of the room and the dresser against the adjoining wall. This took up a lot less space to serve as a spare room until she was old enough to need to claim it for her own. But the 'pièce de résistance' was the new crib in the centre of the room. It was a pink wooden sleigh crib, complete with canopy and a changing table that extended from the edge. Lorien proudly demonstrated it for me.

"One more thing I need to show you," he said, leading me to the little table and chairs. He removed the centrepiece from the table. Concealed within it was a massive xylophone. He picked up the rubber-ended mallets and played out a snippet from 'The Nutcracker Suite'. I burst into tears.

"I love it Lorien. Thanks so much Bree and Simon for staying here to get this done for us."

"Anytime Ash," Simon said, and Bree hugged him to her. Elijah stuck his head in the door, just home.

"Welcome home. Do you like it Ash?" I had my face buried into Lorien's chest and I felt him nod, running his hand down my back soothingly. "Looks like it," he answered and Lorien moved in silent laughter. I drew back from him and looked into his face, smiling. He kissed me lightly and hugged me back to him, swinging me from side to side.

"But why the new crib?"

"Once she's big enough to be out of our room we can sell that one, or leave it downstairs for when she needs to be contained in a gaol cell; like when she starts walking." I looked at him in surprise, and then noticed by his crooked grin he was teasing. I pulled away from him and went to leave the room. "Where are you going Baby?" he asked, capturing me by the hand and stopping me.

"I'm not done crying yet. I need to ring Michael and Glen." Their laughter followed me from the room.

Back to School

"There's nothing I can teach you, nothing you don't know
But teacher, tell me, how can I
Get your heart to tell me so."

L Standish, 'Higher Education'

ON ALAN'S LAST DAY AT SCHOOL, he invited Lorien to come and sit in on the class, getting to know the students and in return, they him. He bounced through our door well after 6.00 pm that Friday night, and alone. I expected to see Alan with him, but assumed from his late arrival that they had completed the handover when the classes were dismissed. He was grinning from ear to ear. "How did it go?" I asked as he dropped his bag near the stairs and came over to greet me properly. Several minutes later, he finally answered,

"It was amazing. He has some really talented students in the various years."

"Did any of those young, pretty girls catch your eye?" I asked mischievously, making him laugh.

"It felt weird being back in that room without you there too." He smiled crookedly and reached into his pocket, pulling out a strange set of keys.

"What are those for?" I asked.

"They're to the Music room." He grinned at me and I understood immediately where he was going with this.

"No way!"

"Why not? Let's relive the past a little... What do you say?"

"No way!" I reiterated. "We never had sex in that room, and I don't intend on starting now."

"Well, I have two weeks to talk you into it."

"Good luck champ!" He smiled knowingly at me, assuming he would eventually get his way. I untangled myself from his grip, not wanting to start a debate on this subject, and he pulled me back to him.

"I missed you all day Baby," he sighed, working his lips softly down my throat.

"I missed you too Lorien. You were all I thought about." He kissed me again and the subject of lewd carry-ons in the Music room dissolved, being more interested in the carry-ons about to take place in the lounge room.

"Is Eli home?" he whispered. I shook my head then angled my ear toward him, which he purred directly into, turning me to jelly. I worked my fingers at the buttons of his shirt, sweeping it down his arms, leaving it hanging loosely from the waistband of his pants. It was still tucked in. His broad shoulders and hard chest were all I could see before me and I feathered my lips across him, savouring the rippling muscles as they contracted under my soft kisses. I sank to my knees and dragged him forward by the front of his pants, leering up at him salaciously. "My, you did miss me!"

"More than you know lover." He smiled and opened his mouth to make further comment when a key rattled in the door. He moaned and helped me to my feet, standing again as Elijah entered, a load of Chinese take-away strung over his arm.

"Hey guys, have you eaten?"

"No, neither of us got around to it," Lorien answered and kissed me softly, taking me back in his embrace. Elijah noted his twin's half-dressed state and worked out his inference, then smiled at us both.

"Looks like I arrived just in time then," he said sarcastically and took the bags into the kitchen, flipping off the lids and grabbing some cutlery out of the drawer. "I'm guessing you literally just walked in too?" He laughed as Lorien pulled a face at him, tugging his shirt from the back of his pants and going to change before eating.

I helped Elijah carry all the containers to the table and grabbed some plates before sitting with him, still smiling at me broadly across the table. "Sorry Ash."

"It can wait," I answered a little sheepishly.

"Since when!" he laughed and asked how our first day apart had gone.

"It was a long day," I admitted and the now descending Lorien agreed with me as he yanked a T-shirt over his head.

"It's going to be an even longer two weeks," Lorien added. "We'll have to make up for some forthcoming lost time this weekend hey Baby?"

The phone rang half an hour later, which put an end to that scenario. It was Nick. Elijah had taken the call and his brow furrowed as the conversation evolved. It appeared he didn't understand what was being said to him. When he finally got off the phone, he told us that they were on their way home and would be here tomorrow morning.

"Great!" I enthused, so happy to be seeing them again.

"What's wrong Eli?" Lorien asked, further reading and understanding his twin's expression.

"I don't think they're coming back."

"But you just said…" I interjected.

"No, I mean I think they're moving. Dad said he'd been given a job offer he couldn't refuse and I'm assuming it's not around here." The three of us looked at each other in silence. If what Elijah had said turned out to be true, we were all going to be looking at relocating; they would want to sell the house. Not that this was the end of the world, but we were all very happy here and it had taken us by surprise more than anything. I didn't think the twins wanted to move either.

We met them at the door on their arrival the next morning, Cara taking us in her arms in turn, as Nick wrestled the bags from the rear of the Range Rover. "How's my little family?" she asked, placing more kisses on her twin's cheeks. Nick dropped the bags and took Elijah, then Lorien and finally me in his embrace, so glad to be home and seeing his family again. Our faces must have portrayed the conflicting emotions of the joy in seeing them and the anxiety of not knowing what was about to happen.

Lorien went into the kitchen to make coffee as his parents made themselves comfortable. "Why all the worried looks kids?" Nick finally asked, surveying the quiet room.

"We're just curious as to what your news on the phone meant," Elijah answered.

"We were going to wait until dinner to give you the good word, but considering the apprehensive faces around here, we might have to do this now." Cara smiled at me and I relaxed a little, hoping there would be a silver lining somewhere in the possible cloudy forecast.

"I've been approached to be the Health and Safety Consultant at the largest coal seam project in Australia. It's anticipated to run for years, which will take me well into a very comfortable retirement. Apparently, my work on lowering the carbon footprint has become well known!" We were all very impressed!

"Where is it and will you have to move?" Lorien asked, cutting to the chase.

"It's near Mackay in Queensland, so yes, we would be moving."

"What about your job Mum?" I asked.

"We've talked about buying a shop in the main street and selling antiques, something I've always had a passion for. I think it's time for a change." I nodded and the twins shared a quick glance.

"We realise this has come as a shock to you all, but we haven't made any final decisions yet, although we have been looking at a property in Mackay. We now want to know what you think."

"It's a bit of a surprise Dad, we didn't see this coming," Lorien said. "I think it's great though that you've been given this opportunity and we'll always have somewhere to come on holidays." Cara smiled at him and ran her hand down his cheek tenderly.

"We'll miss you boys too, we already do, not to mention our new daughter," she said to me.

"How long have we got to find somewhere else to live before you sell the house?" Elijah asked and Cara and Nick shared a smile.

"Do you think we would throw our entire family out on the street?" Nick said and went to one of the bags, unzipping the front section and pulling out an envelope. It didn't matter what was about to evolve, we were a family and would always have each other for support, including

Elijah if he was inclined on coming with us - keeping the unit together. "Open it," Nick said and passed Elijah the envelope. He flicked through the pages and handed it to Lorien who read it just as quickly. They shared another quick glance before asking together,

"You're giving us the house?"

"All paid for and all yours – 50/50. Of course Lorien's fifty percent includes Ashlyn and Mercy too when she comes, plus any future additions, as will yours when you settle down one day son," Nick said to Elijah.

"Why are you doing this?" Lorien asked. I was speechless, unable to form any sentences. Did I just hear right, we now owned our own house?

"Because we can and it will mean you'll never have money worries, not that I assume you would have anyway," Cara said, smiling at her boys.

"We can afford to give you a good start in life so what kind of parents would we be if we didn't do that?" Nick said and laughed.

"Well Bump, it looks like you're a homeowner," Lorien said rubbing my tummy and smiling at me. Several hours ago, we thought we were going to be homeless, and now we owned a house.

"How are you feeling Ashlyn?" Cara asked.

"A lot better now that I'm past the morning sickness."

"Yes, I remember that well, and with two in there..." she rolled her eyes. "And boys..." We laughed.

"Do you want to feel her kick?" Cara's eyebrows shot up and her mouth formed an 'O', coming to lay her hands on me.

"Wow, she's a strong little one. Nick, come and feel this."

"I feel like a ouija board," I laughed, as Lorien and Elijah added their hands to me as well.

"Let's ask Anna and Dom over for a full-on family dinner," Lorien suggested, and I nodded eagerly, happy to be surrounded by my entire family. It was such a rare occasion.

The twins were both wonderful cooks and they deliberated on the main course together whilst I took Cara and Nick upstairs to get them settled. "The nursery looks lovely Ashlyn," Cara said.

"I was a little apprehensive when Lorien told me. He did it as a surprise and I wasn't sure how I would feel about it at first."

"And?"

"I love it, of course."

"Who did the artwork?" Nick asked and I told them about the artistic talents of Glen then showed them the xylophone inset in the tabletop. They were suitably impressed and congratulated Lorien on his choice of colours, on their return to the lounge room.

Mum and Dad arrived shortly after and another round of backslapping and hugs took place, which included Lorien, Elijah and me as well as Cara and Nick. Even though I had only gone out with Elijah for three months, Mum and Dad still treated him as part of our family.

The weekend sped by and it was suddenly Sunday night and I had an anxious husband on my hands. I was sitting on the sofa with Cara, Nick and Elijah watching TV. Actually, I was watching Lorien sitting at the dining room table flicking through Alan's handover notes. I went and stood behind him, lightly rubbing his shoulders. He smiled up at me. "You're nervous?" I asked.

"Yeah."

"Why?"

"I've never done this before Ash."

"You're nervous because it's something new?" He nodded.

"What if I stuff up? I know what teenagers can be like and I don't want to lose them on day one."

"Sweetheart, you are the most entertaining, fabulous person I have ever met, and they will love you. You already met some of them didn't you?" He nodded again. Cara joined us.

"You'll be fine Lori, just remember this is something I've been doing for years. Trust me, if anything, you may end up bored."

"I doubt it."

"Will it help if I come with you to the school in the morning? I have to put in my resignation at some stage so it may as well be tomorrow, bright and early."

"That would be great Mum, thanks." He stood and hugged her. That settled, I marched him off to bed. I was a little disappointed that we didn't make love that night, but it was his first off day, and he was certainly entitled.

"You look perfect," I told him, buttoning his shirt the next morning. "You also look delicious. Think you can get home for lunch?" He laughed and took me into his arms.

"Not today little hottie, but maybe tomorrow..." He leant down and kissed me.

"No breaking any girl's hearts now!"

"I promise Mrs Standish," he said, making me laugh again.

Cara was finishing her breakfast as we made our way into the kitchen. '"Not eating Lori?" she asked.

"I don't think I can."

"OK, just give me five minutes and I'll be ready."

"Take twenty, Mum," he said and rolled his eyes at me. I wanted to cry. It was like sending my child off on the first day of school. I didn't think knowing this would make him feel any better, so kept it to myself.

Watching him walk across the road with Cara, I found I wanted to run after him and drag him back home with me. A thousand excuses ran through my mind, all seemingly acceptable: *we don't need the money, they can get on without a teacher for two weeks, you want to write not teach, I forced you into this, I'm going to miss you… come back to me Lorien.* Nick came up beside me and his arm wended around my waist. "Miss him already?" I nodded and he hugged me to him. "The day will flash by, you'll see."

And flash by it did. By the time Cara came home at noon we had considered what to cook for Lorien in a celebratory first day dinner, completed all the washing and I was about to draw my lead from one-nil to two-nil in Canasta. "How did it go love?" Nick asked as he rose to greet his wife. I spun around in my chair; I had some questions for her too.

"Fine. Mrs Lawper said she was expecting as much when we left, and the temp has been working out well. They're getting the recruitment forms together now and it will be ready for advertisement shortly. What a shame history wasn't your chosen profession instead of music Ashlyn." I smiled at her. "However, the buzz is that Alan O'Dowd will be putting his retirement through shortly. That will be a great opportunity for you or Lori as well."

"He'd want me to take it."

"No need to worry about that now; I doubt it would be until the end of the financial year anyway. He'd be thinking about his superannuation I imagine."

"Shall we break for lunch Ashlyn and then challenge Cara to a game?" I nodded and followed them into the kitchen.

"Cara..." I said hesitantly and took her hand.

"What is it Sweetheart?"

"I think she may want to know how Lorien went this morning. Even though that's all she's had on her mind, she *still* nearly managed to beat me two-nil in Canasta." Cara's laugh bubbled out, and I waited expectantly.

"Dear Lorien. He was so nervous I even got a kiss when I left him. It was like his first day at kindy."

"That's how I felt this morning when he left," I confided to her, making them both laugh.

"I'm afraid I can't tell you much more than that Ashlyn, we weren't together for very long."

"Is he coming home for lunch?"

"I don't think so."

"How am I going to last through two weeks of this?"

"Count them in days Ashlyn, ten in all and you've already nearly knocked over one. Only nine to go," Nick offered. I smiled at him weakly as he handed me a sandwich and we sat down together.

"When do you want to head off, Cara?" Nick asked.

"I was thinking Wednesday."

"We did all the washing..."

"No!" I intercepted. "You can't leave so soon," I said, surprising myself with the abject force in my plea. Cara reached out and patted my hand, both of them smiling at me warmly.

"It's nice to see we're missed," Nick said. "How about Friday, around noon Cara? Spend a few days with the boys and help Ashlyn get through Lori's first week?"

"Why not, we have no real schedule to follow." A smile broke out on my face, glad they had changed their minds.

When the door opened at 4.00 pm, I stood and raced to fling it wide. "What a greeting," Elijah said, pulling me to him for a hug. "Lori not home yet I'm guessing?" he asked sympathetically. I shook my head and peered past him across the road, trying to see if he was approaching in the distance.

"I'm going to the Music room to find him," I said, feeling concerned. I knew he was OK, but my mind and body was calling out for him.

"He won't be much longer Honey. Come on Elijah, sit in as a fourth and we'll play doubles." Poor Cara, it ended up boys against the girls. I'd been OK until Elijah came home, but now all I could concentrate on was my absent husband. Fortunately for Cara, Lorien walked in the door within one hand of finally being whipped by the other two Standish men.

"Lorien!" I cried and ran to meet him, flinging myself into his arms, returning his loving smile.

"Wow, I should stay away more often," he chuckled, and I burst into tears.

"Oh Baby girl, it's OK...shhh...," he soothed me. "She hasn't had a sleep today, has she?" he then directed at his parents.

"Can you imagine her able to sleep today?" Nick answered.

"No," he said, smiling down at me. "I guess not. Come and talk to me whilst I have a shower Ash. I'll tell you all about my day." I was happy to follow him up the stairs, not realising he had *no* intention of showering for a while.

As he made love to me, I found myself crying again. "Please Sweetheart, don't, you're breaking my heart," he whispered into my ear, stopping his motion. He ran his fingers over my brow, moving the hair from my face as he kissed the tears from my cheeks and lids. "I love you Baby, so very, very much...," he crooned.

"I love you so much more Lorien," I whispered and sniffed.

"How do you love me?" he asked, smiling at me as he resumed his rocking.

"Like this," I sighed and moved with him.

"You missed me?"

"You have no idea..."

"I do you know. I'm sure I missed you more."

"You were no doubt too busy to be thinking of anything else."

"I always think of you...," he whispered, and his words threw me into my desire so completely; he caught my mood and strengthened his force.

"Oh Lorien," I moaned, my head rolling from side to side, absorbing the total pleasure roaring through me.

"Hmmm Baby," he purred, his hot mouth at my neck, "I've waited all day for this..." He drew me up and over his thighs as he rose onto his knees, forcing his entire self into me. "Ohhh Baby, hmmm..." he sighed, "Oh God..." he finished in a whimper. I smiled up at him. This was long and drawn out for him instead of impelling and urgent. He smiled down at me, his eyes opening and closing slowly as he lazily moved in and out a few final times before coming to lay with me. "I love you...," he moaned into my mouth before his soft lips coveted my own, his hands taking ownership of my still burning flesh.

I was so happy to lay there with him for the moment before finally getting into the shower, together of course. He laughed when he saw my apprehensive expression. "You're worried we've been up here too long before the shower started, aren't you?" he asked. Damn him, he knew me *so* well! My blush answered him satisfactorily though. "You're pregnant Ash, they know we have sex."

"But not that we can't keep our hands off each other for you to sit and have a coffee with your family first."

"Why the hell would I want coffee when I can have this?" he asked, gesturing to me.

"You know what I mean Lorien!" I admonished as he helped me step into the shower. I did end up getting a full run down of his day though whilst we were in there.

WE ARE FAMILY

Nesting

"The bricks and mortar make the castle strong,
We are mortar, you are the binding bond."

L Standish, 'Build Me'

I WAS FULLY AWARE that what I was doing was 'nesting'. I was now only five days away from my delivery date and over the past week I had managed to rearrange all of our cupboards, including those in the kitchen, detailed the inside of the car, and rearranged some of the lighter items of furniture in the lounge, bathrooms and bedrooms. I was driving Lorien *and* Elijah crazy. They could never find anything. Lorien couldn't write either as I was always hovering somewhere nearby, dusting, moving things or generally being a nuisance by getting him to move the larger items of furniture, only to want them back in their original placement the next day, if not within a few hours. He took it all in his stride though, that was my Lorien for you, but today, he had something to say. "Did you or did you not wash all of Bump's clothes yesterday?"

"I did," I answered.

"So, what are you doing with them back out of the drawers?" Yesterday I had washed her clothes, socks, bibs, towels and all of her bed linen, remaking her cribs from scratch. I was surrounded by a mound of her items once again, ironing and folding them before putting them away...again.

"I can't help it Lorien."

"Has the weather got anything to do with it?" It had been pouring solidly for the past two days and I found that this was lightening my mood, not hampering it.

"No Sweetheart, quite the opposite."

"Do you want to go for a drive somewhere Ash?"

"Do you want me re-detailing the car when we get home?" He laughed; obviously, he did *not* want me doing this.

"Come and sit at the island bench and I'll make us some lunch," he said, leading me by the hand to a stool.

"I just want to repack..."

"You have packed and repacked your labour bag fifty times over Baby. Let it rest for a few hours OK?" I had to laugh. I followed him to the kitchen. We both knew that when nesting started this close to the due date it was a possible sign of ensuing labour. Neither of us had made a big deal about it, although Lorien was watching me even more closely than before.

When he opened the kitchen cupboard, he burst out laughing. "What have you been doing in here?" Not only had I sorted everything by colour, I had also arranged it in accordance with the height of each item as a secondary category.

"Cleaning," was my simple response. He had been enjoying this as much as it must have been frustrating him. When he'd come across me pulling apart all the kitchen cupboard and drawer knobs a few days ago, he was curious as to why. "Disinfecting them," was my simple response on that episode. A myriad of emotions I was giving to him lately.

I eased myself into a sitting position. I was absolutely huge! Where I had been depressed and abhorrent of myself near the halfway mark I was now delighting in my full look, although my poor legs and feet often begged to differ. It had also been nearly three weeks since Lorien and I had made love. I just couldn't get comfortable enough, and every time I stopped moving for more than a minute, Bump wanted to wake and play Guitar Hero in my stomach. Apparently, when I moved it rocked and lulled her, when I stopped, she woke.

It also made sleeping difficult and I was so very tired. I couldn't wait to give birth and the countdown of days was taking forever. The flip side to this was that I was as horny as ever and there was nothing I could do about it. Lorien didn't suffer though, I made sure he was well looked after, rejoiced in doing so in fact, as much as he felt selfish about it. I told him to just hang on and enjoy the ride. "When is Elijah due home?" I asked. Although the air conditioner was on, I still felt stifling hot.

"Not until around 5.00 pm."

"Good," I said and stripped off my dress, naked as the day *I* was born. It felt so much better. Lorien laughed,

"I feel like a kid in a toy store with no money."

"Why?"

"Here you are in front of me, tempting me, and I can't have you."

"We can try Sweetheart, but I can't guarantee anything." He came to me, lunch now on the back burner, and took my breasts in his hands, looking into my eyes and smiling down at me before he kissed me. He eventually drew back, standing fully at attention.

"It's OK Baby. I know it's impossible, but it won't be for much longer."

"I want sex!"

"Do you want me to look after you?"

"No," I sighed, "it won't happen." He looked at me sadly, knowing that this was taking its toll on me. "I'm just so hot."

"You know it lover." I laughed, hugging him to me, as far as was possible at this late stage in the pregnancy would allow anyway.

"I have an idea, come with me." He picked up my dress and led me onto the back verandah. "Here, put this back on," he said, handing it to me.

"I don't want to."

"Please Ash, you'll see why in a minute." I sighed and did as he asked. He then trotted down the stairs and stood to face me, raising his chin and arms to the downpour, instantly soaked. "Come on Baby, come and frolic in the rain with me." Had he lost his mind? "Come to Lorien little one..."

"Little one!" I scoffed as I penguin-waddled down the stairs one by one.

He took me in his arms and danced me around the yard, making me laugh. He tickled me, chased me, pounced at me; I was a willing target and couldn't have outmanoeuvred him if I tried. My hair and dress were plastered to my face and body, water dripping heavily down my arms, coursing from my fingertips, nose and chin. He stripped his shirt off and the hilarity suddenly became serious. He stopped and looked at me, my dress now a transparent sheath. His eyes grew hungry. Our shared forced diet insisted on being fed immediately on a most incredible banquet. I wanted to eat him alive.

He whipped his shirt around my hips and pulled me to him. As he kissed me, I pushed against him, moving him involuntarily backward by the force of my intentions. "Do you want to try?" he purred, his lips working up my throat to my ear, driving me insane. He moved in behind me and ran his hands over me lightly, nudging my hair out of the way as he kissed across the nape of my neck.

"Yes," I whispered and dragged him to the eastern side of the yard, disclosed by bushland, giving us a screen of privacy.

He stripped off his shorts and sat on them, motioning me to him with a finger, which accompanied a cheeky smile. I stood astride him and he took my hands, assisting me to ease down over his thighs. I put my hands on his shoulders and leant down to kiss him as his fingers strummed the irresistible melody that made me ready for him instantly. I had been ready for weeks. I inched back slightly and sunk onto him, feeling fulfilled again. He had to lay back, there simply wasn't enough room for the three of us with him in a half sitting position, and he took my hands again, allowing me to ease the pressure, to use him as a stabilising force. "Oh Lorien, you feel so incredible, I've missed this so much..." I whispered, wanting this to last the longest time, but I soon grew so tired, unable to keep the motion going, even with him aiding me.

"Can you get on your knees Baby?" I nodded and he helped me to stand again. He was so hard Mr Winky was aligned against his stomach as he moved around behind me. "Oh God," he whispered, nearly inaudibly, as he slid into my eager depths, once again taking my upper arms in his hands and pulling me gently back toward him. It was amazing that he could maintain his control after such a long hiatus, but for nearly half an hour he made love to me before I let myself reach my crescendo. He built me slowly and steadily, each and every thrust moved me upwards and reinforced to me the strength of his love, our love. I loved him so much. I felt selfish taking my time but knew this might be the *last* time for God knows how many more weeks... and I wanted to make the most of it.

When he obviously reached the point of no return his force became urgent, a force he knew would also be my undoing. He drove me into the fantastical summit I had waited for so long. With his lips at my nape, holding me nearly vertical against him now, he groaned, driving me upwards and over, the rain driving down upon us in tears of relief and ecstasy.

When Elijah got home, he found us sitting in the rain on the back steps, holding each other, still lazing our hands and lips across each other's. "How long have you two been out here? You look like drowned rats," he laughed. Lorien looked at me and smiled, which I returned, running my hands over his long, rain-straightened hair, pulling his face back to mine. "You're like an open book; no guessing what you got up to out here, hey?" Lorien drew back and smiled. "I'm going to make a pot of tea. I think you should both have some." He walked inside, muttering 'crazy,' to himself.

Lorien grabbed a towel from the bathroom, and I stripped off my wet dress, wrapping its Terrey warmth around me so I could go in and dry off. I used the loo whilst I was in there and walked into the kitchen sheepishly when I'd finished. "Can you have a look at something for me Elijah," I asked. He turned his doctor's eye on me, and I let him know what I wanted him to look at was in the toilet, not on me for a change. He followed me in and when he saw the pinkish residue, he looked at me and smiled.

"It's your operculum Ash." I knew the term; I also knew I was now in the initial stages of labour. "You know it could still be days away?" I nodded, excited though that I was nearly there. I was getting sick of peeing when I sneezed, or laughed... or blinked. He hugged me warmly and I grinned up at him, so very, very happy, not to mention sexually fulfilled. It couldn't have been a better day. "Does Lorien know?"

"Is he racing around the yard in a mad frenzy?" Elijah laughed, knowing that he was therefore not yet aware.

"Go and tell him, I'll be out in a sec with the tea."

I sat on the top step and took Lorien's hand in mine. He was still sitting in the rain, his face glorious in its radiance. I grinned at him. "What are you smiling about gorgeous girl?" He leant up and kissed me, drawing my face to his, pulling me back under the downpour.

"My plug just came away." He pulled back abruptly and gazed at me.

"What?"

"You heard me." Elijah came out, and just in time too as I didn't know what Lorien's immediate reaction would be.

"You're in labour?" he shrilled.

"Lorien, calm down," Elijah told him. "It could be days yet. This is just the initial stage."

"Baby, did I do this to you?" he asked, concerned that our little romp had caused the onset.

"Yeah, about nine months ago," I laughed.

"Be serious Ash!"

"Sweetheart, I *am* due you know."

"I know, but the sex..."

"Enough!" Elijah interrupted, "I don't need to know when, where, in what position or for how long." He and I laughed.

"Couples who are overdue are advised to have sex to bring on the birth, isn't that right Elijah?" I asked.

"Yes, but we don't need to go into that do we?" He looked a little embarrassed, a lot embarrassed. I laughed, knowing that the orgasm itself - Lorien's *and* mine, played a major part in this method of possible inducement.

"Well, I want her perfect, not a day earlier than she should be."

"She'll be fine Lori, trust me," Elijah said. Lorien grinned at me and took off into the yard, jigging, singing,

"I'm going to be a Daddy, gonna be a da-hah-dee."

"Can you believe he's been old enough to vote for four years?" Elijah asked, laughing.

"Aren't you glad he hasn't carried on like this for the past thirty-nine weeks?" I replied.

"God, it would have been unbearable, and Bump would have never known her father. I would have killed him months ago." We both laughed together.

"Come on Mummy, come and dance with me in the rain!" he yelled and threw his head back, letting it pour down on him.

"Is it still OK?" I asked Elijah.

"Go ahead," he said and smiled at me, shaking his head.

He swung me around gently, full of excitement, then dropped to his knees and pressed his face into my belly lightly. "Don't you yell at her again," I warned. He grinned up at me and his face turned into stone when I bent forward and moaned. A small flush of warmth gushed down my legs. My water had broken. He sucked in his breath, about to call for Elijah, but he was already there beside me.

"Lori, help her inside." They took me in, one on either side, and all-but carried me up the stairs. Elijah went to get his bag and told Lorien to dry me off and put me on the bed.

There were no hospital gowns or any other such medical garb in the house and I lay waiting for him, draped solely in a sheet. Lorien sat on the other side of me cross-legged on the bed, holding my hand, a look of worry on his face. "Kiss me Baby," I whispered to him and he leant over and brushed his lips across mine, drawing back, still looking worried. "You can do better than that, lover." He smiled and leant down again, putting in a more sincere effort. Elijah came back in and waited patiently.

"Can I check her out now please?" he asked his twin.

"Go right ahead Doc," Lorien said.

"I'm sorry Ash but I'm going to have to do this manually. It may be a little uncomfortable."

"Is it going to hurt her?" Lorien asked.

"I mean uncomfortable to her ego, not her body. I need to gauge her cervix to find out how dilated she is."

"Oh," he said, a little coyly.

He snapped on a pair of surgical gloves and positioned himself at my knees, asking me to draw them up and apart. "Ready?" I nodded. His bedside manner was wonderful, and I didn't feel uncomfortable at all. As he poked around inside me, he asked whether I had been having any abdominal discomfort over the past few days, of which I had. It took my mind off what he was doing though, and where he was.

"I put that down to Braxton Hicks and didn't think anything more of it."

"You should have said something Ash, just in case, but I think you were right." He pulled off the gloves and looked at Lorien, and then me, smiling. "Well, you're about two centimetres dilated; it could be any day now."

"It could *still* be days?" Lorien asked.

"Possibly, but not probably."

"Typical doctor," Lorien complained. "Never a straight answer." Elijah laughed.

"Just keep your eye on her. I'm going to ring Patrick and let him know what's going on and that I won't be at Uni for a few days. I don't want to miss this." I was glad; his presence alone had a calming influence on me, let alone his stressed-out twin.

When Elijah returned, I was dressed. He sat on the bed and took my hand. "Are you going to do this naturally or have an epidural?"

"I don't know. Which will hurt more?" Elijah laughed.

"Didn't you go through all this in your classes?"

"Well, Mr top student here had all the questions of course." I looked at Lorien and smiled. He grinned back at me. "But now that it's all happening, I'm scared."

"It's natural Ash. Every first-time mother feels this way because they don't know what to expect."

"How is this," I said, running my hand over my stomach of Everest, "going to fit through there?" now pointing at my nether regions.

"Women have been doing this for thousands of years and will be doing it long after we're dust. Muscles stretch... Bones break..." Lorien and I looked at him, mouths agape. "I'm only kidding, sorry. Probably a little inappropriate."

"Damn right," Lorien said, but I saw the funny side of it and laughed. "I need to ring Mum and Dad, Anna and Dom."

"Let me ring my Mum and Dad," I said and Lorien passed me my phone.

Mum was so excited and made me promise I would get Lorien to ring them the *second* we went to the hospital. She was thrilled at becoming a grandmother and had been driving Dad insane for weeks. Poor Dad. I asked Mum to put him on, wanting to see how he was feeling. He was a lot calmer than Mum but was still an expectant grandfather-to-be. "More importantly how are you doing Honey?"

"I'm OK Dad. I just want to get on with it now it's nearly time."

"I can understand that," he said. "You will never experience anything like it Ashlyn. Lorien is in for a surprise too when the time comes." Dad chuckled but was elusive as to his remark when I questioned him further on it. "How is he doing?"

"He's Lorien. How do you think he's doing?" Dad laughed again and Lorien pulled a face at me. I was tired from talking, exhausted, and all I wanted to do was go to sleep. Dad wished me luck and said he would see me at the hospital. Mum got back on for another quick word and I was nearly asleep when Lorien finally took the phone from me. He went to ring his mother's mobile and asked me if I wanted something to eat. I didn't.

"I think you should try Ash," Elijah said. "If you end up in labour quicker than I thought you may not eat anything for a while."

"OK, but nothing too heavy." He smiled at me and left the room.

Cara or Nick obviously wanted to speak to me but Lorien wouldn't allow it, telling them I was too tired. I held my hand out for the phone and he shook his head, moving away from the bed. When he ended the call, he told me they were in Bundaberg and were leaving immediately. It was about a fourteen-hour drive so they would get here in the morning.

"You should have told them to stop halfway and rest somewhere," I said, now wishing I had taken the phone.

"They will if they need to. They aren't going to risk not making it back for the birth of their first grandchild." Little were we to know that they wouldn't make it in time.

New Swear Words

"When you took your first breath I looked at Mum and she smiled,
We had the proof of our unyielding love; it was shining from her eyes."

L Standish, 'Mercy's Song'

IT WAS 3.00 AM and I'd been monitoring my contractions for about half an hour. I was sure this wasn't a false alarm as they were coming faster, now nearly every five minutes, and lasting longer. I eventually woke Lorien, knowing it was time. "Baby, quick, get dressed." He leapt out of bed, dragging on the first thing his hand touched, my dress. When he realised he was trying to force his feet through the armholes he threw it to the ground. Darting into the wardrobe he came out in jeans, pulling a T-Shirt on, back to front.

"Why are you sitting there Ash, get dressed Baby."

"I am dressed Sweetheart," I said and he finally recognised this, and that my hospital bag was sitting next to me on the bed. "Can you wake Elijah?" He took off down the hall and I had one last glance around the room, taking in the end of our days as a duo.

I was already in the lounge room waiting for them when they came bounding down the stairs together. "How far are they apart Ash?" Elijah asked as he hit the bottom step, grabbing the car keys off the dining room table.

"I'll drive," Lorien said.

"No, you won't. You sit in the back with her." To me he said, "Or do we need to get an ambulance?"

"The car will be fine." Lorien then started dragging things from the rumpus area, stacking them next to the hospital bag.

"What are you doing Lorien?" I asked and laughed. He had a music player, various massage items, socks, essential oils; the list went on and on.

"It's all to help you with the labour Ash." I didn't interfere; if this was something he had planned, I was not going to stop him. When he added his laptop to the pile, I had to laugh. "It's so I can send out the emails."

"Won't a text on your mobile do?"

"Crap! I have to ring your parents."

"You can do that from the car Lori, come on let's go," Elijah told him, and we were off.

My bravado was moreso for Lorien's benefit. As we neared the hospital, I was feeling decidedly more nervous than I had when I woke with the first cramping pains. Elijah went on ahead to make the arrangements which left Lorien and I waiting impatiently in reception. He was back within minutes pushing a wheelchair, which they helped me into and wheeled me to a birthing suite. "Get her dressed Lorien. I'll be back with an enema." We had discussed this, and although they were not compulsory anymore, I could think of nothing worse than disgracing myself during childbirth.

Lorien helped me out of my clothes and into a hospital gown, walking me around the room until my next contraction hit. He held me upright, his head swivelling, searching for Elijah.

A nurse came back with him and I went into the adjoining bathroom, instructing her to shut the door behind us. This was something that neither of them needed to see. They were both at the door when I came out and the look on their faces made me laugh. It was a short-lived laugh as another contraction coursed through me. "Why is it happening so fast?" Lorien asked.

"Just give me a minute Lori. Help her onto the bed." He did and then Elijah checked my dilation. "She's eight centimetres."

"What -" Elijah cut him off.

"Get up there with her Lori and give her some support, help her through the contractions." Elijah darted off, to find the doctor I was hoping. The next one ripped through me and I let out a line of expletives, of which the Castlebrook wharfies would have been proud.

"Breathe Ash; come on Honey work through it."

"It's all well and good for you to say Lorien, but I want this thing out of me now!" He took my hand and I squeezed, feeling his knuckles protest under my intense grip. I went to get up as the next contraction passed.

"What are you doing Baby?" I told him in no uncertain terms that I was getting off this bed with or without his help and he decided it was in his best interests to assist me. He walked me around the room again and when the next contraction hit, I leant into the wall and he rubbed my lower back, flicking his eyes from me to the door, waiting anxiously on Elijah's return.

A few minutes later, he rushed in with a doctor in tow. "I'm Doctor Souter. How are we doing Ashlyn?"

"They're getting closer together and more intense," Lorien told him.

"That's fine," he said and asked me to resume the position on the bed. He put my feet into the stirrups and rechecked my cervix. "We're at full dilation Elijah. I believe you're going to assist me in the birth of your niece or nephew?"

"Yes Doctor and it's my niece." He smiled at me, but I could not return the loving gesture. I wanted to push.

"Are you scrubbed?" Elijah nodded and added the surgical gloves to his already sterile hands. "Do you feel like pushing Ashlyn?"

"Yeeesssss," I answered, already pushing.

"This is going to be quick. Elijah, I want you to speak to the nurse and make sure any equipment that might be needed is ready and waiting."

"I've already done it Doctor."

"Excellent, let's have a baby."

"Drugs! I want drugs!" I demanded.

"I'm sorry Ashlyn, it's too late for that, the baby's coming." I looked at Lorien and he returned my gaze with a helpless expression. Him! It was 'him' that had done this to me! In my mind's eye I could see an accusatory finger pointing directly at '*him*', flashing garishly in bands of neon yellow; 'him', 'HIM', 'HIM!!!'

As the next contraction hit, instead of my breathing techniques, I chose to inform Lorien as eloquently as possible that he was not only the result of his parents never being married, but mentioned that he was also a fornicating rectum. I also added for good measure that I would receive a great deal of joy by kicking his testicles up and out through his mouth. His expression did not waiver however; Elijah had warned us of this possibility, and I realised that this is what Dad had been referring to on the phone yesterday as one of Lorien's surprises waiting for him. "I need you to bear down Ashlyn and hold the pressure, good girl..."

The contractions were now one on top of the other and I knew Mercy was coming. "Elijah, would you get your brother a warm washcloth please." He handed it to Lorien and he applied it lightly to my perineum, relaxing my muscles. I was praying that the massaging over the past few months was about to pay off.

I pushed, I swore, I was getting exhausted, and finally Doctor Souter told me I was crowning. "Do you want to see your baby's head Lorien?" he asked. I wanted to see Lorien's head on a stick!

"Oh Baby, she has hair!" he cried and came back to me.

"Alright gentlemen, if you can get on either side of her and grab behind her knees; draw them back as far as you can without making her uncomfortable." They held me in the position and then Doctor Souter said to me, "Ashlyn, I want you to curve around as much as you can when you bear down next time. Tuck your chin into your chest. Now push..." I pushed, I swore. "And again, bear down Ashlyn, hold it..." I forced as hard as I could, grunting with the exertion.

"I don't think I can push anymore..." I said weakly, lying back against the bed. It felt like I had been at this for hours.

"One more good one Ashlyn, come on, push." I pushed and then he had this tiny little red thing in his hands, waving her arms around like Peter Garrett.

"Oh my God Baby! She's here!" I lay back, watching the scene before me through hooded eyes.

"How many?" I asked and Lorien answered,

"Ten and ten," knowing I was referring to her fingers and toes.

"Is she beautiful?"

"She is exceptionally beautiful, Baby girl, just a second..." Doctor Souter cleared her airways then clamped the umbilical cord and let Lorien cut it. He wrapped her in a blanket and passed her to Lorien who carried her to me so carefully, placing her in my outstretched arms. I burst into tears, pulling the blanket away from her slightly so I could see more of her. I could feel a needle go into my rear and I knew that there were more things going on down there, but I was past caring. My role was done.

I looked up at Lorien and smiled through my tears; they were also streaming down his face. He leant down to kiss me and then Bump. I remembered Elijah and searched the room for him. He met my gaze and smiled at me warmly, going back to assisting Doctor Souter. "Do you want to hold her Elijah?" He didn't hear me.

"Relax Baby; he'll get around to it." She was so tiny, so frail. I moved more of the blanket away and counted her fingers and toes, yes, there was ten of each. Her little round mouth was working in random movements and she scrunched up her fists and legs, moving her head from side to side.

"Oh Lorien!" I cried and tried to move over so he could lay with us. He did his best to appease me by laying his arm around my shoulders and he looked at me with so much love my tears freshened.

A nurse came in and wanted to take my baby. I scowled at her, not ready to part with this darling little child. I had heard people jokingly refer to babies' bums and faces being interchangeable when this young, but all I could see in her was Lorien. She was so perfect. Elijah persuaded me to hand her over for a few minutes so they could clean her off, and Lorien took me into the shower to do likewise. I think I fell asleep in there. I didn't recall much after that.

I remembered rousing slightly in the dim light. I was in another room, and could feel a little mouth searching for my nipple. She latched on and started suckling. I hoped it was her, if I were to find out it was Lorien he was seriously going to get it when I recovered full consciousness. The night took me away...

When I woke, I glanced around, immediately awake, looking for my family. Elijah was my first sight. "Where's Lorien? Where's Bump?"

"He'll be back in a second, he's just gone to get us a coffee, and Bump is right here." There was a hospital crib next to my bed and I tried to sit up, wanting my little girl. Elijah picked her up for me. "Time for a feed anyway. Do you remember nursing her last night?" he asked.

"Vaguely," I said, and moved into a better position for her to feed, unable to take my eyes off her. "Did everything go OK?" I asked, still not averting my eyes.

"It was a textbook birth," Elijah told me.

"Would you tell me any differently if that wasn't the case?"

"Of course Ash," he smiled at me smugly, "but talk about your quick deliveries. We got here at 3.30 am and she was born at 5.05 am."

"So today is her birthday?" He smiled and nodded. "The sixth of December; my little girl is a Sagittarius."

"She was always going to be a Sagittarius," Elijah reminded me. He was right.

Mum, Dad, Cara and Nick were all waiting outside and now I was awake, Elijah let them come in. All four of them positively beamed at me and I passed Mercy to Mum first. Lorien finally came back with two coffees as they were mid-way through playing pass the parcel. He grinned and sat next to me on the bed, kissing me openly in front of our parents. "How are you feeling Mummy?" he asked and leant down to kiss me again.

"Wonderful Sweetheart, how are you going?"

"Great. I'm a Daddy!"

"I know it," I laughed.

"Are you ready to go home?"

"Sure, but can I go so soon?"

"There were no complications and both you and Bump are in perfect health; you can leave whenever you like." All five of them laughed as I nudged him out of the way so I could get out of bed. I headed straight for the bathroom with my hand clamped around the back of the hospital gown to retain my modesty.

I sought out Elijah before we left, finding him near reception talking to the nurse behind the counter. "Thanks for everything Elijah," I said and leant up to kiss his cheek.

"It was my pleasure sis," he said, bending down to place a soft kiss on Bump's forehead. "I'll see you at home Mercy," he said, smiling at us both warmly. "I won't be far behind you."

Coming home was a treat. Balloons and flowers awaited me in a flouncy torrent of colour and movement. Cara and Nick had obviously come here first when they arrived as their bags were near the stairway. Lorien led them upstairs to get settled and I took our sleeping girl to our room, Mum in tow, putting her into the crib for the first time. It made her look even tinier when lying in the large wooden frame. I flicked on the baby monitor and sat on the bed, looking at her through the slats.

"She's beautiful Honey," Mum said, and sat next to me, taking my hand in hers. Lorien came in a few minutes later and peered into the crib, then turning to me with a massive grin, came to sit on the other side of me. Mum excused herself, taking the other handset of the baby monitor downstairs with her. Lorien sidled even closer.

"Why are you looking at me like that?" I asked.

"Want to start on number two child?" he asked cheekily and kissed me, laying me back on the bed. My first thought was of Mum and the monitor she had in her hand.

"You aren't getting back in there for a little while longer mister!" I whispered and he sighed resignedly, knowing this was going to be the case.

"I *am* allowed to enjoy my wife alone for a few intimate moments, surely?" I rolled to him, silently assuring that this *was* OK.

"Lori?" Cara was at the door. "Oops, sorry kids." We sat up.

"It's OK Mum, what do you need?" I took a final look at our little miracle before closing the door behind us.

Dad was carting a massive Minnie Mouse under one arm and a giant baby bottle under the other when I came down the stairs. He put the bottle on the dining room table, and I peered into it curiously. Inside was a plethora of baby paraphernalia including more bottles, nappies, rattles, soft toys and formula. "I'm breastfeeding," I said, unsure as to why this item had also been included.

"As good as your intentions are, Honey, sometimes a mother needs a little help. It's here if you need it." I didn't think I would need it.

Cara made coffee and we all sat, Lorien putting Minnie on his knee. "That mouse is in my spot," I said and Lorien laughed, dropping her to the ground so I could take her place. When we were all settled Nick put a box in front of me. I smiled at him and Cara before opening it. Inside was a horizontal gold brooch with a bluebird at its centre and a small matching bracelet, complete with a tiny padlock. They were beautiful.

"Thanks Mum, Dad," I said, getting up to give them both a kiss.

When Bump woke, I went to give her a feed, taking the bracelet and brooch with me. Lorien came too. When I swapped her to my other side, I looked up to see him watching me and a smile broke out on his face. "What?"

"I want to try it."

"Try what?"

"Your breast milk."

"Are you crazy?"

"No," he said, kneeling before me. "Can I?"

"If you want," I said, still thinking him insane. He wasn't there for long, in fact no more than a few seconds, but I could feel him drawing from me, his hands holding me to his lips. "Well?" I asked when he was done. He pulled a slight face.

"It's not what I was expecting." I laughed, jiggling Bump, who came out of her daze, opening her big blue eyes.

"It's still the colostrum Sweetheart; it will change in a few more days." Bump pulled away, she was done, and my breasts now felt a lot softer, drained of the fluid build-up.

"I'll give it another go then," he said, taking her from me to change her. I adjusted myself as Lorien laid her on the bed, changing her nappy. He then dressed her in a cotton jumpsuit covered in little strawberries. She looked adorable, not that I was biased of course. He added the brooch and bracelet, and I grabbed the bassinet on the way out, which was pointless. She was not out of a pair of eager arms again all day.

The End of the Drought

"Believe me Baby when I say I want you morning, night and day
It's permanent now in my heart, don't stop! Please start."

L Standish, 'The Words I Want to Hear'

I COULDN'T BELIEVE that at the age of twenty-three I first realised that my father was part clairvoyant. Bump was now four weeks old and was not getting enough nutrients from my breast milk alone and I had started to wean her onto a formula bottle intake for the past week. This was also done via Elijah's recommendation and it was now him who I was seeking out. I found him on the verandah, asleep on one of the sun lounges. I had no intention of waking him, so laid out on the other lounge, waiting for him to wake up. The whole house was currently asleep; Bump in her Daddy's arms on our bed. I closed my eyes and revelled in the silence that surrounded me. I couldn't remember the last time there was not one noise to be heard, and with the exception of an occasional car making its way down Bridge Street, all was quiet. I also slept.

I woke when the lounge shifted under me and I opened my eyes to find my husband and daughter sitting on the edge. "Hi Mummy," Lorien said quietly and leant down to kiss me, lowering Bump so I could kiss her too.

"Shhh," I said, motioning to the sleeping Elijah.

"I know, but someone wants her morning tea," he whispered. "Do you want to try and feed her, or will I give her a bottle?" I sat up and held my arms out for her, willing to give it a first attempt before going in for the reserves. She latched on and watched me as she fed. She'd been focussing well for the past two weeks and was even able to lift her head. Of course we thought she was some kind of genius, but Elijah assured us it was all part of the natural development. I traced my finger down her plump cheek, causing her to let go of my nipple and smile at me. When she had first smiled, we knew it was wind; the last week we knew it was now the real thing. I smiled back. It was all very sweet and smile worthy, but she would not go back on my breast. Lorien went to get a bottle ready. Waiting on his return, I sat her facing me on my knee and sang softly to her. She smiled again.

When Lorien returned, he took her from me and assumed the position. She was hungry and took to the plastic nipple as if it was my own. We were lucky she didn't mind the fake boob or the taste of the formula, and since we'd started her on it, her weight gain had been impressive. Lorien was watching me when my gaze returned to him. "What?"

"She only fed from one, right?" I nodded. "So can I pleeeease try again Ash?" I'd told Lorien two weeks ago he was not getting another taste of my breast milk until Bump was weaned; she was barely getting enough without him making a hog of himself. I'd initially come out here to ask Elijah how I could stop my milk production, and after her current abysmal attempt, knew there was no point in prolonging the inevitable. I smiled at him and he moved in closer, balancing Bump and the bottle in one hand, reaching for my dress to pull the still milk-hardened breast from it.

"You just hold her, I'll get it out." He waggled his eyebrows at me and sat back, waiting for me to do just that. "Give her to me," I said and took our baby girl from him. I was sure he wouldn't drop her, but when Lorien was faced with my still-huge breasts, I couldn't be one hundred percent sure he would be concentrating as well as he should. We also hadn't made love since she was born, and it was taking a toll again on both of us.

He was at it a lot longer than the first colostrum attempt and he finally drew back, smiling up at me widely. I felt a lot better as he had relieved the pressure marginally. "It's sweeter than I expected."

"It *is* milk," I told him, laughing quietly.

"I know, but I thought it would be more like the formula. She's going to miss the real thing."

"She doesn't seem to be," I said, looking down at her, sucking up the last of the formula. I handed Lorien the bottle and leant her forward to tap and circle over her back, bringing up a prize-winning burp.

"That's my girl," Lorien said. Elijah stirred and Lorien quickly tucked me back into my dress. "I'm glad he slept through the second feeding," he said, grinning at me lecherously, before going inside to change her.

"Hey sis," Elijah said when he was fully conscious.

"Hey bro," I said and smiled at him. "Want a coffee?" He rubbed his hands over his face and nodded, standing and following me into the kitchen.

"Where's the rest of our family?"

"Lorien's changing her, she just had a feed. Can I ask you something?"

"Without him around, anything you like Ash." I laughed, he was right though; these conversations were always easier when it was just the two of us. Lorien seemed to embarrass his twin adeptly, although rarely meant intentionally. He was simply unable to keep the personal aspects to himself when his questioning became more pointed and specific.

"She only fed off me for a few minutes today and wouldn't go back on."

"So, you're looking at weaning her altogether?"

"Is there an issue with it?"

"No, she's taken to the bottle and formula, and even you can see what a difference it's made to her development." I could.

"What do I do now?"

"It depends. Do you want to try it naturally or take tablets?"

"I'd like to try naturally first. How long will it take?"

"Anywhere from a week to months. Each case is different." I handed him a mug and headed to the dining room table to drink them. I sat thoughtful for a few minutes, mulling it over in my head when he continued. "You can try first and then take the tablets if it's stressing you too much."

"OK. What should I do?"

"These are not medical suggestions, but methods tried and tested by other mothers. Putting cabbage leaves into your bra helps. You aren't allergic to cabbage, are you?"

"No."

"OK, try that, and also wear a snug bra. You'll need to avoid nipple stimulation and will definitely have to keep Lori off them. As long as they're being drawn on, your body will continue to make milk." That in a nutshell is why we could discuss these issues more effectively without Mercy's Daddy around. Right then and there was when it would have all fallen apart if Lorien was privy to the conversation. He would have wanted to make suggestions, attempt scenarios and pose rhetorical questions at him. I was happy to just take the advice and work with it.

Lorien came down with Bump and laid her on the bunny rug. He positioned the Sesame Street baby gym over her, and she batted and squeezed at the toys happily.

Cara and Nick had left two weeks ago, and I was missing them already. I didn't know what I would have done without Cara and Mum for the first few days; their advice and experience with an actual baby far outweighed Elijah's medical knowledge at times as it was the real thing. He had never given birth to a child and then had to raise it, whereas both of our mothers had. Mum had also been onto me for a week now, insisting we bring Mercy over to spend the night or weekend with them, giving Lorien and I time to be alone. I was sure this was not in relation to us having sex, but simply to be Lorien and Ashlyn again. So far, I had said no. I was unaware, sitting there sipping my coffee, how quickly I was about to take her up on the offer, as a knock was heard at the door. Elijah went to answer it. "Hey guys!" It was Michael and Glen, Simon and Bree.

"Hi twin," Michael said and moved past him, straight for Bump. "How's my Goddaughter?" he asked, picking her up and lifting her into the air. She rewarded him with a smile. We had a small Christening for her whilst Lorien's parents were home, knowing this was the only chance we would get for some time. Elijah and Michael were her Godfathers and Bree her Godmother. They were all tickled pink when we asked them, and they accepted immediately when the offer was made. There would have been no other choice than to have Elijah as her Godfather, regardless.

This also brought Lorien and I to a difficult decision. We had sat Elijah down when we made out our wills and told him if anything was to happen to both of us, that we wanted him to become Mercy's custodian. His answer of yes was immediate, so I reminded him of all that it would contain: loss of his own personal life, difficulties with work schedules, lack of female companionship if she was still very young; the list was endless. He acknowledged all of this and was prepared to make those sacrifices. We were both pleased that our little girl would be well looked after if tragedy was to ever strike us both down. It wasn't a pleasant conversation, but one that had to take place.

Michael pulled a present from his back pocket, taking a seat at the table and setting her on his knee. He passed it to Bump and she tore at the wrapping. As per the norm with babies, she received more pleasure from the paper than the actual gift inside. Several times Michael had to stop her putting the paper into her mouth. "Michael, you don't have to bring her something every time you come over."

"It's not like I'll be having any of my own. I like to spoil her." He had bought a T-Shirt, the words across it reading, 'My Godfather is as Spunky as Me'. He laid her across the table and removed the current shirt she was wearing, putting the new one on and turning her around to show us all.

"Thanks Michael, I didn't know you felt that way about me," Elijah said, laughing.

"I was referring to myself, not you twin!" he admonished, and raised the shirt to give her a bout of raspberries to her tummy. We all delighted in making her smile and took every opportunity to do so, now she had started for real. It surprised us all when a laugh emitted from her rosebud mouth. "How long has she been doing that?" he asked.

"It's her first that I know of," I said and looked at Elijah and Lorien to see if I had missed one previously.

"Nope, first one," Lorien said, and Elijah agreed.

"Well, there you go Uncle Michael, you've created a milestone."

"How could you not laugh, looking at that face?" Simon added and we all laughed, looking at Michael.

"My turn," Bree said and reached for her.

"What are you guys doing this weekend?" Glen asked.

"No plans. Why, what are you thinking of doing?"

"Snipers is closed. They're renovating and didn't finish in time so we thought you might be up for a social occasion."

"Your timing is perfect Glen. As of this moment I am taking her off the boob." I was rather excited at finally being able to relax and enjoy a drink with my friends. Other than the two I had on my wedding day, and one other glass when Alan was here, alcohol had not passed my lips for well over ten months and I was looking forward to it immensely.

"When did you decide this Baby?" Lorien asked, pulling me to his knee.

"You saw her feed before Sweetheart, there's little point in trying anymore."

"But I was just getting used to it. You can't take *me* off the boob yet." I laughed and kissed him, and he grinned up at me.

"You've tried it?" Bree asked, taking Mercy back to the gym. Elijah intercepted and took her for a nurse.

"Twice. Once when she was first born, and this morning. Ash wouldn't let me near them again until today." Elijah made a face.

"I don't blame her," Michael said, "I've seen you eat!" We all laughed at this.

"What did it taste like?" Bree asked.

"You can try it if you like, it might be your last chance," I said.

"Do we have to take it from the original carton it comes in?" Michael asked.

"No, I have some expressed in the fridge," I laughed.

"But the choice is yours," Lorien said, and I smacked him lightly. I got up and took the bottle from the fridge, squeezing the nipple and shaking it.

"Who's first?" Now that the option was in front of them, no one was as brave as the humorous conversation had suggested. Finally, Glen took it from me and sucked for a few seconds. Bree looked at him with a grimace on her face and he said,

"What? It's not like I'll ever get another chance to try it." Taking his point into due consideration, Michael then reached for the bottle as Glen let out a massive burp, making us laugh again. "It's sweet!" I smiled at him.

"It's pretty good stuff," Michael said and then squeezed some into his coffee.

They all ended up relenting, perhaps because the opportunity would be few and far between, with the possible exception of Bree and Simon who would one day have their own baby. They both still ended up trying it. "An excellent year," Simon announced, then handed it to Elijah.

"Ahhh, will you be offended if I don't?" he asked me.

"Of course not," I said.

"Don't be a wuss," Lorien said and handed him the bottle. "You're not sharing *my* bottle," he said, running his hand lightly across my breast. Elijah rolled his eyes at his twin and apologised to Bump for stealing her food before finally trying it. He shrugged and handed the bottle back to Lorien.

"A rather rich bouquet, delicate flavour, full bodied..." We laughed again. Michael started to guffaw loudly, reminding us of the communal tasting of our chocolate body paint several years ago.

"I'd like to think there's no foreplay juices involved in the mix this time," Michael said, closing his eyes and drawing his hands together in silent prayer. It *was* rather reminiscent...

"So, tonight. What do you reckon?" Glen asked again.

"I can ring Mum and get her and Dad to have her for the night. She's been bugging me for weeks for a private visit with Bump." Lorien smiled and handed me the phone, drawing me down to kiss him. He whispered in my ear,

"I can think of a few other things we can achieve whilst she's gone too." I smiled down at him; I was in total agreement. In fact, my body had been ready for a few days now. I was no longer sore and thankful that I hadn't needed an episiotomy to aid with Mercy's delivery. Tonight was *definitely* going to be the night.

Mum picked Mercy up around 4.00 pm and it was harder letting her go than I thought it would be. I nearly called the whole thing off when we had the back door of the car closed, but Lorien reined me in. "Come on Ash, this has to be done at some time, and no, I'm not thinking about sex, we can do that whether she's here or not. Let your Mum and Dad have her Sweetheart, we'll see her tomorrow." I relented and cried as Mum drove off.

This was everyone's cue to go to the bottle-shop, leaving Lorien and me alone for a few minutes to adjust to the new situation. We'd decided to stay here for the night as we were set up for guests already and nothing needed to be done.

By the time they got back, I was over my sook and took the three bottles of champagne Michael passed to me, putting them in the fridge. Glen dumped a mass of snacks on the table and Lorien told me to go join our friends on the verandah; he'd do the grunt work. They'd also brought ice, and Elijah filled the esky outside after putting all the beer bottles in first. This time-saver of alleviating the need to go into the kitchen had become a favourite within the group. "Christ, how much did you buy?" I asked when I saw Lorien coming out of the kitchen, performing a balancing act with the platters. Pretzels, dips, deli meats, various cheeses, corn chips, fruit, kalamata olives, pickled onions, capers and gherkins.

"There's more," Glen said. "We're going to make our own pizzas later, much better than the frozen pies and sausage roll crap."

"You brought more pot didn't you Glen?" I asked, knowing another bout of the munchies was coming.

"Are you going to try some this time Ash? You aren't pregnant or breastfeeding anymore." I looked at Elijah. Could I? Should I?

"It's up to you Ash."

"What about if there's schizophrenia in my family? Isn't that supposed to trigger it?"

"Is there schizophrenia in your family?"

"No." He grinned at me. "I don't know if I'll be able to stomach the smell any better than when I was pregnant though."

"Trial and error dah-link," Michael advised. We would see...

The pool table in the rumpus area had been a cause of disagreement with the twins for a few months now. Lorien wanted to get rid of it so he could buy a baby grand piano and Elijah was adamant about keeping it. When Simon suggested a game of Kelly Pool, Elijah smiled at his twin triumphantly. "I still want to get rid of it Eli," Lorien said, and Elijah shook his head.

"No, put the piano somewhere else."

"Like where?" Lorien asked, making a face.

"Not my problem bro," he answered officiously. I wished there was somewhere we could find room to have a piano, even an upright would be OK by me. I would love to sit and watch Lorien play. The acoustics and timbre of the real thing pitted against a keyboard was compelling in itself. And, to watch him get lost in the movements and melody made my heart flutter at the thought of it. However, it was not going to happen without a major shuffle of the downstairs furniture; not that Lorien didn't keep trying.

I had drawn the 2 ball. The hard thing about Kelly Pool was to keep your cool when someone was shooting at your ball. If they were to find out which one you were hoping to pot, they would sink it on you, and it would be game over Ashlyn. We were such a competitive little bunch and I had to admit that my eyes were keen to spot which ones they were taking deliberate and difficult aim at, trying to sink their own. Bree was out - number 11, as was Simon - number 15. So far it had been Glen who managed to knock them out of the game by sinking both of their balls. I was sure he was the black ball - number 8. On my next turn, it was positioned near the centre hole and with careful aim, I shot, taking it out. Regardless of whose ball it was, there was now one less on the table, making it easier to shoot at mine. I looked at Glen to see whether I had knocked him out, but he smiled and motioned to Michael who scowled at me. It had been his.

There were six balls on the table and four of us still playing, so odds were favourable that we'd be sinking each other's from hereon in. I couldn't get a clear shot of the 2 ball and didn't want to make it obvious that it was mine, so went for the 9 ball and sunk it. I looked around the room to see who was now pouting. None of them were, damn it. I still couldn't get a clear shot of my ball and the 5 ball was hanging over the corner pocket. I would be an idiot to ignore it, ensuring yet another turn at my own after sinking it. I hit, I missed, I was pissed off!

Lorien aimed for the 10 ball and due to the bad angle he was shooting from, I assumed it was his. However, he miscalculated the shot, which sent it flying around the table, knocking the 6 ball in. Glen moaned and put his cue down; a lucky shot had put him out of the game. Lorien fired the 13 ball in, and neither Elijah nor I flinched. There were now only three balls left on the table and therefore all three balls belonged to one of us. Lorien lined up my 2 ball. "Don't you dare Lorien, or I will cut you off for life!"

"Well, that means the 5 ball is Eli's!" He swung his cue toward it, unable to shoot at his own 10 ball cleanly.

"You suck Lori!" Elijah told him.

"No, I want her to keep doing that to me, and if I sink her ball it will all come crumbling down."

"Lorien!" I said as he took the shot, missing.

"You did that deliberately Ash, didn't you!" he chastised and chased me around the table.

"No! I didn't!" I laughed crazily over my shoulder. "It was because of what you said!" He didn't let up and finally caught me trying to bolt into the bathroom. He grabbed me around the waist and crab walked me in there, locking the door behind us. "Let me out Lorien," I warned.

"Nuh huh, you have to pay a penalty fee."

"And what might that entail?"

"Suck me," he said and laughed, unable to keep a straight face.

"Nice try Lorien, now let me out."

"No, some form of payment will need to exchange hands before I free you little one..."

"How about later?" He opened his eyes wide and growled as he launched himself at me, biting and sucking on my neck. His fingers probed and prodded into my sides, making me laugh.

"It's your go Ash!" Bree called from outside the door.

"Coming!" I called.

"We gathered that!" Michael retorted and I pushed a wriggling Lorien from me, opening the door.

"Did you miss, Elijah?" I asked, taking my cue from where I'd left it.

"Only yours Ash, I managed to sink Lori's."

"Great!" Lorien said and watched me line up Elijah's ball and then mine, gauging which was easier to pot. With this shot, assuming one went in, I would win the game.

"No Baby," Lorien said, coming over behind me, "pot Eli's. If you miss, yours will be hard for him to pocket."

"Do you want me to use this on *your* balls?" I asked, waving the cue at him. He laughed, taking a step back, allowing me to take my shot. I aimed for my own... and sunk it. Yay for me!

"Rack them back up?" Simon asked. We were all ready for another game. I was feeling rather cocky after the last round and more than a little pissed.

We played a few more rounds before Glen suggested sparking up. I still wasn't sure but followed them outside, knowing if the smell assaulted me, I could pass. "Are you going to try some?" Lorien asked, snuggling up behind me, taking the joint from Bree.

"I guess so," I said, and he drew my face toward him, exhaling the smoke into my mouth. I puffed most of it immediately back out; I'd never smoked anything before, and it was a coarse sensation. "Let me try again," I said, taking it from Lorien's hand.

"Suck it straight down your throat Ash, don't inhale and then suck it down, it will make you cough," Michael advised. He was wrong and I spluttered everywhere, feeling that my lungs were coming up through my throat; the acrid smoke burning its way out of my respiratory tract.

"Cough and you're off!" offered Michael. I glowered at him and leant back against Lorien, allowing him to hold me upright. I wasn't sure I could trust my swimming head.

"How do you feel?" he asked a few minutes later, once I had regained my control.

"OK, a bit woozy I suppose."

"Can I have a kiss?"

"I suppose," I said and turned in his arms, smiling up at him, drawing his face down to mine. "Hmmm, that's nice," I sighed, fully feeling every part of his mouth against mine. His hands running over my back were so soothing and it felt like we were an extension of each other, moving as one force.

"Knock it off you two," Michael interjected. "Enough of the pot pashes!"

"Not yet," Lorien whispered to me, and then said more loudly, "Come with me Ash, I want to show you some of my speciality pool shots." He led me to the kitchen doorway.

"And what might those be?" asked Elijah.

"Masse shot, jump shot, bank shot..." he shot back, and dragged me to the pool table, handing me a cue. He lined up a few balls and I had no idea what he was doing. I thought we'd come in here for another kiss, not to learn trick shots. "Now lean in over it, that's it..." As I horizontally aligned myself over the ball, I felt Lorien pressing into me from behind, placing his arms around mine, helping me hold the cue. "Now this is called the bank shot, as I won't bank on you letting me have my way..." He ran his hands up my thighs and tucked his fingers into my briefs, tugging at them lightly. I realised what he was getting at and tried to move away from him. He had me trapped.

"Lorien, no!" I whispered. They would all be back inside within seconds and I didn't want to be found in a truly compromising situation. Playacting - fair enough, actual intercourse, no way!

"It's been so long Baby," he mumbled against my nape, dragging my briefs mid-thigh and getting busy with his curious fingers. He chuckled quietly and pushed against me again, making sure I was aware of the raging hard-on he had working for him back there.

"You had every intention of this when you pulled me in here didn't you?" I threw at him.

"Uh huh," he admitted. "I am no longer responsible for what happens now..."

"Oh yes you bloody well are!" Michael said from behind us. The way I was pinned to the table, I was unable to turn and face him.

"Lorien, let me up!" I cried. He laughed again before surreptitiously pulling my briefs back up my legs, leaving them in a most uncomfortable position.

"It's OK Michael. I'm just teaching her a few of the finer points."

"Twin, your finer points are nearly bursting through the front of your pants!" This made me laugh. It was nice to see Lorien on the receiving end for a change, not that it flustered him any.

"Lorien! Get off me!" I called again and started to wriggle under him.

"Oh Baby, yeah! Work it Baby!" I pulled his arm closer to me, the only thing of him that I could get a grip on, and I sunk my teeth in.

"Holy shit!" he cried and backed off. "You little sadist!" he laughed, looking at me and rubbing his arm. I didn't think I had bitten him *that* hard. "I have some major things in store for you later missy!" he threatened, and I believed him.

"Did I hurt you too badly?" I asked, taking him in my arms.

"No Baby, I'm just teasing..."

"It got you off me," I smiled up at him.

"I was more interested in getting off!"

"You pig!" He just grinned at me. The rest of them were still outside. We re-joined them, leaving the sexual antics for later when we got to bed. I seriously did *not* want to have a late night tonight!

Making our own pizzas was more fun than I expected, and creating your own choice of flavour was the ultimate. We fought over the toppings and elbowed each other out of the way in a playful manner. We were all famished and warded off the munchies with large greasy bites, Lorien kissing me with a face full of grease. "Ewww!" I said, wiping my face off on a napkin, instigating him to kiss more grease onto me. "Stop it Lorien, it's gross." He smiled at me lewdly and passed me my glass of champagne.

"My plan is to get you drunk and disorderly, and you are already disorderly..."

"I hate to pop your bubble, but I *am* a sure thing you know." He waggled his eyebrows at me and grabbed another slice.

I was pretty pissed by the time we all went to bed, but not so drunk that I wasn't able to race him up the stairs so we could race each other off. He grabbed at me as we closed the bedroom door behind us, "Get your gear off Ash!" he whispered urgently, pushing me backwards onto the bed. He lifted my legs in the air and had my briefs off in one second flat, tossing them onto the floor as he knelt between my thighs.

"You're still hungry?" I laughed breathily.

"Hmmm," he purred against me, sending a thrill right through me.

"I've been waiting weeks for this..." I sighed, working with his flow and ebb, working into a long-awaited body scream. There was no one better at this than he. Even though I had never experienced anyone else, I couldn't imagine that he wasn't one of the best.

As I peaked, he lifted my knees up and over his shoulders, going in deep and infiltrating me to my very essence. I held onto his head, forcing him into me further as my moans rocketed into rapid intakes of breath, loving him so totally.

When I opened my eyes, he was looking up at me, still lapping softly, nuzzling and invoking, keeping my arousal on the edge. I smiled lazily at him and he returned my gesture, drawing back and licking his lips, still gliding a searching finger within my confines. "Worth the wait Baby?"

"Always lover, you are my erotic soul-mate." He laughed and drew me to a standing position in front of him as he worked his boxers off. He sat on the edge of the bed.

"Sit," he instructed and as I went to turn around, he swung my hips, preventing me from doing so. "No, sit facing away from me. It's something I want to try..."

"What's this called?" I asked softly as I sunk down onto him. It felt so wonderful to be full from him again.

"A reverse cowgirl," he said, making me laugh, "but I want to add a twist..." He could do what he wanted; I was content to ride him like this until morning broke through the windows. He lay back for a while, his hands lightly on my hips, allowing me to use him for my own pleasure. When he asked me to stop, I assumed he was nearly there, but was surprised to see him hook his feet against the edge of the bedframe and push himself further up the bed, pulling from me in the same movement.

"Lorien!" I groaned, and scooted up the bed, reclaiming my former position.

"This was what I was getting to," he sighed, and he lay me down, my back on his chest as he took control from beneath me. It was the most incredible thing... His hands were free to roam and tease over the front of my body; there didn't seem enough areas for him to remain at for any given amount of time. My nipples were coaxed, and my vertical heat assaulted as he worked his magic on me against every angle of my body. The great thing about him having a large penis was we could make love in any position, and this new one was rapidly becoming my favourite.

"Oh Ash, you make me so fucking hot!" he whispered against my nape and I moved my face sideways, wanting to kiss him. He couldn't reach me, but blew lightly into my ear, sending me soaring again. "Oh fuck Baby," he gasped, sitting slightly forward, taking me with him. His hands shot to my hips and held onto me as he blasted his way through his orgasm, finally dropping back to the bed, shuddering.

I hated to break our seal when we finished making love, loving the continued full feeling for a while longer. But this time I needed to be against him, and I climbed off and went to lay in his arms. He smiled at me, his breath still erratic and I leant down to kiss him. It wasn't a soft kiss, but one full of heat and fervour, wanting to eat him alive. "Hmmm Baby," he murmured. "You're hot all over again?"

"Still," I told him and was ready to go again immediately.

"You'll have to give me a few minutes," he said, and I lowered down his body.

"You've got exactly sixty seconds," I warned, and his laughter was silenced the instant I took him into my mouth.

Life Goes On

"The rush and push and pull of life, I'm done with,
There's only what I want from life, I'll deal with."

L Standish, 'Your Choice, My Life'

I'D BEEN AT MUM AND DAD'S for most of the day, finally going through all the old school papers and junk, clearing out the last of my stuff still at their place. It was all quiet when I returned home. "Where are you all?" I called up the stairs and when there was no reply, I went in search of them. They couldn't be too far away; the car was in the driveway.

All searches of the bedrooms proved fruitless and with no other place to look, I entered our ensuite, and there I found them. I watched silently at first, my heart melting for the two people I adored most. Lorien had Bump in the spa bath with a mountain of bubbles, and he was singing The Jackson Five's 'ABC' to her, dipping her into the water as her chubby little legs kicked and splashed her Daddy. She was smiling and giggling in joy to the attention her father was bestowing on her. I quietly backed out and grabbed the camcorder, filming them through the ajar ensuite door.

"How long have you been there?" Lorien asked several minutes later.

"Long enough," I smiled at him. "How's our girl enjoying her first big bath?"

"She loves it. Are you coming in Mummy?" I turned off the camcorder and put it on the vanity, stripping off to join the rest of my family. Lorien passed her to me when I was sitting comfortably, and she proceeded to splash water over me too.

"You're a little water fairy, aren't you Bump?" I asked and she responded with a joyous screech; the sound travelling well in the acoustics of the large bathroom. I hitched my knees up and laid her across my lap, her little feet digging into my stomach as I blew raspberries on her tummy.

"I feel left out," Lorien pouted at me, so we changed places. I climbed onto his lap, holding Bump in the same position across my knees and we formed a family sandwich. "That's better," he said as he made a silly face at Bump and held us both in his strong arms.

There was a knock at the door a few minutes later and I quickly covered myself in bubbles before Lorien told Elijah to come in; not that he hadn't seen the most private parts of me during delivery, but this was a little different. He smiled at us widely and took the camcorder from the vanity, capturing us in the moment. "This is so sweet," he crooned, "I wish I could get in there with you. I don't suppose you have swimmers on?"

"No Eli, sorry."

"You're home early," I said.

"Teachers are on strike until Monday, I have the rest of the week off. Well, from classes anyway. There's still plenty I can do here." It was currently Thursday, and I had a wonderful idea.

"Let's see if we can arrange for Michael, Glen, Simon and Bree to come with us to Wally's weekender! Maybe Melayne would like to come too?"

"I can't Ash, but you guys go. It sounds like a great time," he sighed.

"Can't smarn't" I answered, already planning the weekend, hopeful that it was possible to organise. "Go to Daddy," I said, sliding off Lorien's lap and passing Bump to him. As I went to stand, the twins were looking at me, smiling, realising I was about to announce myself totally to Bump's Uncle Elijah in full-frontal nudity.

"Oh yeah, right," I laughed and resumed the position. Elijah smiled and said,

"I'm going to start dinner. Any requests?"

"Whatever you like bro," Lorien answered, dunking Bump playfully up and down in the water again, another shriek emanating from her little mouth.

"Give me a sec and I'll help you," I said and waited for him to leave so I could get out of the spa.

"I'll have a kiss first," Lorien said, and I leant over to press my lips against his, the mood finally broken by another resounding screech. I smiled at him and got out, drying myself and dressing, all under Lorien's lustful gaze. "I'll get back to you later Baby!" he growled.

Sitting at the table after dinner I grabbed the book of poems I'd found when cleaning out my room. "Are you guys ready for some insights into the young mind of Ashlyn Mercy?"

"What have you got there?" Lorien asked.

"I found an old poetry book when I was cleaning out today and I couldn't bring myself to throw it away. Want to hear some?" They both nodded and I flicked through to the ones I'd earmarked for their amusement.

'Can it be said often enough?
Can it be said at all?

Can it be whispered to me?

And when it does, it tells me... nothing changes.'

They both laughed. "That was from my deep period, here's another,"

'Standing on the empty stage,

Trying to recapture that moment of glory.

No spotlight. No audience.

And there never was.'

"And this one is my personal favourite,"

'The mirror cracked and I cried as it can no longer reflect my image.

It now reflects my future; to crack and fall like so much toxic waste.

What happens to stars in the sky when they fade?

Where do we come from and who is it to say we ever were?

Someone who knows little, but of themselves, thinks a great deal.'

"What the hell does that even mean?" Lorien asked, wiping the baby food goo off Bump's cheeks.

"I don't know, but it sounded good at the time."

"Give us a poem Ash," Elijah said, and I launched into the next one.

"Here's one I wrote for Scott Markham in Year 8 when I was *so* in love with him." The twins laughed again, they both knew Scott. He was a year above us and a bit of a dork, but my pubescent eyes held him in such high regard and the irony of it was, he was also a very talented musician. It was why I had taken up the violin in the first place, so I could be near him at band rehearsals. I was also a bit of a dork...

'I sit upon a lonely beach
As I've sat upon before,
Tossing stones into the wave-wash
Having nothing, wanting more.
The dark and dismal weather
Plays emotions in my heart,
But I never heard it beating
It's torn asunder, torn apart.
The cold, it beckons to me
And I turn to it in fear,
For I know my life is destined
To never hold another dear.
The sun's rays seem so distant
Falling weakly to the sea,
Falling like the tears of Heaven
For they know you don't love me.'

I finished and looked at them, laughing, expecting them to join me. "So, were you still writing these when we came along?" Elijah asked, smirking.

"Yep."

"Are there any about me?"

"I refuse to answer on the grounds that it might incriminate me." I hadn't thought about that when I started to read these to the twins, but there *was* one about Elijah in there and I was hoping he would never get a chance to read it. Total embarrassment!

"You actually went out with this guy?" Lorien asked.

"No, but I sure wished at the time."

"You really had a thing for him huh?" Was he jealous? Was he *kidding*? He picked up the book and started flicking through random pages. I looked at Elijah and raised my eyebrows; he smiled and shrugged his shoulders. Neither of us knew what the change in his mood had resulted from. I was fourteen for Christ's sake. "These are *all* about love," he said. "Who were all these guys? I thought Eli was your first real boyfriend?"

"He was Sweetheart. Please don't get yourself upset, they're only poems from the mind of a young girl who wanted to be loved."

"You told me you were a virgin," he said quietly, his eyes never leaving the pages. I realised now that this was a horrible mistake. I should have burnt this book, but I had no idea how it would affect him when I found it.

"I am, I mean I was," I said laughing. "Elijah didn't even get past second base."

"It's true Lori," he said. "Why are you getting so worked up over this? Ash had a life before we moved here."

"Well, this poem describing sex sounds right on the money. How would you know that if you hadn't already had sex with someone else?"

"Lorien, I was fourteen or fifteen when I wrote most of those. I wanted to share something with someone that was beautiful. It's simply how I envisioned it would be at the time." He read it out aloud,

'As the flame of lust ignites and your pupils dilate
Heat and tension fills the air as you succumb to your fate.
You can feel your bodies drawn; it's electric to the touch
Sparks alight your very soul and you're wanting this so much.
Caresses played upon your lips as you're lain down on the bed.

Erotic thoughts race through your mind and your legs begin to spread.

"Stop it Lorien," I said, "you're being ridiculous." He ignored me, continuing,

Working slowly with his hands moving down with expertise
Erogenous zones are being sought and he finds them all with ease.
Then he hits the target spot, you can feel you're going numb
First relaxed and then so tense, whispering magic with his tongue.
And now I am in control gently kneading with my hands
So soft the piper blows, playing music to his glands.
Painful pleasures linger on until you're clutching desperately
The bonding moment has arrived to consummate the urgency.
As penetration takes its course you're feeling hot as well as cold,
And you shout obscenities as he spills his liquid gold.
You lay back into his arms - recall the passion of the night,
Turn and look into his eyes and once again the flame ignites.'

"That's pretty good Ash," Elijah offered. Lorien's face was a brewing storm.

"Does it sound like it was written by a virgin though?" Lorien asked viciously.

"You can't seriously be jealous Lorien," I said. He flicked through to the final hand-written page and I stiffened. The last poem was Elijah's, and I knew Lorien understood this as he read it.

"Here," he said eventually, flinging the book to his twin, "this one's yours and what a gem." He stood up and grabbed Mercy from the highchair, taking her upstairs.

"What's wrong with him?" I turned to Elijah and asked.

"Hmmm?" He was reading the poem.

"Give me that!" I said and snatched the book from him.

"Sorry Ash, curiosity and all that." He grinned at me. I rolled my eyes at him and took off up the stairs in search of my bereft one, darting back to the table to get the book as Elijah went to open it again. He smiled at me and I said,

"You aren't helping!" He chuckled as I left the room, hearing him murmur,

"Liquid gold..."

Lorien was bent over Mercy's crib singing softly when I entered her room. I didn't interrupt and certainly didn't want to wake her now she was settled. I stood quietly, waiting for him to turn around and find me. The singing eventually stopped but he still stood there, not moving. I didn't know what to say to him, didn't know how to repair the damage when I wasn't even sure why I needed to, why this had upset him so. After several moments, I approached him and tentatively put my hand on his arm. He turned and looked at me. I didn't know what else to say to him, "I'm sorry Lorien." He took me in his arms and held me tightly, kissing my forehead.

"What are you apologising for?"

"I don't know but I felt like it needed to be said."

"It's not your fault. I'm just so insanely jealous to think of you caring about anyone other than me. Makes me a bit of a selfish prick hey?" He drew back and smiled at me.

"You need to remember, I love you with all of my heart. A heart that didn't know what love meant until you came along. All of those words are just silly schoolgirl fantasy, being written about you; not even knowing you existed then."

"I owe *you* an apology."

"No, you don't. Knowing how much you love me is enough Lorien, and I know you love me so much."

"I'll certainly never be able to look Scott in the eye the same way again," he laughed. "What a fool to never see how much you cared for him."

"I told him once and it was so embarrassing. He wasn't interested though, which is why I had such a hard time discussing it when I realised I'd fallen for you. I didn't want rejection and I knew it was a possibility, a very likely possibility."

"You were wrong though, weren't you?" He took my left hand and thumbed the wedding ring on my finger.

"I had no idea that a love could exist like this, and I think we're the lucky ones. Not everyone loves as passionately as we do."

"I wish I knew you when you were fifteen and you secretly loved me enough to write a poem about me."

"For all you know, hundreds of girls did, you just weren't aware of it. Do you think for one second that any of the boys I lusted after in lower high school had an inkling of how I felt about them?"

"Except for the foolish Scott," he corrected me.

"Yes, except for Scott," I agreed.

"Will you write me a poem Baby?" I laughed quietly, thinking he was kidding. His face showed no sign of mirth however and I realised he was serious.

"I don't think I can conjure up that kind of teen angst anymore Lorien."

"Will you try?"

"I'll try if it makes you happy."

"It will." He leant down and kissed me. This made me happy.

Going to bed that night I handed him a sheet of paper. "Now it's not Shakespeare, but I think I've captured all the uncertainty of youth."

"You're finished?" he asked as he took the paper from me, unfolding it. He read it to himself.

'As I look back upon my past
To such a lonely place,
Only blacks and whites, no colour
To match my drawn and ashen face.
Every day was like the winter
Every dawn, as black as night,
Every song without a melody
Every bird without its flight.
Without rain, there are no rainbows
No stars, without the black,
The birds sing ever sweetly
Bringing dreams and hoping, back.
Now I sigh and lean back in your arms
As my enamoured heart doth sing
For I do trust that you love me
And with what the future brings.'

"I love it Ash, I really do." He read it through again. "No one has ever done anything like this for me before." I couldn't believe such a simple thing could bring him such joy and I was honoured that it had been me to give him such a gift, albeit a pretty lame one.

"It's how I felt, and how you made me feel, when we first got together. I knew I loved you from our beginning and hoped you felt the same."

"You know I did, longer than you did, remember?"

"I know, but it's still hard when you're a teenager. We should be given all those driving hormones when we know what to do with them, not when we're still emotionally unequipped."

"You were hurt a lot though, weren't you Baby?"

"Weren't we all? It wasn't so much that I was ridiculed and stoned to death, it was unrequited love more than anything."

"I love how your 'enamoured heart doth sing'."

"Pretty weak huh?" I laughed.

"No Baby, it made me feel like I was fifteen again."

"So, you're happy with my meagre attempt then?"

"Delirious."

"And how come I've never been the recipient of one of your poems?"

"What about my biography in English about you, not to mention 'Ashlyn's Song'?" I was so stupid. I hadn't even thought of his essays and music, never stopped to think that he'd written plenty for me over the years. I then understood what he meant about never having received one; he had always written them for others.

"Did you ever write songs or poems for girls before you met me?"

"Not specifically. Used a pinch from this girl, a smidge from another to form a separate person. No one ever inspired me enough to write one for them solely… until you came along." He looked at me with so much love in his eyes. It made me want to cry. "And now I write them for Mercy too…"

"The proof of our love projected back at us."

"Yes Baby, and what a wonderful projection."

"Know what rhymes with projection?" I asked, taking him in my hand as I laughed.

"Know what rhymes with stupendous?" I thought for a second and his stiffening member brought an excellent answer to mind.

"Humungous?" He laughed,

"I was thinking cunnilingus."

"That doesn't rhyme!"

"It does if you say them with a French accent." I tried it and he was right. "Speak French to me Baby."

"Je t'aime de tout mon coeur. Je flamber pour tu, je suis une demi-vie sans toi."

"God, you could recite a recipe to me, and I'd get horny over it."

"Baby, I could do that in English!" He laughed with me.

"What did you say?"

"I love you with all of my heart. I burn for you; I am a half-life without you."

"Ich werde dich immer Lieben," he said.

"What's that about your dick?" I asked playfully. He laughed,

"German doesn't sound as romantic as French does it?"

"No."

"I will always love you."

"I know," I told him and reached up for a kiss.

"That's what I said to you in German."

"I know. I did German in Year 7 too."

"Whitney's greatest hit from 'The Bodyguard' doesn't carry quite the same emotion when sung in German, does it?"

"Nein!" We laughed again. "Je veux faire l'amour pour vous," I whispered in his ear and he moved down and kissed me deeply. "Did you understand what I said?"

"Hmmm," he purred, "but I'm going to make love to *you* instead." He had understood... and did it *so* well...

THE END

EPILOGUE

WHEN ALAN CAME TO VISIT US again over the Easter school holidays, he finally told us what Cara had mentioned several months before; he was retiring as of the first of July. He wanted Lorien or me to act in the position until permanently recruited, with the option of us to apply for it if we were so inclined. I wasn't ready to be away from Lorien yet, but I was ready for a little reality; to be back among the land of the living and to know the lyrics to some real songs, not just the usual pre-school selections. Lorien was delighted with my decision as it let him off the hook, not that anyone had a gun to either of our heads. My first job! It turned out to be a week of firsts...

I was about to go on my first motorbike ride behind Lorien and with great excitement I was putting on my gear in the bedroom. Lorien had arranged for Elijah to look after Mercy for a few hours and I couldn't wait to get on the back of that bike. I trusted Lorien with all aspects of my life, including his ability to ride. I knew he wouldn't let me get on it if he considered it in any way unsafe.

I was having a bit of a problem getting the jacket zipped up, realising I shouldn't have put my gloves on first. But now I couldn't get them off, so went in search of Lorien to help me. I nearly dropped my jaw when I saw him in our bedroom, also dressing. His Draggin jeans were on and he was in the process of putting on his boots when I walked in. He was so incredibly hot. The armoured pants had a sexy heavy cut to them and a wide waistband that sat just above his navel. When he stood, it reminded me of Zorro; all he needed was a cape and mask. "What's up Baby?" he asked when he saw me standing there staring at him.

"My heart rate for one..." He tilted his head and looked at me with a confused expression. "You look edible Lorien." He laughed and ran his hands over his chest quickly.

"Does something for you hey?"

"Oh yeah!" Boots on, he reached for his jacket, not bothering to put a shirt on underneath.

"I'll leave it off this time so you can use me as your playground when we stop for lunch." I smiled at him and noted this offer; I was ready for lunch now. "Having trouble getting your gear on?" he asked, noticing my semi-dressed state.

"I can't get the jacket zipped up with these gloves on, and I can't get them off either." Lorien helped me get the gloves off and then zipped me up, handing me my helmet.

"Are you ready Ash?" I was. "Well let's go."

I stood next to the bike whilst Lorien climbed on. Elijah had Mercy in his arms watching our departure. Apparently, he was not going to miss this. "Eli, give Mercy to Ash and climb on, show her how to do it." I held Mercy and watched Elijah step on the foot peg and throw his leg over the seat, sitting in behind Lorien on the small pillion seat. He showed me where to put my hands and how to lean into him, for cornering especially. None of it was sinking in. Lorien fired the ignition and gave it a few revs, waiting for it to warm up as Elijah climbed off. He leant down and kissed the front of my visor where my mouth was positioned behind it.

"Just in case I don't see you again," he said forlornly.

"Don't say that!" I said and whipped the visor up so I could speak more clearly.

"You'll be fine Babe, you know Lori would never hurt you." I gave him a watery smile and handed Mercy back to him, looking nervously at the bike.

"Hop on Baby!" Lorien instructed gleefully, but I think I had changed my mind.

"Here, take my hand," Elijah offered, standing beside the bike to help me on.

Once settled, it didn't feel too bad. Elijah ran me through the bum and hand placements again and I thought I was ready. "Is she right?" Lorien called to his brother and Elijah gave him a thumb up. We were off.

"AAAAHHHHHHHHHHHHHH!" was all that I could get out of my mouth for the first few seconds. This was nothing like I expected. When we reached the end of Bridge Street, Lorien paused at the intersection and we shot off to the left. I hugged in behind him so tightly; all I could see when I peeked was the back of his jacket. My arms were a strangle hold around his waist and my thighs were starting to ache from gripping onto him.

I assumed we were going to Glassread as he pulled over just before the turn-off, dragging his helmet off. "You OK Ash?" I nodded, and flipped up my visor again so he could hear me.

"Baby, sit back a little, you're in my seat with me." I laughed and squidged back a bit and felt myself sink into the formation of my actual seat. "Relax and enjoy it."

"I'll try." He smiled at me and put his helmet back on, kicking the bike into gear and we were off again. This time I relaxed and looked around at the passing scenery we both knew so well. I kept myself aligned to him so when he cornered, we went as one. I was disappointed when it was all over, and we pulled up next to Glassread Reserve.

"What did you think?" Lorien asked, lying on the blanket we'd bought, tucking into a sandwich.

"I loved it, that was like... flying... like sex!" He laughed.

"You're a natural Baby, an excellent pillion, once I got you onto your own seat anyway."

"Can you teach me to ride?" I asked, thinking how wonderful it would be zooming around together on our own bikes.

"If you like Ash." On second thoughts, I preferred being in behind Lorien, it was so exciting and romantic. "Are you going to have some lunch?" I took the sandwich from his hand and put it on a plate before lowering myself to his bare chest.

"I thought you'd never ask," I murmured as I leant in to kiss him.

GLOSSARY OF AUSSIE SLANG

- All together: in the 'all together' is nude, naked.
- Arse/d around: delay something by behaving in a silly or unproductive manner.
- Bloke: guy, man. 'Blokey-bloke' – manly man.
- Bloody: completely, entirely, truly, very, purely, damn. An adverbial mild expletive used to emphasise the word following it. Bloody brilliant! Bloody thief. Bloody good! Bloody bad! Bloody angry!
- Bolt / ed: took off, moved with great speed.
- Bottle shop: A place to buy alcohol. Also known as the 'bottle-o' or 'grog shop'.
- Broke: as in go for/went for broke. To gamble everything.
- Cracked a good one: effectively accomplished.
- Cup (the): see Phar Lap.
- Dig (constant): to deliberately insult or annoy.
- Dill: idiot. Someone who does something without thinking.
- Full-blown: to the maximum extent of, the nth degree.
- Full on: intense.
- Full stop: As a rule a full stop marks the end of a sentence, known as a period in the USA. In this instance it equates to 'that's it, no more to add'.
- Gash: female genitalia.
- Gob-smacked: amazed.
- Good on you: well done, congratulations. Can also be used in a derogatory/sarcastic sense, 'You broke the last plate? Good on you!'.
- Goss: short for gossip.

- Grew very thin: became more difficult to deal with. 'My patience is growing very thin due to your behaviour'.
- Have a go: (at someone) to attack or criticise.
- Huff (in a): in a snit. To be angry, miffed or offended.
- In the buff: naked.
- Jelly: a gelatine based dessert, known as jello in the USA.
- Kindy: Kindergarten. The first year of school in Australia, and follows pre-school.
- Knock it off: stop it.
- L-Plates: to be on your learner's permit which is the first stage of learning to drive in Australia.
- Let it drop: stop talking about something – let the subject slide.
- Loo: toilet.
- Milo: is a chocolate and malt powder mixed with milk to produce a hot or cold drink. Loved by kids and adults alike, with the kids often sneaking the raw powder straight out of the tin by the spoonful!
- Nappy: diaper.
- Out to it: unconscious, asleep.
- Pass the parcel: a children's game at parties where a parcel is passed around to music. When the music stops the child holding the 'parcel' gets to remove a layer of wrapping, hoping to find a treat. The final removal of the wrapping will hold a prize, like a toy.
- Phar Lap: Australia's most famous prize-winning horse of the annual Melbourne Cup. 'The Cup' is the 'race that stops a nation' and is held the second Tuesday in November.
- Reckon: think, as in - What do you reckon? What do you think?
- Right: as in 'is she right?' Is she OK, is she ready.
- Sec: second. Not necessarily a literal meaning of one second. Hang on a sec could refer to as long as it takes, and definitely not only one second.

- Slag: a contemptible person. When referring to a female, equivalent to slut.
- Smart-arse: see dickhead. Smart-arsed (as in grin): a very wide grin, usually showing smugness, self-satisfaction, or inner humour.
- Spinning out: freaking out. To be extremely surprised, upset, angry or confused.
- Stitch: as in stitch of clothing. 'I didn't have a stitch on'. I was naked.
- Stuff up: make a mistake.
- Take-away: take-out. Place where you buy a variety of ready-made meals such as hamburgers, fish and chips, chips (aka fries), plus an assortment of other deep-fried food. Carries ice creams and soft drinks (soda), chips (crisps) and often lollies (candy), milk, bread, etc. In the USA this would be a 7-11 or an AM/PM.
- Trackies: track suit pants. Sweat pants.
- Tucking: eating vigorously.
- Up the duff: pregnant.
- Wuss: weak, cowardly or timid.

This glossary of Australian slang was developed to assist non-Aussies with any terms they find confusing in the novel. This could range from another country having a different understanding of the same word or phrase, to not understanding the term whatsoever.

The glossary outlines the reference to how the slang is used in the novel and is not all encompassing of every use of the word or phrase in Australia. Slang can also vary from state to state, which is why immigrants who have lived here for decades still look at we born and bred Aussies in total confusion when we speak. Who can blame them! ☺

A special thank you to my dear friend Jennifer D McLaughlin, my USA mate and pen-pal since we were 13 years old. Her input into this glossary from an American perspective has been immeasurable. Thanks Jen!

About the author

Cassandra Ann Frew (nee Souter) was born on a July winter's night in Hornsby NSW. At the age of three, the family moved to a dairy farm outside Lismore NSW where she spent the majority of her childhood. At ten years old, the family moved to Lake Macquarie NSW.

Cassie found her love of romance writing during her high school years, and her first several 'novels' were hand-written exercise books, passed around for her friends to read.

Her career in business and administration has led her into further self-education including web design, IT, professional proofreading and editing, creative writing and industrial psychology. She is also a Justice of the Peace and a Civil Celebrant.

Her most rewarding achievement to date is what she has in common with the residents of the Standish household – their love of music, playing an instrument and the 80s. What a decade!

These stories belong to my readers, and to Ashlyn and the Standish family. This is how love should be, can be, is.

www.ingramcontent.com/pod-product-compliance
Lightning Source LLC
Chambersburg PA
CBHW050500260626
47157CB00004B/1122